THE
COLORMAN

THE
COLORMAN

Erika Wood

TATRA PRESS LLC

Library of Congress Control Number: 2009930600

Contact Chris Sulavik
Tatra Press LLC
292 Spook Rock Road
Suffern, NY 10901
www.tatrapress.com

Text composed by Heather Marshall.

Book design by Kathleen Lynch, Black Kat Design.

To Seth

and to Ronan and Freya

Color is my day-long obsession, joy and torment.

—CLAUDE MONET

*Vibrating, colors peal like silver bells and clang like bronze bells,
proclaiming happiness, passion and love, soul, blood
and death.*

—EMIL NOLDE

Most of the animals James Morrow had begun to collect since his illness were small and all of them were already dead. He didn't kill them, even though for his purposes, the carcasses were better fresh than days-old and bloated. He could always use the bone from a creature left long on the roadside. Though Morrow had lost his sense of smell by then, he did leave the skunks to the proper authorities. He kept thick, construction-site trashbags and rubber gloves in his car for drives along the country lanes near his manufactory. So it was that some raccoons, an unfortunate opossum and numerous squirrels donated their little bodies to his work.

Working in the evenings after his employees had left, he skinned the animals, separated fat from flesh, and subjected this portion or that to the tools of his trade. The bones he then dried and burned, some charred to matte black, others all the way to ash white. Still others he dried slowly in a kiln until light and powdery. Fat was cooked down, skin and sinew were tanned, muscle and certain organs were salted, dried and wrapped in thick, tar-soaked cloth strips. Cennini had recommended sheep's feet for bone black and whites, but Morrow believed he'd chosen that particular beast simply for its easy availability at the time, though it could have been for the thickness of the bone.

Considering this, Morrow rubbed his arm and squeezed it to the circumference of his wrist. He stared at his hands with curiosity.

At that time he had not yet met Rain Morton; in fact, he had forced the memory of her existence from his mind. Though the probability of his early demise had been explained by the main oncologist his HMO had assigned to him, and though it had prompted him to get on with this project he had vaguely been planning for decades, the doctor had failed to fully impress upon him any tragedy or finality to his diagnosis. In fact, all the various doctors and nurses James had contact with projected an interest in the cancer itself. But, having not met him before he appeared with his symptoms and damning bloodwork, the doctors had made little contact with James Morrow's well-protected soul.

Overlooking the deepest part of the Hudson, just south of its bend at Constitution Island, at the dead end of one dirt road into another, sat Highland Morrow Paint and Pigments Manufactory. The Highland Morrow factory was built early in the nineteenth century by practical men who would never have dreamed of depriving a building of charm or warmth just because its purpose was manufacturing. It was practical for the time, which is to say invitingly scaled to humans, with its red-brick facade, wrought iron gates, small courtyard and leaded windows. The views it commanded over the downward slope of trees, past the train tracks and the river beyond, toward the dramatic peaks of Crow's Nest and Storm King across the water, caused private homes, estates really, to be built right alongside it. Old Mahican Road had become tony and exclusive except for Morrow's modest little 1830s house adjacent to the factory. The other structures that had sprouted along this old dirt road were nothing if not immodest, dream homes designed and then built without compromises. Their money kept the area some-what private, though every few years Morrow had to fight off some new resident's concern over the "dangerous chemicals" he used in manufacturing paints. Dangerous indeed. Thankfully, Morrow's grandfather had been forward thinking enough to ensure that his business had rights in perpetuity against all those who bought land around it.

Inside, brick pillars divided the factory's soaring casement windows and long metal and glass work tables held clusters of arcane-looking tools and bottled unctures. The work that took place on the main factory floor was hardly dangerous. Not to the neighbors, anyway. Under each window, mulling stations were manned in turns, fresh workers replacing those worn out by the literal grind. Workers were rarely neighbors, though Morrow often found that job-seekers came to him from art schools, the children of people like his neighbors. He tended not to hire them, however, preferring to hire men and women who were supporting families—folks who had no one else to pay their bills and who were more likely to stay with him long term.

Alvaro Montoya dumped a tall heap of red ochre-pigment powder onto the glass slab on the countertop and stabbed his large palette knife into the center, forming a neat crater. Into that he poured in a measure of first-press linseed oil. With the same palette knife, Alvaro scooped the raw pigment from the outer slope in—out in, out in, pressing down into the darkening center. He worked quickly so as not to lose any oil in rivulets off the side, collecting up what had quickly become a thick paste and pressing off to the center again. He scraped the excess from the palette knife onto the bottom of the crystal-clear muller and placed it down on the center of the lumpy bright red heap.

A muller is a thick, up-ended mushroom of solid glass weighing about ten pounds, the wider bottom flat up to a rounded edge, the upper part round and fat to Alvaro's hand.

Alvaro moved the muller round, round, round, round over the glass surface to a count of twenty-four, causing the brilliant red to flatten out, a wide circle like a bright red vinyl record staining the glass. Then, tilting it up, sometimes having to break the suction with his palette knife, he skimmed around its edges and across the glass surface with practiced gestures, troweling the fresh paint into the center again. The grinding, Alvaro found, always released unique aromas depending on the pigment he was working with. Linseed oil had a sour nutty strong note that most people couldn't smell past, but Alvaro found that the unique qualities of each pigment began to assert themselves as his muller broke up and incorporated smaller and smaller particles of pigment into the oil. Red ochre, he found, gave a desert scent with a little metallic top note. A hint of something familiar, wet and sleek. And back into it he went: round, round, round, round to twenty-four again with his other hand on top.

Morrow had decorated the factory space with a series of large prints of famous paintings. Turner's "An Artist's Colour-man's Workshop," surprisingly tame, nonetheless reflected the work carried out at Highland Morrow. It was the other prints, including Degas' "Le Tub," featuring a woman's back and long arm extended downward toward her feet, and Caillebotte's "Floor Scrapers," showing the leaning, intensely physical pose of pulling scrapers along a wooden floor, which mirrored perfectly the physical nature of mulling paints. The muscular backs in Caillebotte's floor-scraper paintings, in his "Oarsmen," and in various Degas bathers reminded the workers where these mate-rials might end up, and the physical nature of what they gave toward that hope.

The yoga teacher James had engaged to train his staff in occu-pational and physical-therapy techniques encouraged Alvaro and the other employees to count grinds and switch hands and direction every twenty rounds or so. Alvaro counted to twenty-four since it was a nice musical number. Montoya was from Argentina, Spanish-speaking as most of his factory colleagues, though the others were from desperately poor circumstances in Mexico, Honduras and Colombia. Alvaro had been the beneficiary of a decent education and opportunities in his home country. He'd come to New York to be a musician, but found himself lumped together with the cleaning staff and delivery people by the privileged Americans he had met there. Morrow, on the other hand, though gruff and diffident most of the time, seemed to see Alvaro for who he was, more than just another pair of hands. Still, Alvaro's off-hours were spent at his piano, writing songs and composing tunes, so taking long periods of meditation to a four-four beat was the perfect job for him. One with private side-benefits.

After an hour of mulling, Alvaro took a turn on the machines. Most pigments were ground by hand, but Morrow had two triple-mill grinders for the more voluminous whites and the harder pigments.

The triple-mill grinder rolled its buttery paint, a green malachite this time, from drum to drum. Looking like icing in Oz, the mound of paint folded and bucked between rollers, turning and tucking in on itself like a living thing. The thin sheet it pulled down between the first two rollers was slid over and slurped up by a third roller, whose same direction of rotation pushed the gathering paint back upward where it grew into a silkier fat slug than what had been troweled in. Alvaro dug up the heavy stuff with a wide spatula and wiped it back up onto the first roller for another go through the mill. As the thick paste worked its way around the drums again, it was finally collected with a sensuous push push push into a wide-mouthed bucket below.

Highland Morrow specialized in artists' oil paints. Not just any oil paints, but handmade versions of a classical palette. Ultramarine, Olive Green, Yellow Ochre, Burnt and Raw Sienna and Umber, Venetian Red and Alizarin Crimson. Real Flake White and Lamp Black.

A list of colors at the art supply store. But those colors were cooked up, mixed, treated and tubed in very specific and sometimes quirky ways.

The term "Flake White," for example, struck fear into the heart of many an artist, though its dangers were not always well-known or heeded. Van Gogh was said to have adored his lead white paint so much he ate it. This, of course, would have explained the intractable melancholy of his last days in Arles. Lead poisoning can cause blindness, deafness and kidney damage but, most uniquely of all, nerve disorders, muscle spasms and *irritability* (one of those charming medical euphemisms similar to discomfort as in "you may feel a pinch and then some discomfort during the extraction of spinal fluids"), all this leading, of course, to total loss of mental capacity and death.

Mercury, sulfur, lead and cadmium—materials making up many important pigments—are almost all deadly to humans in large enough doses. Artists have always been vulnerable to their effects by breathing their vapors hours upon hours in treacherously fragrant studios or frequently by absorbing them directly into the skin—on fingers used to smooth and correct, on the back of a hand used as a palette, into the palm while washing a paint brush and, of course, accidentally splattered, wiped on brows and spilled.

Highland Morrow Art Materials folded small-print health warnings into every box of their paints, but James Morrow, artist's colorman, owner and operator of the business his great-grandfather had started in England in the 1840s, and whose family before that had served as colormen to some of the great portraitists of the realm, refused to update his materials. No water-based oils. No fume-less turpenoid. And absolutely no pthalo, quinacridone, dioxazine, napthol or hansa pigments would ever synthetically tint Morrow's colors.

Highland Morrow wasn't for all artists. High prices and a fairly limited selection of materials put many painters off, but to conservators, forgers, and a growing number of artists who thought of their materials as a meaningful contribution to the final product, Highland Morrow was the only source.

Morrow, in his uniform of charcoal sweater, black jeans and boots, moved among his employees dressed in theirs of white jackets and paper hats. He checked the texture of the malachite, stabbing a clean palette knife into the bucket and rubbing it across a card lying in a stack kept nearby for this purpose. He tilted the card in the light, eyeing it for hue, texture and covering power. He jutted his chin at Alvaro. "You put it through again?"

"Yeah, boss," Alvaro said, smiling.

"I think you got it. How about the ochres?"

"They're holding steady. I laid you out all the cards over here." Alvaro went back to the mulling table where a dozen cards were carefully arranged, each with the same cryptic brushstrokes. On every card a single red stroke smeared downward from thick to thin over a printed line, dark to light like a stormy red sky above the sea and a milky orb of the color, fifty-fifty with titanium white, hovering next to it.

Morrow pulled his dark eyeglass frames down his long nose and checked the cards. He rearranged them a little. He held two up under a lamp and then angled them toward the window.

"Looks like you have it, Alvaro," he said quietly. "It's good."

Alvaro looked up at Morrow. He noticed that Morrow was unusually slow moving, standing still, not looking at anything in particular.

"You need something, boss?" he asked.

Morrow appeared not to have heard him. He didn't move and Alvaro didn't either. All the employees were accustomed to Morrow's brief "holidays," a term housepainters use for missed spots. If these got to be too long, Alvaro would ask again, but this time Morrow came back repeating what Alvaro had asked him. "Need something?" he murmured, sounding vaguely present. "Uh, there's a bottle in my office, Alvaro. Prescription bottle by the lamp. I'd appreciate that, my man."

Morrow continued around the room taking readings from thermometers, stirring thick oily liquids and checking inside the doors of enormous room-sized kilns, while Alvaro hopped lightly up the spiral staircase to Morrow's perched second-floor loft office. The room was dark except for a small lamp on the desk, but bottles and jars of detrita lined the walls on narrow shelves. Blown-glass and metal contraptions crowded the room's corners. A large, black-leather couch lay against the back wall, mostly obscured by stacks of papers and books.

Alvaro found the bottle on the desk, and picking it up, noticed a photo behind it, illuminated by a little halo of light by the desk lamp above. It was a yellowed picture of a beautiful young woman. She was lively and hopeful, her long hair cut in thick bangs hanging over her pretty face, partly hiding what looked like a smile. She held a couple of paint brushes toward the camera, accusingly.

Through the office windows, the view down onto the factory floor was broad, and from this vantage point the well-worn antiquity of the place was enlivened by fields of pure pigment lying in trays, buckets and bags all over the room. Powders, liquids and oils of contrasting hues created a sharp counterpoint to the calm of the browns and grays of the equipment. Alvaro saw them as can-can dancers cavorting in a monastery.

Sliding back down the railing of the spiral staircase, Alvaro bounded over to his boss to deliver the bottle.

GWENDOLYN BROOKER GALLERIES was painted in subtle tan Helvetica caps on the plate glass window. Behind the glass stood a bare white wall with a single large white canvas hanging on it. Blank mostly, until closer inspection revealed that the meandering marks were purposeful; they were what the artwork amounted to. A freshly gessoed canvas manhandled with haphazard smears and gouges.

A three-person show was opening that night. The artists' families and friends crowded the place, along with the usual varieties of New Yorkers whom art openings attract.

There were the shabby art students hoarding free wine and cheese, and there were the citizen art fans whose interest in art was far deeper than their pockets. There was the occasional collector or critic intensely sought by gallery owners, but whose appearances at openings were rare. They were easily identifiable; they never touched the wine or cheese.

Rain Morton Madlin wandered around the various species and genuses in attendance, trying to see the works through their eyes and eavesdropping on conversations. Looking about a decade younger than her years, Rain had a raw-edges openness about her and was pretty in an unself-conscious way. Her hair hung long and clean but carelessly unflattened; untrimmed bangs dipped into her large, liquid eyes. Her wide mouth betrayed a sadness floating around her that she buoyed with a resolute positivity.

Rain neared a couple, the man clearly here under protest, the woman attempting to hold her ground against him.

"...total crap. I mean I know it's a cliché, but my kid—no, my DOG could do this," he blurted.

"But the question is *would* your dog do this?" the woman asked.

"Exactly my point!"

"I think that was MY point."

Rain allowed a smile to creep up on her face, letting on she had heard them.

"I mean, right?" the man said to Rain, just before she passed by.

"What's that?" Rain asked politely.

"I'm saying, who really likes this? Bodily fluid art, porn, preserved animals. Art that the artist never lays a hand on. It's like a big joke."

"I like them," Rain remarked, surveying the space.

The man and his companion laughed as though she were joking.

"I do, I like them and I don't think the amount of effort that went into a particular piece has anything to say about its value." Rain kept her tone light. "I know it's unfair, but I think it's true."

"Right, right," the man agreed. "You can't convince me it's any good and I can't convince you it's crap. Eye of the beholder. But you would spend your hard-earned—I mean you're okay with the obscene amounts of money spent on these when, you know, starving children and all that?"

"Yes," Rain said.

The man shook his head wearily.

Rain pressed on, "I think the prices are reasonable. It's expensive to sell art. The gallery owners spend tons on space to show the work, and on events and overseas art shows and catalogs and ads. Then, of course, there are the artists, spending their lives—"

"Still seems high," the man interrupted.

"If you're asking do I think it's worth spending large sums of money on art, I'd have to say yes."

"The diamond skull?"

"Oh, I can name better ones than that. I like the two-million dollar, mile-long pole speared into the earth," she said, "with only a small inscribed disk visible." Rain laughed. "At least you can *see* the diamonds, huh?"

Rain knew it was one of those conversations not much worth having. Most art-world people would just have moved right past. It's nothing they haven't all heard before, loudly, angrily, sometimes drunkenly, but usually self-assuredly as if these objections were original. She wasn't sure why she had engaged the guy, but despite being so steeped in the art world, Rain could see how it looked to people on the outside. She was deep enough in not to have to make bristly excuses for it, but she'd also thought a lot about the merits of spending her life doing something that few, if any, would ever be able to appreciate. "I assume you go to movies?" she asked.

"Mmmm," the man answered.

"Think about the money spent on those. Each has its audience. The millions spent on some of those—and some of them everybody agrees are total turkeys—that money eclipses any one of the craziest sounding art prices. Ultimately, I think engaging people's minds is worthwhile."

The woman piped in. "And the very fact that it isn't mainstream, that it *is* quirky and odd and provocative, for some people that's worth something right there."

Rain smiled at the woman, understanding her meaning, but not quite joining in. "And really, some of the pieces were incredibly time consuming to make, if that's what interests you."

"You're probably one of the artists!" the man said with a laugh.

Rain smiled.

The woman put her hand over her mouth and the man blushed. "Which ones?" he asked.

Rain pointed across the room and as the man started to speak again, saying those, those he liked, those weren't the ones he had meant, Rain just moved along nodding and waving, heading toward the back room.

In such a fresh, clean space, Rain's paintings looked almost unfamiliar to her. She was proud of them, but they were like her movie star clients, and she their plastic surgeon. She knew them in their becoming, in their guts and raw vulnerability.

Nothing in the man's criticisms particularly bothered her. If he'd been dragged to almost any art school in America, any biennial, any contemporary art institute, he'd realize Rain was actually laughably antiquated in her use of actual paint. Actual pigment in oil applied to actual canvas on stretcher bars. For most critics, her own husband among them, Rain's work was almost quaint in its attachment to these materials. But for Rain, ultimately, making art was never a matter that required defending. It was what made her feel most human, most alive. Marking canvas with silken paint globules took her out of herself and her mind and into the materials and smells and the textures of the weave of canvas, the skim of gesso, the landscape of oil and pigment. It was pleasure and meaning and hope and acceptance.

In the back office of the gallery a bottle of decent scotch perched on the desk between Gwendolyn Brooker herself and a gentleman dressed in an Armani suit and cowboy boots. He was laughing and easy; she was leaning toward him, trying unsuccessfully to cover her tension. Gwen pointedly set down her glass.

"Joss, Joss, Joss," she said, speaking fast but low. "How many years have we known each other?"

Joss Harp took this as an invitation and grabbed her knee in his big, fleshy hand.

Gwen went on as though he'd answered her, "And in all those years have I ever steered you wrong?"

Harp winked, and then patted and released her tiny knee. "Not so as I can tell, you haven't."

"Then trust me on this one: it's an important piece, a smart inv—"

Harp interrupted her. "Not prepared to buy just today. Having to be a bit more conservative in these *times*." Harp downed his scotch and then plunked his empty glass down on the desk next to Gwen's.

"But Joss…" Gwen began energetically, refilling his glass as she spoke.

"Just gonna slow down there a little, is all. Just a little risk aversion thing, you understand. But you must be doing okay, Gwenny, huh? What with all them foreigners you been selling to past couple of years?"

Gwen screwed the top back on the bottle and cradled it in her lap. "I can't help feeling sorry that our best works are flying overseas. There used to be important collectors in this country. Passionate people, visionaries."

Joss picked up his refilled glass, drank it down in one go and stood. He adjusted his belt over his full belly, shoving his shirt deep into his pants. "Honey, begging doesn't suit you," he said with a sudden turn in tone. With that, he screwed his hat onto his head and exited on big confident strides. As he passed through the viewing room, the big man noted Rain standing there. He touched the brim of his hat and took her in unabashedly. "Be seein' you," he said and strolled through the crowds and out of the gallery.

Rain pivoted around the doorway and into Gwen's office. "*Gwenny?*" she said incredulously.

Gwen looked down to find the bottle of scotch still in her hands. She returned it onto her desk. "You know, I USED to be good at this," she commented with vague irony.

"Come on, now," Rain said, gathering the glasses and bottle and putting them away.

Gwen didn't notice what Rain was doing; she was so accustomed to being served.

"That man is a boor," Gwen declared, smoothing her Missoni dress and rubbing a hand down her fine, still-shapely calf.

"No sale?" Rain asked.

"Twice a year I shipped out crates of important works so he could *view* them," Gwen complained. She stood and came through her office door with Rain. "Funny how he always shopped for art right before one of those famous parties of his. All very impressive, showing off dozens of important works on your vacation home walls. He even had the nerve to invite me once." Gwen shook her head. "And I actually went! The Hamptons. Everyone there thought I was raking it in."

"I always thought he bought."

"One. He'd return all but one. Now he won't even do the one," she said. "I'm getting out."

"We've all heard that before," Rain said.

"I'm serious. Rain, you should really forget about painting. It's not a smart move right now. Don't do it if you don't have to."

Rain rolled her eyes and said flatly, "I have to."

Gwen insisted, "I mean it. Don't do it. It's a disease."

"Yes, it's a disease," Rain echoed with a sigh.

Gwen smiled tiredly, "Alright. I'm getting senile. Just wheel me out into the storage space and cover me in bubble wrap."

They lingered in the doorway looking out at the milling crowd.

"Thanks for this," Rain said.

"Summer show," Gwen said, shrugging. "Why shouldn't you be one of them?"

"But it's a big deal for me," Rain replied.

"Well, I can only do it once, so don't get too worked up about it," Gwen said, dismissing Rain's gratitude as if it were a kitchen moth.

Important artists never showed in the summer months in New York City. Those months were often given over to a gallery's junior directors to curate as they like. For many artists these group shows were second-tier, but still added an important name to the resume.

"It's changing, Rain," Gwen said quietly. "It's always been hard, but it's getting harder. We had an awfully brief renaissance in this country."

"That was a renaissance? I thought it was a *will-it-go-with-my-couch*."

Gwen laughed, "It was a *will-it-go-with-my-stock-portfolio*."

"And you're sure the Medicis weren't thinking the same thing? Do we really care why they collected?"

"Collectors shape art," Gwen said, shaking her head lightly. "Come on, Saatchi? And yes, when collectors' motives go off-kilter there are odd bends in the market." She gestured out to the gallery goers. "Still, what are vacations and clothes and diamonds going to mean to generations to come?"

Rain had heard Gwen rue this same thing during all of the fifteen years she had known her. "You're right. There won't be much for the kids to fight over."

"Rain," Gwen turned away from the gallery and leaned back against the door jamb looking at her. "Don't do it. Get a sensible job at an ad agency, raise babies and don't torture yourself with this. I'm serious, Rain. It's all falling apart. Even Sotheby's is feeling it. It's nothing about what you deserve, or your promise. Nobody cares if you make good art. Nobody can stand still long enough to see it."

Rain shook her head, still smiling. "Gwen, I've heard this so many times from you. Sometimes I actually think you're trying to talk me out of it."

"I AM."

"And other times I think you're just testing me—" Rain interrupted herself. "Hey, isn't that Esterow?"

As Gwendolyn unceremoniously left Rain's company, and Rain watched her go, she felt her fond smile fade slowly as she wandered into the crowd.

"*Rain drops keep falling on my head!*"—the ruckus erupted behind Rain and she knew exactly who it was without turning around. Quinn and Stan, trailing their impossibly stylish entourage. "*But that doesn't mean my eyes will soon be turning—RED! Cryin's not for me!*" Rain turned and dipped her knees.

Stan, the singer, was, as always, sore-thumb, low-rent cool in his pork-pie hat and bowling shirt.

Quinn thrust a crazy bouquet of sticks and scraggly wild flowers at Rain.

Stan, making no effort to greet Rain, kept singing as she kissed and shook hands with their friends—an assortment of new girlfriends and boyfriends, among them three models, a writer, a cartographic conservator and a bagpiping firefighter whom they had intercepted while he was walking home from a parade.

Stan finally ended his serenade and took his turn to hug Rain, *"Nothin' worryin' me..."*

"How are you, Gee?" Quinn asked. "Good gig!" he added, taking in the scene with a nod.

"You did it," Stan echoed.

"Stepmother..." Rain reminded them.

"No, no," Quinn argued. "Professional hard-ass stepmother who would not risk reputation without seeing something real there."

"Yeah," Stan agreed. "You'd have gotten it eventually. Nepotism is underrated."

"I'd be jobless," Quinn shrugged.

"No apartment for me," said Stan.

"I'm not ungrateful," Rain said. "I just want some to sell and I want to get my own show somewhere else."

"Not here?" Quinn asked.

"Nah, she can't."

"Why not, where is she? Let me talk to her," Stan cried.

Rain put a hand on Stan's shoulder. "Down boy," she said. "She's got her stable of artists. They're all well established. Certain number of shows a year, all that, you know."

"Ah, the gentleman arrives," Stan said, poking out his hand. Karl Madlin took it in a firm handshake. One for Quinn, too. Karl, Rain's husband, was good looking, in a very youthful-slash-successful way. And he knew it. He clashed with Stan and Quinn in his Paul Stuart, French-cuffed, dress shirt and black Crockett & Jones monkstraps. His trousers hit at the all-too-current, high-water point.

Karl was aloof around her old friends, who seemed to stiffen up around him. Rain had never gotten used to seeing her friends act that way around Karl, and she knew they didn't like him.

"Nice to see you," Karl said, placing a hand on the back of Rain's neck.

Stan waved toward the rest of their group. "We're going to mix," he said.

"Can I put these somewhere?" Quinn asked, lifting his bouquet.

"Behind the desk, please," Rain said, "and thanks for those."

When they had left, Rain ducked out from Karl's hand. "There are some people you should be talking to," Karl said before she could speak.

The crowd had thickened to capacity now, friends and family waiting smilingly in clusters for the artists to greet them. This swirl of sociability, chatter and strained decorum made Rain tense and unsteady. She preferred being alone, sealed in her small, messy studio, living inside the sinewy lines she painted. This clean space, the dress skimming her body and baring her arms, her hair loose and all the talking and posturing. All of it felt wrong. Too much. It felt like it could all dissolve into nonsense.

"I'd be one of those people," a man behind her said and Rain turned at once and buried herself into a broad, fragrant, barrel chest. The scratchy blazer at her cheek, the perfectly pressed dark shirt by her eye, the tie, one she knew, and the ever-present PEN lapel pin she had always played with as a little girl.

"Alright," he said. As Rain stayed pressed into his chest, John Morton wrapped his arms around his daughter and Rain closed her eyes. "Take me to your paintings, show me something," he said. He understood the moment she was in and helped her cover for it.

Rain took her father's arm and led him to her canvasses.

To her, his famous face was no different than any father's— just as perfect, just as familiar, just as hers. She couldn't look at him now: he had appeared just at that moment of fear and uncertainty. It was like looking into the face of the sun—the man who had been both mother and father to her.

Her college roommate had exclaimed upon discovering she was the daughter of John Ray Morton, "Oh, my God! He's the reason I knew I could never write a novel!" Pressed to explain, her friend had simply described him as though it were that obvious: "Big white guy? Fisherman sweaters? Wild white hair? Wire-rimmed glasses? Pipe?"

But John Morton had never been intimidating or iconic to Rain. He was all present, all available, all focus, speaking with her from before the reaches of her earliest memory in fully adult conversation: open, questioning and respectful. He had always made her feel complete and secure.

That's not to say he had always been there. Rain was raised by a succession of nannies while her father worked or occasionally traveled without her. But somehow he gave her the feeling that he had been there all along when he returned or emerged from his study after long hours away from her.

With her father there for her, Rain finally understood what was good about an opening.

From across the room, Rain's works were large dark strops that looked stretched across the face of each canvas. The square construction and white of the canvas seemed like the only aspects of the artwork wrought by human hand. Instead of being tucked around the back of the work as was the convention, the canvasses just reached around to the edges, rippled, ungessoed and shredded past thick brass nails. The wood of the supports was stained and beaten to look like the surface of railroad ties. The markings on the face, however, appeared to be formed by some nesting creature—organic and random—each meandering, splitting and rejoining in its journey along the surface.

Though from afar the forms appeared to be made out of glimmering charcoal, closer inspection revealed they were built up with strands of oil paint in layers of color. What was monolithic and singular from afar became busy and suggestive up close. Rain led her father to the piece and positioned him at a close angle to it.

"It looks found," her father commented.

"Thanks," Rain said, adding, "I think."

"Found in a good way, Rain, like things you'd want to gather up."

"I think I like to make them because I want to have them around."

"That's one approach," John said cryptically.

"What do you mean?" Rain asked, a tiny bit defensive.

"An approach," John said. "Your approach, Rain Morton Madlin."

"John Ray Morton," Rain said right back at him, "I know you."

"Alright," John gave in to his daughter. "Plain and simple representation-abstraction question, that's all," he said. "I'm old school. I'm stuck with representation, but I see all the joy and meaning and discovery in that."

Karl approached. John tended to make Karl slightly deferential, but never enough to completely relinquish his claim on Rain's attentions. "Rain, can you come talk to some people over here?"

John benignly ignored Karl. Consistently. Like he was Rain's private dalliance his good manners didn't allow him to acknowledge. It wasn't disapproval. Far from it. Just a polite, knowing, couldn't-care-less. This, of course, drove Karl crazy, but the older man's status didn't give Karl the slightest opening to express it.

John gave Rain a light double pat on the shoulder while continuing to study her work and Rain turned to Karl, as though from one world to another, and said, "Sure."

Though clearly young, the woman was angular and looked slightly bent. Rain couldn't help but notice the dark circles under her eyes. She was dressed quite stylishly and her hair was razored and gelled, but she wore no makeup on her worn-looking face. Was it an aesthetic? A way to flaunt carelessness while projecting supremely confident attractiveness? Rain wasn't fussy about her appearance but she wore a minimal bit of makeup, which she strangely thought a favor to those who had to look at her all day. A little coverup, some lip gloss, mascara, nothing too noticeable. This woman's sunken eye sockets were like a dare.

"Rain, you know Penelope Caldwell-Worthington. And this is…"

"Peter," Penelope said indicating the young man with her. (*Pee-tah*: she had a British accent.) Peter shook hands and shoved them back under the strap of his messenger bag.

By "you know," Karl had meant by reputation. Penelope was an art star. An impressive persona he had enlisted to elevate Rain's opening. She had won that year's Turner Prize, which ranked her right up with the biggest celebrities, monstrous for the art world. Penelope's art—gallery performance—consisted of recitations of current pop songs in earnest, energetic, slam-poetry style in front of caged monkeys. During these appearances, while wearing nothing but Manolos, she peeled bananas and hurled them beneath her feet. She shouted the lyrics, streamed through an ear piece, atonally into a microphone at her jaw, à la Janet Jackson circa 1990. She riffed on the lyrics, now aggressive, now pleading, now robotic. She would then stomp through the bananas and repeat some of the refrains of the songs at the monkeys. She would keep this up for hours, switching lyrics, even mid-stanza, depending on what song was ranked number one on the pop charts at the time. Though Rain didn't catch her New York show, she saw it on YouTube and was perfectly unmoved by the theatrics. She did acknowledge, however, that the concept was appealing enough for those art-world arbiters only too ready to adore such pandering to human weakness. *Naked girl. Bananas? Heels? Score!* Rain thought.

Rain met Penelope congenially enough but felt both defiant and intimidated in her presence. Part of her admired Penelope's ambition. And she respected the rather long-lensed, utopian-based cultural criticism and the depth of self-assurance that Penelope's performances required. She was Karl's ideal, really, and though Rain knew that, there was a part of her that kind of relished her own NOT being Penelope. It was liberating to be faced by her ultimate rival. Rain had never been an art school "alternachick." Proving herself an artist never seemed to require hair dye, eyeliner and safety pins. But, at the same time, she had never felt the need to lay public claim to her sexuality. Naked, this Penelope looked as though she were wearing a tight Barbie wetsuit, her figure was so elongated and plastic looking. Even her geometrically shaped bush seemed glued on. Unreal. A little gross to Rain, though she understood it was a sort of ironic ideal.

Karl and his colleagues were talking about artists, dealers and curators. They traded players and inside knowledge like baseball fans.

Though she fully acknowledged to herself that she might have been reacting against this woman more strongly than she would have liked, Rain's attention wavered as she watched people circulating around the gallery, trying to keep herself from tallying viewers in front of her pieces against those in front of works by the other two artists. She couldn't help but feel the buzz of eyes as they brushed by her work—the little pangs as they exchanged comments she couldn't hear.

Rain didn't know the other two artists showing. They were chosen by Philip, Gwendolyn's new director. There was one other painter and a sculptor. Or rather, one wall-based artist and a dimensional artist. The sculptor's pieces were actually just vague swellings in the gallery wall, painted over with the wall paint from Gwen's back room, used to touch up between shows. The sculptor had worked for three days in the place, fitting his plaster forms to the walls, spackling them in and then using Gwen's paint to camouflage them back into the scenery.

The other painter—the one from the front window—had the scratched gesso schtick that seemed to be getting a lot of attention. But then Rain figured most of the admirers were his own recruits. Sometimes, when witnessing the enthusiasm surrounding this sort of work, Rain felt as though she'd missed some entire micro-culture in the art world. Was it jealousy she was actually feeling?

Rain understood that the art "world" was like a network of veins. There were large and small ones crossing each other with absolutely nothing in common. They appeared to perform the same function. They pulsed at the same rate and were moved by some of the same influences. But their players coursed on independently, never mixing or even feeling anything about the other.

One of Rain's jobs at the gallery was dealing with the unsolicited submissions heaped upon them daily. Large manila envelopes addressed in all their variety, some even arriving via FedEx, to the Gwendolyn Brooker Gallery, West Broadway, New York, NY, 10012—printed labels, cartoon-like sharpie, scribbled messes, ripped and retaped.

Mostly artists sent slides in stiff plastic sheets, though increasingly it was CDs along with printed pages. Then, of course, there were the occasional actual paintings, something that always felt vaguely embarrassing to Rain. A desperate flinging. None of these had much to do with Gwendolyn Brooker Gallery, however. Rain couldn't understand how so many people can have missed day one of art-representation-search 101: *Know what the gallery represents.* Gwen Brooker showed a very particular vein of work: social realism. But, however narrow her area of interest, Gwen always managed to commit to the tradition of the summer show, which helped keep the mountains of slides coming in. That, and her irritating habit of sometimes grabbing a pile of submissions and writing carefully considered advice back to the artists, listing galleries they should approach and other avenues they might pursue. Invaluable information for those who were able to recognize what they had been granted when facing, ultimately, her rejection.

One of the great art dealers who dominated the New York art world during the latter half of the century, Gwen had emerged from a line of powerful professional women in New York: Edith Halpert, Betty Parsons, Terry Dintenfass, Joan Washburn, Louise Ross. Some were mentors, some competitors. But characters, all of them. Confident, intellectual taste-makers who appeared to be passing into history. Even Gwen was beginning to talk more frequently of retiring to England with John, though both John and Rain laughed at her whenever she said that. The art was part of her, the artists like her children, even though most were her own age or older. She would never stop promoting them, never undersell them or resist buying up their works when they became available.

If the submissions included the required Self-Addressed-Stamped Envelope, Rain would open it and push the whole sad packet right back in, sliding a card in after it with Gwen's polite pass and heartfelt encouragement regarding their efforts. It fascinated Rain to see the range of work out there at which so many people were earnestly plugging away. Much of it was just plain bad. Some of it was alright, though her standards slid downwards as long days of this task dragged on. But, most sadly of all, sometimes she came across work that was actually very good, which was of course rejected, anyway.

The part of her that just loved the visual was made hopeful by finding interesting work out there. She delighted that a human mind and hand had conspired to create something refreshing and thoughtful. But there was that little part of her that was nervous when she came across work she liked. Such a tangle of feeling. Hopeful yet left behind. Hadn't she missed something? Wasn't she making that classic neophyte mistake of misinterpreting her own beginner discoveries as interesting for other people to see? The burst of pleasure she found in good paintings was always followed closely by those dark fears. Fears she willed against blooming into jealousy or paranoia.

Practicing serious effort in art meant excluding things. The moment brush or stick or finger or knife hits canvas or wood or masonite or stone or object, exclusions have been made. Materials, scale, subject, style—these are all mostly determined from the first mark. But these exclusions are not always comfortable. It is the decision made, the selective leavings behind—that is the dirty work which we admire in artists.

"Where are you, Rain?" Karl smiled uncharacteristically.

"Sorry," Rain said, coming back.

"You know Penelope is here jurying at Pollack Krasner."

"Is that right?" Rain asked. "How do you like it?"

"Quite disappointing, I should say," she replied archly.

Karl interrupted, "Rain knows all about that, don't you Rain? She handles the slush pile around here."

"Oh, my God," Penelope effused. "It's simply amazing to me the shit we have to slog through in there. It's like none of them has any idea what's going on in the art world. Honestly, I have no idea how these people can believe that their chalky-looking portraits of nudes with their Cezanne brushstrokes and their Matisse colors are just going to jolt us out of our seats," she laughed. "It *is* despicable. Or the glowing candy-land treacle storybook scenes… I'm not joking." Her words piled out one on top of the other.

Rain waited until Penelope had concluded her offering. Rain was unsurprised that none of them had said a word about her work. It just wasn't done. The most you might get was hearty congratulations, never comments about the work to your face.

"Yeah," Rain said non-committally. "I don't know; I guess I find it heartening."

"Heartening?" Penelope's accent was elevating as she got more animated. "It's absolutely depressing!" she moaned, allowing herself a good look up and down at Rain in her thrift store dress. "Rather pathetic, I should think."

Rain smiled at her. "I guess I see it as a good thing—people making art at all. I don't think about it from a business point of view, I guess. Gwen just isn't going to take on anything new, so it's not even a matter of that. I just see it as something people are doing and getting pleasure from."

"Yes, well…they might keep it to themselves," Penelope quipped cheekily.

"We better get going," Peter said. First thing out of his mouth. American, evidently.

"It was a pleasure," Penelope said to Rain, as though she'd been thanked. Rain was left a little rattled.

Rain watched her kiss Karl on both cheeks. She was irritated by Penelope, but resisted the burden that disliking a person requires. How this person so homely of face could be so supremely confident and superior? But Rain refused to engage in those sorts of judgments. She didn't believe in them and so tried to nip them off before they could bloom into a whole thought about this woman's skeletal thinness and wide, high breasts and perfect slope of hip all shown off in draped linen and ruched silk. Something in her ashen, unprimped face was belligerent. Something in her embrace and exploitation of popular culture, her exploitation of the utterly unexploitable. Nope. I can't go there, she demanded of herself.

Rain rejoined Karl in the increasing crowd.

"I'm going to head out for drinks with them. You want to join us later?"

"Uh, Gwen's?" Rain asked.

"Oh, God, yeah," Karl said. "Totally forgot. I'll…uh…"

"Go ahead. Just meet us there around nine, okay?"

"Hey," Karl said. "Did I say congratulations?"

Rain gave him a single peck on one cheek.

PURPLE

Purple haze all in my brain
Lately things just don't seem the same
Actin' funny, but I don't know why
'Scuse me while I kiss the sky.

—JIMI HENDRIX

Purple is richness beyond measure, the sensuousness of wine-stained lovers' lips and the quenching sweetness of grape and berry. Purple is also injury and death: the florid purple of a bruise, the darkening face of a choking victim, the opalescence of rotting flesh.

The term "purple prose" was coined by Horace, referencing the pretension of sewing bits of purple into garments to feign wealth. It is fussy, overwrought, and nobody's falling for it, anyway. Purple dyes were more precious than gold at that time, so faking it in this way was the ancient equivalent of dripping in cubic zirconia and gold plate. There's a double layer of humiliation. That it's fake, and that you're working so hard to appear to be something that is false to begin with.

Purple is royalty, a connotation that has everything to do with the extreme value of the pigments available for cloth-dying in antiquity. Tyrian purple was the original purple dye, created from tiny, snail-like mollusks. Only the super-rich royalty could afford such expensive stuff. It was the true holy grail the pigment-making alchemists worked toward—the gold created from the "philosopher's stone."

Though found in nature both in flora and precious stones, purple was the most difficult to reproduce as a colorant. Thus purple as a moniker persists to this day in its air of rarity and oddness, per purple cow.

Some theories hold that the earth was once more purple than green, that a purple-appearing, light-sensitive molecule called retinal was more commonly found than our familiar green chlorophyll. Could this explain the "wine dark seas" of the Odyssey and the many other confusing color terms in ancient languages? Perhaps this explains the more intricate delineation of indigo and violet after blue in our essential, and older, breakdown of primary colors in Newton's R.o.y. G. B.i.v. spectrum as opposed to the more current-day color wheel's triad (red yellow blue) and hexagonal wheel (adding the complements orange, green and purple), with it's one simple "purple" now comprising the stretch at that end of visible energy.

The Greeks described colors ranging from dark to light, rather than hue to hue along the rainbow. Was this simply a matter of descriptive terms, of translation? Like the proverbial dozens of words the Inuits use for snow compared to our own single word? Perhaps we are color Inuits, lovingly distinguishing shades where ancient peoples just didn't see meaningful distinctions. Could we have evolved out of color blindness over the millennia? Or did our color sensitivity just shift toward another end of the spectrum?

Left over from the days when the river and then the train were the only reasonable modes of industrial transport in the Hudson Valley, the riverfront still sported oil yards, abandoned factories, chain-link fences and unusable super-fund sites all along its banks. Even as economies picked up, many of these sites were slow to be transformed into waterfront beauties, though a few spots are notable exceptions: the old Nabisco factory in Beacon, now home to the fabulously minimal and grand scale Dia:Beacon; a number of green spa and condo sites in development and the ever-increasing number of "open space" projects reclaiming river properties as their prior stewards die off and their heirs can't afford to maintain them.

This type of economic fluke had allowed James Morrow, grandson of founder James Birch Morrow, who had brought the works over from England in the 1920s, to inherit and resuscitate the business his father had failed at so desperately. Morrow still owned a little property around the small factory building, but in the thick woods immediately surrounding Highland Morrow were properties his grandfather had collected, and his spendthrift father had sold off, including an insane asylum (erstwhile rehab clinic now uninhabited), a defunct monastery and no fewer than five churches. Watching his father fall dangerously close to losing the business, James finally quit college in England, married and brought his young, beautiful, Norwegian wife with him. In 1964, at the tender age of twenty-two, James took the helm of the foundering little company and all its mysterious recipes and equipment. The land was nearly all sold off by then, only the small caretaker's house remaining, and the new country estates were beginning to pop up in the woods around them. James, his wife and father installed themselves in the little house where James' father set about drinking himself to death with a good deal of efficiency.

James was young enough to have been a part of the hippie generation, but his father's destruction of everything his beloved grandfather had built made him uncharacteristically practical and unsentimental. Rather than wallowing in the utopian ideals of a better world, James' energies were honed and focused on keeping alive a centuries-old craft and business. Even through the sorrows and tragedies that dogged his young life, somehow James managed to make the business a success.

Gwen and Rain stood in the kitchen of Gwen's loft. Even though Rain's father lived there with Gwen, Rain still thought of the place as Gwen's. She had owned this cavernous and exquisitely decorated loft since the earliest days of Soho's gentrification in the early 1970s. Gwen and John had dated for several years before marrying ten years ago, at which point Rain was already on her own.

Gwen's loft blended outsider art objects with sleek, modernist furniture and, of course, her own artists' works were peppered throughout. The narrow hallway into the kitchen was crowded with portraits of Gwen by most of them. Gwen sitting demurely in Henry Chilton's distinctive elongated style. Gwen laughing in Rip Goulding's dark, splattery markings. Gwen's hands by Jacob Houseman, her lover for many years. And Gwen dancing with John by Stephan Carr, her youngest artist who was most like a son to her. In it, Gwen looks directly at the viewer, her chin raised proudly and her arm crossing possessively in front of John. He holds her passively, his arms wide to her and the viewer. His demure smile and his downward gaze give his expression a kind of benign satisfaction. Rain always loved this portrait of her father and Gwen. It spoke so lyrically and gracefully of the happy and evenhanded aspects of their relationship.

Karl sauntered into the kitchen having let himself in. "How are the *gallerists*?" Karl said. He took Rain's head and gave it a possessive peck. Karl seemed to think a slight sarcasm was the same thing as easy-going flirtatiousness.

Gwen grimaced slightly with her back to him. "Karl, you always know just what to say to cheer me up." She busied herself opening boxes of crackers for the party she was throwing that night.

"Ah, come on, Gwen, if anyone can make the art bubble last, it's you," he chuckled.

"You're lucky I adore your wife or I don't think we could be friends," Gwen said in a chipper voice.

"Don't worry, Madam, you may have seen the last of me for a while. I'm off to London—the academy calls." This was a fellowship they both knew well. A tiny flicker of appreciation of what this meant flitted across Gwen's face, but only Rain caught it.

Gwen set her face into a natural smile and turned it toward Karl. "How wonderful for you."

Turning her back to him again, Gwen muttered, "How convenient…"

Karl shrugged, finished with his mission, which was simply to let Gwen know this piece of his good fortune. He picked at an hors d'oeuvres platter and left the kitchen, passing John Morton in the doorway. Karl watched the older man enter the kitchen, seeming to want to turn back. But then he appeared to think better of it, choosing the effortless, breezy exit over the awkward double back.

John gave Rain a warm smooch and, passing around Gwen, took her hand and sat down on a kitchen stool just behind her. He played with his wife's hand lightly while the three of them talked, ignoring the dozen or so people out in the living room.

"So Dad, I was thinking about what you said at the opening about artworks and books and I just really don't see it. Unless you're talking about those massive, storytelling, narrative, formal paintings with troops and generals or tableaux…or maybe diptychs, triptychs…"

"No, no, no," John said. "I'm not talking at all about how they're read, or how they're received…or, or their *literary content* for God's sake. I'm talking about the experience of making the thing. The discovery and the pleasure I'm talking about is the artist's."

Rain was stopped short by this, realizing that she approached her work acquisitively. She painted what she liked to see, shapes she found appealing and mysterious to look at. She painted like she was shopping.

John watched his daughter and twiddled Gwen's fingers.

"And what will you be doing this fall?" Gwen asked.

Rain sighed and looked away again. "Yup," she said, gathering up a tray and poking at the crackers on it. "That would be England. That's what the man said, Gwen."

"He's going. I'm asking YOU."

"Well, Gwen, we're married—remember that whole thing?"

Gwendolyn took a long, quiet look at Rain. "You come see me on Tuesday," she said. "We're going to order lunch in and we're going to talk."

Rain looked past her. "Daddy…what is she up to?"

"Good job tonight, girls," John Morton said innocently. "The show was fantastic. It looked great."

"Are you on her side?" Rain asked.

"I don't side. My single priority is happiness. And love. And trust. And another scotch."

He held out his empty glass.

The storage warehouse of the Museum of Modern Art in Queens was made available to scholars, critics and historians both for viewing art and for reading the impressive collection of papers— not just letters and journals of the artists, but those of important collectors, curators, critics and contributors as well.

Rain had developed the habit of coming along with Karl when he had access to places like this. Even though his paternalistic teacherliness had eased up over the last couple of years, the habit had remained and it was an easy partnering they played out in this space. A nice relief from the progression toward the matched judgmentalism and rebellion they'd begun to develop.

They stood before a great, looming Frank Stella. All neon colors and cartoonish black outlines, it was sculptural and dwarfing. Karl was checking notes, distracted and only glancing at the artwork. Rain was respectful and transfixed.

"It's just so huge," she said.

Karl closed his eyes to cover an eye-roll. He pinched his brow and said with a sigh, "Very insightful."

Rain was nicked by his sarcasm, but pressed on nonetheless. "No, I mean he's almost doing something with the sheer size of it. I feel like it's a dare."

"There's plenty written about Stella," Karl said impatiently. "I can lend you some Danto if you like."

"I know that stuff," Rain defended herself. "It's just occurring to me looking at it. Being swallowed up by it."

"'All that *stuff*'," Karl quoted her with clear exasperation. "'*All that stuff*', yeah…"

Rain was taken aback. "Jesus, you're mean lately."

Karl let the arm holding his notebook flop against his leg.

"Well how else do you expect an art critic who is about to give a lecture this evening on Derridas and the End of Millennia Politics of the New to respond to a comment like that?" He picked up his prop again, studying it as though in a pantomime. "Honestly, Rainie," he said, shaking his head rather dramatically.

Rain walked away from him momentarily, then returned to the enormous painting. It was monstrous, bright, jutting out at the viewer aggressively, while the sloppy expressive brushwork and cartoonish forms maintained a degree of humor. It was almost slapstick, on an aggressive scale.

Rain cocked her head. "It's just…I can't articulate what I'm thinking. I'm just not getting it across."

"Uhm-hmmm." More note taking. "The most famous novelist of this century for a father and she can't put her thoughts into words," Karl looked up at her and grinned, happy again. "Poor kid." He chucked her chin with his notebook.

Rain gave a little crumple, like a slight release on a marionette.

Karl had her back where he felt most comfortable. Rain slightly self-conscious and embarrassed, himself jocular and generous toward her.

"Just keeping you honest," he said, unable to suppress an enormous smile.

"Okay," Rain assembled her thoughts. "Okay. It just makes me think about how art…making the physical objects that are art… and then valuing them in the way that we do in museums… It all seems such a stab at immortality. Such a gut response against obliteration."

"I mean, Stella being important enough to be in the Modern and the Hirschhorn and wherever else—even when he's wrapped up in plastic and shoved into the sub-basement, his work is something formidable. Something somebody is going to have to deal with. Do you see what I mean?"

Karl's smile had shrunk almost imperceptibly. From the inside. "Sure. You're concerned about the janitors around here." Back came the smile.

"Know what? You're an asshole lately," Rain turned away from him and started walking toward the door.

Karl laughed. "Now that was articulate," he said, lunging toward her. "Jeez, what happened to your sense of humor, Rainie-lee?" Reaching her, Karl gripped her shoulders and jiggled her out through a side door into the next room.

They passed into an enormous gallery in the display area, a room presently filled with a monumental Franz Klein.

Rain stopped in front of it and whispered, "Oh, I adore this. It makes me so jealous."

Karl's expression turned professional. "Yes, well, your little, sloppy, dark tracks, those are… You keep at those, make a few important ones, flesh out the ideas you've been stabbing at and you'll get your first real show at Shuldenfrei."

"You think he'd give me a show?" Rain turned. "Really?"

Karl nodded. "Black, scrubby, angsty, maybe a little bigger. A BODY of them and sure…"

"It sounds pathetic, but I really want that, you know?" Rain said. "My own show."

Karl took her by the shoulders from behind. "Just don't go this big."

"Are you speaking as an art critic?" she asked playfully.

"I'm speaking as an art critic who has to live with this stuff. You are my Frank Stella…" he intoned, nuzzling her, "and I am that janitor!"

Rain finally joined him laughing.

If you had asked Rain why she switched from representation to abstraction in her artwork, she would have described a process of distillation, a feeling of discovery and fresh attention that the abstractions provided her, and just plain liking the results. She might have even dug around for some theory and history depending on who you were and how much you were aware of the conversation of art and the continuing progression of it through time.

She would never have mentioned her husband's response to her work, never would have acknowledged the extremity of her reaction to him when they first met, particularly since she had excused herself with the fact that she'd alighted upon abstraction just *before* she met him.

Rain had gone directly from college to art school the following September after her graduation. It seemed like something she'd always meant to do. The next step. Her work was good. She had built a decent portfolio in college even though her major was philosophy, not art. She just moved on to the School of Visual Arts after college as though following elementary school with junior high. It was just what happened the next year.

Some of the classes were good, and she was glad to have the opportunity to get in a little bit of art history and theory that she'd missed in college, not having wanted to sully her direct experience of art-making with too much academic tooth-gnashing quite yet. So of course, partly in response to the truly naïve and almost charmingly blind enthusiasm of manifestos like the Futurists (*Number 1. We want to sing the love of danger, the habit of energy and rashness. Number 2. The essential elements of our poetry will be courage, audacity and revolt.*), which actually made her feel that she should bring a little more courage and audacity and less irony and sly wit to her art. There had been too much of that rebellion among her peers in school, she thought, it being the basis for all their humor and the way they dealt with each other. In that art-school-mobius-strip kind of logic, Rain took what she knew, inverted it, laid it up against the past, inverted both and then indeed inverted the inversions until she'd emptied content and emotion and the human hand from her work. All this reading and critiquing and looking caused Rain to revisit the whole question of what she'd set about to do with all those brushes and paints and flat surfaces.

What resulted, rather than the very competent and increasingly individualistic portraiture she'd been engaging in previously, was a nesting instinct, hiding the unprotected open portraits she'd produced while in high school and college and painting in utterly unrepresentative feeling-texture and dehumanization. An insectification, if you will, of her results on canvas. At first she knew that it was a matter of hiding, of trying to be more cagey, more opaque than the slightly vulnerable faces she used to paint. It was during a show called "floors and ceilings" to which Rain had submitted two large works involving a great deal of impasto and encaustic on corner-shaped triptychs, that she caught the eye of the very cultish professor of Post-Modernism. His field was of course the faddish perpetually "new" European philosophy, which was satisfyingly tricky enough to make it the perfect mainstay of art philosophy in academia.

Karl Madlin was thirty, about the same height as Rain. He wore his hair long and bound in back. His tiny, wire-rimmed specs played against the athleticism of his body to sign *intellectual*. He liked to play the nerd with his students and frequently broke into very pleased smiles to reward the most imitative thinking. But he graded hard, which, bad-mommy-style, just deepened his students' attachment.

Having Karl Madlin show up at your group show and spend a lot of time in front of your work was, in that very sealed and particular society of art school, the precise equivalent of stumping the physics professor. It was impressing the unimpressable. And it gave all of Rain's formerly uninterested colleagues a slow, shocked head-turn toward her, metaphorically speaking.

Meeting Rain finally, later in the evening (Rain had fervently avoided that side of the room at the opening), Karl took her hand in his and looked deep into her eyes saying he just wanted to see what was in there. She later thought he might have been high that night, or possibly being sarcastic, or both, even though he smoked very little in the time she knew him. But he invited her along with some of his doctoral students to Cedar Tavern, the famous abstract expressionists' bar, saying that he wanted to see what she soaked up out of the place.

Rain knew, of course, that this Cedar Tavern, while furnished with much of the same worn-out looking furniture and bar as the old place, was actually a few blocks away from the original Cedars where deKooning and his wife fought, where Pollock was banned from the place for tearing down the men's room door, and Kerouac likewise for peeing into an ashtray. But she kept this close to the vest, watching the acolytes fawning desperately and feeling grateful she didn't need to impress Madlin for grades so that she could freely appreciate his unusual manners and sharp mind. There was a lot of studiously relaxed art banter that evening, Rain purposefully opting out of it. The excuse of being an art maker and not an art talker being eagerly swallowed by those theory students who believed artists were rarely regular, living, breathing human beings, but rather historic figures. That is, dead.

Madlin, on the other hand, kept trying to draw out her opinions. Rain knew he was flirting with her, but she couldn't tell whether he was really interested in what she had to say, or was just trying to tease her among all these well-rehearsed, walking art encyclopedias.

"So Rain," he said, ignoring some or other pithy remark aimed at him by his worshipers, "I want to understand what your piece was saying, why I was so drawn to it."

"'Why not try to understand the song of a bird...?'" Rain quoted with an embarrassing directness.

Madlin widened his eyes at her. Although he knew this was a quote and remembered that there was something charmingly mischievous about it, he did not recall that this was how Picasso had impishly insulted a critic, while elevating art to a natural phenomenon. Nobody else knew the quote, and would not have been able to place it, this being before the days of Google and wireless PDAs. They didn't dare actually ask, and since Madlin ran with it, they all nodded knowingly as though they knew it well, too. This marked a turning point in the evening. Madlin would later tell her it cemented his attraction to her, but perhaps it was his slight discomfiture in not knowing the source on the spot that linked him to her so tightly that night.

"Indeed," Madlin said. "Indeed! 'We love the night and flowers without trying to understand them...' something like that, right? Mmm-hmmm, very good. Tell that to the astronomer and the botanist!"

"I agree," Rain said, smiling down into her beer, a watery lager in a thick, heavy mug. Madlin poured her some more. "But their equivalent would be the academic critic, wouldn't it? Not the artist?"

"Touché!" Madlin bellowed. "But why, oh, lord, why," he intoned, very Orson Welles at this point in the evening (it was getting late and there had been a number of pitchers and as many defectors), "why would anyone want to mark canvas without a thought as to why they were doing it? Really, I want to know."

The most fawning of the students, a guy named Thom who left the program soon after Rain and Karl hooked up, sat forward and continued on that line. "Honestly, the horror of the *everyone can be an artist*," he sneered. "The disservice it metes on the world. I'd like to take every high school art teacher and force some Derridas down her delicate little throat. Just a taste. One lit-tle taste, dearie!" He ground a fist into his other hand sadistically, and Rain noted that he failed to meet her eye every time she spoke.

"I'm not sure what's wrong with that," Rain said. "Why not let the infinite number of monkeys keep on typing if you might get that one Hamlet?"

"That's what I'm saying! You'll never find it!" he exclaimed, literally hopping in his seat but speaking to Karl rather than to Rain.

"Again, that's *your* problem, isn't it?" Rain asked, also directing her comments to Karl. "That's your job."

"That makes no sense," Thom continued, whining now. "No sense at all. You cannot possibly be part of the conversation of art if you have no idea what you're saying."

Rain plunked her heavy mug down, empty. "Okay there," she said. She'd been there a long time too. With the bang of the glass, everyone at the table focused on her, and Rain plowed on ahead bravely.

"I mean, yes, I want to join in that conversation, that's who I'm listening to, that's who makes sense to me, it's them, the artists from history that I'm aiming toward in a way. But think about it. There you are at the table with Rembrandt, Titian, line 'em all up, all up through Picasso, there's Pollock, deKooning, Schnabel! for God's sake, whoever, the shark guy, you know, earthworks, all of them, and suddenly it's your turn to speak," Rain paused dramatically. "All heads turn to you. Burning gazes, the whole thing. But to have it count, to actually make a meaningful contribution at *that* table it would *have* to be original, wouldn't it? And honest? Something you were brave enough to blurt out, all your own, coming from what makes you original and unique…and so if you succeed… If you succeed, wouldn't it have to make NO sense to them at all? Wouldn't it have to be new in some sense? So it's really not up to them or the people who study them to know if what you're making now has any relevance or matters or *ranks*…with them, you know?"

"So, then nothing matters, whatever goes, whatever you want to slap on a canvas…" Thom began.

"No, no, no," Rain was saying, finally having to raise her voice to interrupt him. "NO! Honesty and originality are the most essential qualities a human being can muster! Those qualities make us human, provoke passion and awakening and when they are first articulated, they are invariably…" she cast around, sputtering, "*insipid* and *false* to the establishment!" Rain was practically yelling now, the bottomless mug of beer finally having gone to her head. And she couldn't have cared less what these people thought of her, that she was lecturing basics to Ph.D. candidates. "Every loosening in art that we value with millions at auction today was seen as utter dreck when the paint was still wet. It's whoever was honest enough to hear you, it's whether THEY put you at the table or not. Whether anybody then has anything to say to YOU."

"Relativist bullshit," Thom was muttering, but Karl was smiling at her charmingly.

It was just the three of them left at the table now and Karl turned to Thom pointedly and said, "Well, I'll be seeing you tomorrow, then," and just waited for him to leave. His leaving, of course, being a little more thorough than Karl meant it to be, but no less than he intended right at that moment.

It wasn't long after that night that Rain dropped out of art school and moved in with Karl. She'd found all she needed in terms of art instruction and support from him. His fierce narcissism and self-centeredness widened to include her for many of their years together, so she mistook his self-regard for support and his snobbiness for belief in her. He made her dizzy with his attention and his passion, but in front of her friends and other people who loved her, he was always a bit strange and jealous.

The very fact that Rain rented a studio outside her home was an enormous luxury. Even its marginal neighborhood and ugly five-story walk-up couldn't mar the over-indulgence it represented. Most artists in the city lived in their studios, with the more successful ones perhaps earning walls between the bed and the easel, sometimes only a few more feet of space.

That she had one was enviable enough, but that her father paid for it was something that Rain would never admit, even to her closest friends, though most of those who knew about her studio suspected it. Few of her friends even knew about the place since she never brought people there. It wasn't that Rain was shy to show her work; in fact, she brought most finished pieces back to the apartment she shared with Karl and even hung some of them there. It had nothing to do with the state she kept the studio in or the unfinished works. It was simply a sense of proportion. To most of her friends, it would be have been like screeching to a stop in a Lamborghini right in front of their lopsided old ten-speeds. They would have been impressed and complimentary, but some part of her suspected they might wonder if she deserved it.

The studio rental was a wedding present from her father, arranged by Gwendolyn, who could always perfectly carry out whatever her husband conceived. John Morton knew Rain's fiercest wishes. Though Gwen disliked Karl from the very beginning and held dark and pessimistic ideas about pursuing any aspect of art as a career—art-making darkest of all—she dutifully found and stocked Rain's first studio magnificently. She thought it would provide a soon-to-be, much-needed escape from the controlling and small-minded man Rain insisted upon marrying so young.

Though Gwen had told Karl that the gift was really just for Rain, he was emphatic about coming along to see it. The appointment at the courthouse was still days away, but Karl and Rain had both taken time off from work to get ready and have a few small gatherings in preparation for the big day.

John's heart condition counter-indicated the five-floor walk up, so he waited for them in the car while Gwen led them to the over-painted glossy black door. It and the jamb were bejeweled with odd buzzers, locks, a tiny camera lens and a peephole.

As Gwen pulled open the door to the tune of its soon-familiar metallic sigh, Rain took close note of the air. It was a smell she would come to associate with working there. A fragrance that would unknot her stomach and loosen her shoulders. It was clean and faintly aromatic and yet had a kind of fresh antiquity to it. Like an opened pyramid, the small entry and stairwell suggested untold riches inside maybe this chamber, maybe that one.

Gwen pointed out a mailbox.

"Why would she need that?" Karl asked.

"I'm sure it just comes with the place," Rain said.

"That's right," Gwen said, heading up the stairs at her usual quick clip.

It was the first door on the fifth floor. The flight above was just a small landing and a door onto the rooftop. Gwen worked her way through the array of keys and pushed in the door to the freshly painted space. It smelled of spackle and latex and looked like a miniature of a Hitchcock set. One of those north-facing, slanted walls of paned windows with a narrow balcony outside it. The view of the airshaft was nothing to speak of, but the wall of windows itself was breathtaking. The interior space was tiny. About ten by twelve feet. There was running water, a small counter over a cabinet, and a bar-sized refrigerator.

"Gwen!" Rain breathed as she walked into it.

Karl followed silently.

"Gwen, it's so beautiful!" Rain exclaimed.

Gwen walked over to the easel that Rain hadn't even noticed yet. It reached right up almost to the top of the ten-foot ceiling. Well oiled and substantial, it had a metal rack arching overhead with three spotlights fixed on it. A high tripod with a board atop it and an adjustable padded stool stood with it. "It's used," Gwen said, smiling. "That's good luck."

"Oh, my…" Rain stammered, struck speechless as she examined the complicated workings of the easel, taking in the impossible perfection of this little space. A tall set of shelves stood by the door on a short expanse of wall, but the other two walls were left bare. Another bank of spotlights dropped down on wires from the ceiling in front of the easel, which could be swiveled in any direction. Rain tried the light switches. "Gwen!" Rain said again.

Karl shook his head.

Gwen opened the little refrigerator and retrieved a half bottle of Veuve Cliquot from it. The little fridge was stacked tight with water bottles, this thoroughness being a Gwen trademark. Two plastic champagne flutes stood on the counter. "You two can share one," Gwen said, working the wires on the top.

Karl let out a little laugh. He sat on the stool, swiveling back and forth. "Don't you think she should be sure this was what she wants first?"

"I have no idea what you mean, Karl," Gwen said dryly as she handed Rain a glass of champagne.

"I mean, she quit art school to work for you and suddenly a studio? Studios don't make the work, artists do."

"Karl…" Rain said.

"No, Karl," Gwen said. "Artists who are more than just conceptualists, and even sometimes those, need space in which to work. They are, after all, dealing with the corporeal. Objects take up space."

Rain interrupted them. "It's more than I ever dreamed of, Gwen. Thank you so much!"

Gwen didn't look at Rain and said, "You do good work in here," with a pleased smile on her face.

"Is there a bathroom?" Karl asked.

"In the hall," Gwen replied.

"I just hope it doesn't jinx her," Karl said.

"The bathroom?" Rain asked.

"The big, intimidating studio," Karl said, mock innocently. "It's like the prize before the work has begun."

"These are tools…" Gwen began, in a tired voice.

"I'll be fine, Karl," Rain interrupted her. "You'll see."

Much to Karl's pressed-mouth surprise, Rain worked long hours in her studio. In a strange way that she didn't like to acknowledge to herself, Karl's disapproval fueled her focus and perseverance. It provided something her father's uncritical and constant approval didn't; motivation and a desire to prove herself. Really, she thought she was trying to prove herself to her father who so unwaveringly approved of everything about her, that she almost felt selfish in her push to achieve this.

Karl's charms were reserved for Rain alone. He was abrasive and contrary with other people, but could be quite unabashedly loving and worshipful when they were alone. Their intimate life was a lazy game for her, Karl's passionate enthusiasm doing the work for both of them. The fact that her friends found Karl prickly and uncomfortable provided Rain with the perfect barrier between herself and the entertaining assortment of good friends she adored. It was a way to separate herself and give herself the time and devotion her art demanded, without having actually to make those claims about her time's value herself.

Rain found Karl's irritability merely curmudgeonly and amusing and only very occasionally did his condescension touch her at all. Sometimes she wondered if this meant she was hugely egotistical, but she knew that her friends (and probably most strangers who encountered them together), saw her as a victim to his superiority and control.

Years of work had left Rain's studio filled up and richly messy. The shelves were piled high with supplies, the fridge held a more motley assortment of food and drink and the walls were covered with images ripped from magazines, postcards collected from museums, her own sketches, fields of color taped up next to each other.

Though she'd known about it for several months, the reality of the end of this studio was fast approaching. The building had been sold and was slated for destruction. The entire block had finally been purchased by a single developer who had patiently fought years of rent-stabilized apartment dwellers and a little old tiny sliver of a building whose owner wouldn't budge for decades, leading him to consider incorporating the little shoe repair shop's building into the plans for his high-rise. The old man had finally died heirless, and the plans fell into place quickly afterward. It was part of the reason Rain had so readily agreed to go to England with Karl for the fall. She would move out of the studio, take the few months in England and then deal with finding a new space when she got back.

Now there was an air of tragedy around her studio. This place she'd been most herself. This home.

The smells: turp, mineral spirits and the earthy-nutty scent of paint glopped straight from the tube, along with the high note of linseed oil that lays over all the others—these were home. Even when Rain was low and uncertain and sure that she had nothing whatever to offer to the world, there were seventy-five things she could do in her studio to soothe her and make her feel like she was doing something right.

If she was not already in the middle of a piece, there was the pleasant busy work of stretching a new canvas or gessoing.

Gessoing was Rain's favorite. The craft elements of the work were so satisfying. They had built-in and easy-to-achieve goals. She knew with certainty whether she'd succeeded at her task. Bubbling and rippling were failures. Slack fabric, off-square corners, missed spots—all these were clear failures. Success became humbly invisible, but once achieved, gave her a sense of a proper arena within which to freely take risks.

This started with simply gathering up her materials; poking at the hardening lumps of paint on her palette with the palette knife, adding fresh dollops of whatever colors were low or too dry, picking this and that brush, round tapered filberts, flat square brights, tiny rounds and riggers, pouring out solvents and supports into little metal cups, adjusting lights or angling the canvas to catch the daylight from the big windows, changing the music. This last was key, a big part of creating the mood of whatever piece she was working on. She could still hear what she was listening to when she saw her old paintings. She'd typically crank up all the albums that Karl couldn't stand when she was alone in her studio. King Crimson. The White Stripes. The Tom Tom Club. *La Traviata*, extra loud. The Sugarcubes. All her yell-along music. Music she rode during the hours she worked.

When she felt intensely anti-Karl, Rain got out the series of small self-portraits she had continued making over the years she had known him, despite his deep disdain for realism. These, especially, she knew he'd have hated, paintings of herself looking odd, dark, angry and lopsided. Somewhat Lucien Freud, with a bit of Ralph Steadman. Not quite Francis Bacon, but getting there. It was something she considered a peculiar little habit, for those days when she needed to exert something individual and independent. Paintings of a woman no one would want to own or control. Paintings of a need-free quirky character, each on a six-by-six inch block of wood, each one created wet, in one session, with little planning beyond whatever gush of emotion she might have been coping with that day, they were beginning to add up in the drawer where she tucked them away to dry. Rain didn't consider them any part of her "real art" so she didn't allow them to amount to anything; they were more a kind of diary.

On the wall behind her easel, Rain had tacked up the encrusted paint she occasionally peeled off the glass of her palette. In the three years she had inhabited her studio, she had produced eight such constructions and they told the story of her materials. Alizarin Crimson, True Ultramarine, Cerulean Blue, Hansa Yellow Deep, Raw Sienna, Burnt Sienna, Burnt Umber, Viridian Green. These were arrayed along two sides of the rectangle and then blended, bent and zagged toward various browns and blacks in the center and toward the larger globs of Ivory Black and Titanium White on opposite ends.

They were abstracts, worked in an honest, time-consuming and organic way. Rain sometimes stared at them in wonder. There was a kind of perfection in a palette. A purity of potential and intention unsullied by intelligence and effort. Free of the ruin of concept or affectation but full of the richness of human touch.

Once on her "real art" canvases, Rain's colors all tended toward mud. She worked the paint like a sculptor, adding, shaping, pushing, contouring, adding some more. So the palette had something she tried to achieve in her intentional work. An honesty and a purity that her hand ruined.

The work was not going smoothly. She was distracted thinking about Karl and the fall. Heading off to England. How she'd do there. Rain never liked England, though Gwen and John went almost every summer and she had visited them there often.

From home Rain loved England and all things English. She had watched the Royal Wedding at two o'clock in the morning with one of her nannies when she was only five. She loved tea and biscuits, Jane Austen, all the BBC shows and British movies, loved Shakespeare and many of her favorite authors were British or at least partly so. But somehow every time she went to England she found herself speaking her American accent with a self-conscious exaggeration, flinching at the derision that seemed to flow toward her from even the most charming of citizens. Brits she met had such a good-natured way of delivering their condescension, like they just wanted to watch how well you could bear it. Not well in Rain's case, it turns out. Rain never particularly thought of herself as an American—it just wasn't high on her list of self-modifiers— but abroad she found she took it on as a fierce mantle. More abhorrent to her than the way Americans were treated in Europe, however, was the smarmy, effete denial many of them affected regarding their own ingredients while they were there. Like they had baked up a lobster with eggs and flour.

Rain liked the French better. They were less interested in Americans and more interested in all things American, which added up to a grudging respect with a cover of utter disregard. This contrasted wholly with the disdain masked by teasing attention usually dealt her by Brits, especially during her teen-aged tan-and-blonde years. France was a much more comfortable arrangement as far as Rain was concerned. Having grown up in New York City, she found a similar gruff positivity in their manner and treatment of tourists.

It had been almost eight years since her last trip to England. And really, she wasn't sure she wanted to experience that treatment while being there as the *Mrs*. It seemed wrong to stay in New York while Karl spent months away in London, though, and too depressing to deal with the end of this studio. But the more she thought about it, the more she grudgingly admitted to herself that Gwen might have been right.

Rain was washing out her brushes. It was no use trying to work when she was feeling this out of sorts. It was too sad knowing this would be one of her last days working here.

But four months without her husband? That seemed awfully long. She wasn't sure if their relationship was strong enough to put up with that stretch. They'd been together now almost eight years and yet she still found Karl attractive. He had an itchy pull on her; she was not sure what it was. His needling and then the sudden odd and unexpected throes of passionate attention were some kind of addictive combination to her. He was a skilled and purely attentive lover, but he kept her guessing and often played games with her expectations. Rain wondered whether this was maybe a formula for a long-lasting, healthy intimate life. However passive her friends might have considered her role, had they known anything about it, there was nothing formulaic about her and Karl's connection. Nothing boring or predictable.

Karl, bare-chested, half covered in a sheet, his twinkling eyes large and strikingly blue without his glasses, his lips full and moist, like fat plums.

Rain covered her palette with a sheet of waxed paper, screwed on the tops of a few open tubes of paint, dried off the brushes she'd left in the sink with paper towels. She checked and buckled up her leather backpack.

Karl smiles and rolls on top of her, going in for her neck.

Rain tugged her bag up over one shoulder and strolled through the West Village. Their apartment building was at Lafayette and 4th Street. Just about equidistant from Parsons where Karl taught and the School of Visual Arts from where Karl had plucked her, had directed her work, narrowed it, taught her so much more than art school could have, challenged her, pushed her, gave her passion and focus and clarity without the suspect motivation of running a business—art school being, he always said, useful for graphic artists, illustrators and technicians at printing companies (oh, his disdain for his employers ran pretty deep) but pointless for someone with something real to contribute to art history.

Karl strokes the curve of her waist, down along her jutting hipbone...

As she pushed open the door to their apartment, Rain could hear a rustling from the bedroom. She dropped her keys on the table by the door and her bag on the floor underneath. Maybe the sound was coming from the back elevator next to the kitchen. It was an old building and the back elevator still worked for half of the apartments. It was used mostly for trash and deliveries, but otherwise not very often.

"Hello? You home?" Rain called out, heading toward the kitchen.

Karl groaned from the bedroom.

Rain turned back toward the bedroom. There Karl was, lying all rumpled in the bed. He rolled over huffily as she entered the room. He wasn't wearing his glasses.

"Oh, you poor thing..." Rain said. She leaned in to touch Karl's face and he turned crankily away.

Rain was used to his behavior by then. He was such a baby when he got sick. She smiled at him, anyway. "Do you need anything?" she asked him.

"Where have you been? I'm dying here," Karl said, invoking the blame-equals-innocence effect.

"At the studio," Rain said, giving him a look. "Was that the elevator?"

"I thought you were supposed to have lunch with Gwen today," Karl said.

"I am," Rain said. "I'm heading over there in a few minutes. I just couldn't concentrate this morning—I've got this strange feeling. I'm anxious or something. I can't think why."

As she sat down on the bed next to him, Karl rose abruptly. "I'm going to take a bath," he said.

He stood naked from the bed and tromped into the bathroom. His rubbery, aging behind stayed in her mind. Images sometimes sparked their meaning in ways she didn't grasp immediately—little things like Karl didn't normally sleep naked—but the image bestowed itself instead simply as an image: an aging man whose work was not physical, his yellow ass cheeks heading south, darkened unpleasantly with black hairs between them, but the graceful beauty of still loving the man who bears them. Wasn't that the contradiction? It was an image of multilayered subtlety and Rain wasn't raised to see the obvious. Karl slammed the bathroom door.

"You know London?" Karl said, shouting from behind the door to her and then he was silent. Rain thought the air in the room was musty and close and started to straighten the bed.

He hadn't said anything else, so Rain shouted back, "Yeah?"

Karl poked his head out of the bathroom. "I was thinking London was going to be a huge bore for you. Maybe Gwen's right: maybe you should just stick around the States and set up a new studio this fall." He watched her as she smoothed the sheets, looking around for the top sheet. "You know, get that show ready?" he said.

Rain stopped and straightened up, looking at him. He'd said magic words. Her show. But she asked, "You don't want me to go?"

"No!" Karl shouted in exasperation and slammed the door. And then he opened it again. He paused and said, "I thought you wanted to be an artist."

He must really be sick, Rain was thinking. He wasn't usually this frustrated without some precipitating event. Every little thing was irritating him. This was what his intense involvement in her career had come to. No longer pulling but pushing. The challenge of hope he created in her morphing into a threat now.

Rain grabbed up a pillow, turned her back to him and muttered, "I guess that I thought what I…"

Karl interrupted her. "I mean, how much work can you get done in London, anyway? And here's your last chance to be in the studio and instead you come home…" Karl left that one hanging, playing with the door handle. "I just need to know, are you really going to be an artist or do you just like talking about it."

He may have purposefully been trying to start an argument, and with this he succeeded gloriously. Even though Rain knew he was stomping on all her triggers, she had been kicked in her most sensitive spot now.

"YOU talk about it," Rain said, turning back to face him.

"Yeah, well, Rain, criticism is my job and what you talk about is making art and that is just not the same thing, is it?" Karl took hold of the door again, ready to shut it, a tight smile gripping his face. "Honestly, I'm just trying to help you. Most artists would gnaw off their left arm for a summer group show at Gwendolyn Brooker. If you're just going to let this show drop…"

"Look, just SAY if you don't want me in London, alright?" Rain threw down the pillow she was holding. Just as it hit the floor, the phone started to ring.

Rain was momentarily confused by the sound. She didn't usually fight back with Karl and it gave her a terrible feeling of vertigo. It was as if the pillow hitting the floor had burst into rings. The second ring snapped her out of her daze and she grabbed the phone.

The little green screen on the phone read a familiar number and Rain purposefully plastered a smile on her face as she answered it, "I'm on my way! I'll be right there…"

She listened.

"What happened?"

Listened.

"When?"

Listened.

"Well, what did they say?"

Listened.

"How long?"

Listened.

"I'm coming. Which hospital?"

Listened.

"Sit tight, Gwen, I'll be right there. Do you need anything?"

BLUE

No ocean deep could hold this sorrow
No midnight sky could wear this hue
I bow my head, pray for tomorrow
and I cry the deepest blue.

—AL HEMBERGER

W hile "the blues" is probably the most easily identified color emotion, blue in art can often have the opposite effect. It can burst from the canvas in a clean field of beauty. Blue is, of course, the heavens, but it is also the well-established color of the Virgin Mother and all of the purity and innocence that she embodies. In language, blue has its connotations of innocence. A reliable friend is true blue. A flash of innocent eyes are baby blues, since babies' blue eyes might only last a couple of months before they go green or gray or brown. So blue is innocent, genuine, holy and clean, but also dark, depressed and violent.

Blue has had one of the most dramatic of histories in art materials. Egyptian blue, which kept the murals in Pompeii grand and bright over millennia, was made from a simple enough recipe of copper, calcium, sand and salt, heated to 830 degrees Fahrenheit. The all-important specific methods of its preparation were lost some time between 200 and 700 C.E. However, once discovered, other blues took its place. The blue of the Madonna's robes in all the most spectacular frescoes in Italy is the precious crushed lapis, Ultramarine. *Extreme blue.* Lapis lazuli is a beautiful stone, streaked and mottled with gold. While this works to advantage in jewels, bringing a complementary depth and glint to the stone, in paint, that silica will dull the blue. In 1437, Cennino Cennini, the Plato of art materials, described the method for purifying Ultramarine: the powdered lapis should be kneaded under a weak lye solution in a dough of wax, pine rosin, linseed oil and gum mastic. The dough hangs on to the silica, the calcite and the pyrite of the beautiful gold streaks, while the purest blue particles settle out in the solution.

Yves Klein eventually demonstrated that there was a blue bluer than blue, but his was more a method than a new hue; pure Ultramarine in a resin medium of his invention which avoids the previously inevitable contamination of the pigment by its supporting oil, egg or glue. There are, of course, dozens of distinct blues we can identify, though many artists create them from nothing more than one good Ultramarine combined with whites and breaths of other tones to pull from it. A standard palette will include at least two blues, the cooler Ultramarine and perhaps a Cerulean, the warm, greenish blue made from cobaltous chloride and potassium stannate. Combined with silica and calcium sulphate, washed and heated, it becomes the only blue without any violet, and thus an important player on any palette.

Lucy Wilkinson enjoyed her body more and more as she aged. Turning fifty that year had been strangely liberating. Strange only since she'd been so unhappy at the turning of her last two decade markers, both occasions having been the crux of one crisis or another. The birth of her son on the first and the devastating split of her third marriage on the second. But now, stretching out on her lover's empty bed in his quaint Hudson River house, she thought she must finally have gotten this thing right. She even suspected there was a little bit of the masculine sense of freedom and, *bien sûr*, an ultimately Buddhist spirit of non-ownership in her relationship with James Morrow. The things that were meaningful to her—her yoga practice, her ongoing healing with her grown son, her various women's groups—these were her true heart's connections. They took a place apart from her sexuality, though of course, the yoga did sneak into it a little.

She might say she was just here for the sex, but it seemed to her that she and James had a beautifully "skillful" relationship, to use another of her yogic terms. Evolved. Lucy's maturity was thrilling to her, especially since her carefully minimal food intake and her vigorous teaching schedule kept her body toned like an eighteen-year-old's. This physical confidence and pleasure was something she hadn't been blessed with as a teenager or a young woman. Finding it now, even though her face had loosened and her hair was wiry with grays, was like a consolation prize worth far more than the dangled carrot you were supposed to have wanted in the first place.

Better, since the pleasures of attractiveness were such a double-edged sword for a young woman. By spending her teens, twenties and even up through much of her forties increasingly plump, Lucy suspected that she'd taken down one of the pillars of her beauty on purpose since all it ever brought her was insult and pain. Uncaring lovers looking only for conquests, jealousy and insults from other women and that leering false interest and utter dismissal from elders. These last two were attitudes in which she always promised herself she would never indulge. The respect and directness she employed when dealing with others in the studio where she taught may have been partly responsible for her elevated status there, where most of the other teachers and students were much younger women.

Now that she had little jowls and crows feet and those unruly gray curls, Lucy could embrace her sexuality and attractiveness. Age brought her another pillar down, societally speaking, but this demotion somehow made her feel braver and stronger, rather than simply shut out, the way her fat had.

Though James was not her only partner, he was her most regular. She kept her other relations to one-night stands, usually with other yoga teachers on retreat, those opportunities for combined enlightenment, tantric practice and the "letting go of attachment" being too good to pass up. Those isolated incidents were a bit of a game, she knew, both for her and for these men, who were invariably quite a bit younger than she—usually married, vaguely homosexual or in committed relationships. There was plenty of experimentation and the occasional group session, but she didn't go on retreats too often, as maintaining that perfectly balanced detachment was sometimes difficult in the face of the dangerously contagious exhibitionism so rampant there.

With James there was nothing to have to pretend. They had an ease together, James expecting so little of her, and allowing her to conquer him at each of their twice-monthly meetings. Once she came on to him, he would come back at her voraciously enough, but he was passive until she'd moved on him. In fact, he had been quite unperturbed by the one companionably unsexual evening they'd spent together. Lucy had done it to test him, to get a feel for what he might do, and though by their next date he did seem particularly energetic, James was so easy with skipping the sex, that Lucy wondered whether she needed to complain. But then she brought her awareness to yet another level of appreciation for this relationship. No attachment. No expectations or whining or games or demands. Just what it was.

They had the routine whittled down to dinner at his place once a month when she came up to perform onsite physical therapy for his employees and in the city at her place between those visits. Their assignations were easy, slipped into like favorite slippers but no less energetic or pleasurable for that ease.

James would always rise early, make coffee, and get the Sunday paper from his porch or down at her corner deli, while Lucy committed her series of morning poses in the bedroom. When she joined him, James would poach them each an egg, his taken with buttered toast, hers with a teaspoon of wheat germ instead of the yolk, and they would indulge in another hour or so of the *Sunday Times*, "that great public bath," as Wolfe called it.

In the city, they might go to a movie or a play, walk around the Village or Soho, take in a few galleries. In the country, they might take a drive, go to an apple orchard or a regional food or antiques festival. Sometimes they planned these Sundays ahead, but mostly they would just flow into a day of companionship, suggested lightly by one of them from something they'd come across in the paper.

Always they'd take their leave of each other with a kiss and a date for their next meeting, rarely the following week, rarely more than two weeks on.

Lucy's sense of their detachment from one another was exaggerated, however, and this became clear when she came downstairs on this particular morning to find James looking stricken at the breakfast table, no coffee, no eggs or toast. He seemed suddenly old, his jaw slack and his eyes watery and red.

"Oh, my God, are you alright?" Lucy asked, genuinely worried. He looked like he'd had an attack of some kind, and Lucy struggled to put down the very attached and unenlightened selfish worry that she'd be stuck caring for him if he'd had a stroke or something. *Be here now, be here now*, she chanted in her mind.

"Lucy," James said vaguely.

"Yes, James?" she asked.

"No, it's nothing, it's…" He trailed off here, rose and started to make the coffee and eggs. "I just lost track of time."

Lucy sat at the table and slid the paper he'd been reading over to her. The paper was folded to the obituaries page, with the headline *John Ray Morton, 72, Pulitzer Prize–Winning Author, Is Dead (From Page A1)* at the top. "Oh," she said, uncertainly. "Did you know him?"

"What?... Yes," James answered, unconvincingly on to the next task.

"He wrote *Danville's Mission*, right? And *Shoes...*? Something about shoes?"

"*Shoes of the Trumpeter.* Yes—"

Lucy sat in silence for a while, calculating what she knew of James' age. She was pretty sure he was still in his sixties. That number, that "72," coupled with the very *Times*-ian, rather bludgeonly "Is Dead" were indeed chilling, and Lucy was feeling a distinct distance growing between embracing getting older and her revulsion for that which age ultimately brings. She spent so much time around her younger colleagues, so careful to ignore their generational differences, that she had embraced, she realized, her age merely as a fashion statement, like dressing down pearls, rather than any kind of reality about time. After all, Lucy had achieved something of a rare feat by leaving behind the bodily unease of her youth, the aches and injuries her large body had foisted upon her, and had therefore fooled herself into appreciating this onset of age.

So James looking suddenly old, his colleagues beginning to appear in obituaries, this brought such an unwelcome feeling of fear and disgust upon Lucy, that she could feel the kitchen turning into a morgue. What she'd always seen as a peaceful Zen-like antiquity started to look gray and elderly, washed out and airless. She stood. She paced a moment. James seemed not to notice her agitation, perhaps being involved in his own thoughts of his lost friend.

"Was this..." Lucy began. "Was this a good friend of yours?" she asked.

"I wouldn't say…" James paused. He didn't turn around, but he ceased moving. "No. No, he was someone I knew once. He… he used to live up the road here."

Lucy's irrational fears began to abate just enough for the room to return to its normal hues. Though she'd successfully averted the panic attack, she surprised herself by being so thrown off by James' display of emotion. She'd flattered herself, in a way, that all of the routine and careful integrity of roles played were something she maintained for James' sake, rather than her own. But he seemed perfectly open to her in his silence and stillness, so unlike her catlike pacing and jittery nerves.

Deep breath. Sit again. Be with the feelings. Make note of the panic and let it pass on by. Another deep breath.

Rain and Karl waited in an elevator. Rain rested her head against the cool marble of the elevator wall. Karl was preoccupied. His eyes darted around.

"I don't want to talk about it," Rain said, tired.

"Asshole lawyers," Karl spat.

"His estate is complicated. They'll sort it out eventually," she said and then added a prickly, "Why do you care?"

"Rain," Karl began and, as the doors opened, he fell silent again. They walked out into a modern, all-glass lobby. The flat brilliance of the late summer day was magnified in this vast clear box.

As they left the building, Rain said flatly, "I want to walk."

Karl rolled his eyes. "Seventy-five blocks? Jesus, Rain."

"Seventy-five blocks," Rain said.

"I want to talk to you about the fall," Karl said taking her arm possessively. "I was thinking you might want to spend those months up at the cabin."

"You…" Rain stopped walking, but didn't look at him. She stared down at the concrete beneath her feet and said, "You what?"

"It's supposed to be valuable, and it'll be too cold to work on it by the time I get back…"

"Why?" Rain said. "Why would I…?"

"I just thought now that there's the cabin…"

"The *cabin*?" Rain sputtered. Now she looked at him. Karl reflexively let go of her arm. "It's not a *cabin*; it's a rotting shed out in the woods. I don't think anybody's lived there since I was a baby."

"So you'll spend some time chasing the raccoons out of the place, and by the time I'm back you'll have the perfect studio, and a nice little weekend place for us."

"I was going to paint in that place in London…"

"And why can't you paint there? Look, Rain, most artists…"

"Karl, please please please don't start with the lecturing right now. PLEASE please. I really can't take it." She started walking again.

"I was just going to say…"

"Please." Rain stopped and put her head into her hands, bracing herself for her husband's all-the-more-intense lecture. She knew asking him to spare her was futile—backfiring, most likely, but she couldn't stop herself. She knew what was coming: generous, superior instruction.

"Rain," Karl began with a cozy sigh, "most artists don't have cushy studios to work in. If you're really an artist, you're just thrilled just to have some time—to carve out every spare moment…"

"Most?" Rain demanded, uncharacteristically letting her irritation show. "Most you've ever heard of actually are supported, are helped and financed if they're going to make it at all."

"Oh, yeah, so they can produce a bunch of shit colorful la-di-da LANDscapes, right?" Karl said, heating himself up now. "I respect work that just HAS to be made, that the artist doesn't make just to show. Ambition, Rain, ambition is like a poison to art. All those things you want, that image you have of yourself preening around a pretty studio, it's poison, Rain. It gets you nothing. Maybe that's all you want, though, huh?" She knew he was pushing her in two directions at once, but the heat that it generated in her head didn't allow her to name it, to point out his double standards, the push-you-pull-me he foisted on her.

That familiar vertigo was beginning to wash over her, but Rain was grounded by the emptiness left in her father's absence. It kept her feet firmly planted in the New York sidewalk. Right there on the Upper East Side, in front of his lawyer's office.

"You…" Rain began, purposefully maintaining control in her voice, "haven't got any idea…what you're talking about. You don't know ANYthing about making art or being an artist or art or even being—" Rain waved bunny fingers in his face, "*arty.*"

Karl shoved his hands into his pockets, set his feet like he was getting comfortable and turned his face skyward in a here-we-go kind of pose.

"No," Rain said, keeping a finger up in his face. "Listen to me."

Karl looked at her past the finger.

"I tell you what, have a *great* time in London this fall and *don't* tell me what to do with my time!" And with that, she turned and walked quickly away from him.

"Oh, very good, Rain," Karl called after her. "Nice!"

Rain wore a black dress with a high-buttoned collar and short puff sleeves. It was a "not" dress. Not frumpy. Not revealing. Not too stylish. Not awful. Not the way she felt right now, however. She was in a daze, wandering through the National Arts Club alone among mostly elderly literary types who were chatting and munching hors d'oeuvres and sipping cocktails. She was moving around as though she was searching for someone. It kept people from trying to talk to her for the most part. The speaking to her that got through this grate seemed muted to her. Her own responses felt mute and flat, like she was speaking into a pillow.

Somebody, an old friend of his, more of a colleague probably: "He had a good life. It's a blessing he left so quickly— no pain…"

Rain looked at this old guy. Should have been him instead. "I wish he wasn't dead," she said at his face.

Another one: "You were very lucky. He adored you, you know," like he knew what the hell John Morton ever felt.

Rain said, "I do know, yes."

Another goddamn sad-sack but the bright-side-of-it-all face: "At least he didn't suffer."

Rain finally said, "I don't want him to be dead."

Everybody knew her Dad and now that he couldn't defend himself, they seemed to know all about the value of his life: "He lived such a full life, enjoyed it so very much. We should all…"

Rain said, "He shouldn't have died yet."

Different person, same goddamn thing: "It's alright, honey, it was his time. His life was good and it was long and he accomplished so much."

Cold, stoic, to all of them. To none of them. Not caring how raw this sounded, Rain said, "But I still need him."

Same lady, seemed to be under some delusion that this was an actual conversation: "You'll be alright," and actually patted Rain on the arm. "You'll be alright. Your mother…?"

"Died in childbirth," Rain said. "Excuse me." Rain realized she was enjoying making these people uncomfortable. Not a healthy sign of coping. Very immature on top of that. She left the room.

Stepping out onto a balcony, Rain looked down and saw Karl talking feverishly into a cell phone, pacing on the street in front of the building. Rain, numb from it all, turned and looked back into the room only to find Gwen laughing into the face of some overdressed man with that kind of glowing tan rich-guy skin complexion. Metrosexual and seventies. Ick.

Tears filled Rain's eyes as she watched her. Gwen caught Rain's glance and excused herself. Approaching Rain, she brought her familiar fragrance, a dress she'd worn with him, her makeup and her hair done beautifully and effortlessly as always.

"Rain," she gently scolded.

"He's not even cold yet," Rain blurted.

Gwen smiled and looked down. Patiently, she said, "I won't let you judge me. I'm very clear about your father and me. I adored him. I am who I am and one of the greatest things your father did for me was to love me as I am."

Rain snapped, "He had bad taste."

Gwen smiled and leaned against the stone wall of the balcony alongside Rain. "It's going to get better, Rain. Appreciate what you had of him. Don't be so angry you lost him."

Rain was crying now. "It's stupid."

Gwen took a pressed handkerchief from her small purse and handed it over. Rain took it without saying a word. "Did they deliver the keys to the cabin and the papers?" Gwen asked her.

Rain was silent for a moment until she realized she couldn't care less what Gwen did with her affections now. It was her father she wanted.

Rain wiped her face, cleared her throat and asked Gwen, "Had you ever gone there?"

"Only once, a long time ago. We just stopped in to see it. It might need a little work, but it's an architectural gem," she sniffed knowingly. "Valuable," she said.

Looking down, Rain said, "I thought he'd sold it after I was born."

Gwen looked out over Gramercy Park; its high, wrought-iron fence held in the bursting lushness of the late summer foliage. "He said too many memories. I think he wrote *Mission* there." Gwen said. She removed the tiny purse from her wrist and ran her fingers over its curves. "I believe he loved it, but he'd somehow sealed off that era."

"Well, I'm going up next week," Rain said casually, feeling like she was crashing over a threshold. "We're renting the loft out while Karl's in England for the fellowship."

Gwen smiled over toward the park. "So, you're not going," she said quietly.

"No," Rain said. "I don't…" her voice trailed away. She didn't want to be doing things for anybody else's approval today.

"Smart girl."

"What do you mean?" Rain asked, looking up at the sky, trying not to sound defensive. The old argument about Karl had begun when she had started seeing him. Rain would not divulge to Gwen that this plan hadn't been her idea.

"Nothing. Going to work up there?"

"I'm going to set up a studio there, spend some time painting and fix the place up a little, much as I can."

They stood in silence for a few moments, Gwen's presence finally soothing Rain. Something of her father was still left in her company. Rain feared that the bantering, easy, friendly bond between the two women could not bear the snivelly, grab-on, sink-down, sob-fest that Rain felt on the perpetual verge of these days: it was just not that sort of relationship. Gwen claimed not to have raised her own children. "Nannies and boarding school did that for me," she liked to say, and she had entered into her relationship with Rain with a lot of respect but very little physical affection. Rain was already twelve when they first met and that sort of thing had just never felt right.

Gwen looked at Rain now fondly, but with a little regret flickering across her face. It seemed as though she'd have liked to reach out and put a hand on Rain, but she didn't. Instead, she offered, "Your father told me that you were the only pure thing in his life."

"Pure?" Rain turned uncomprehendingly to Gwen and met her eyes for the first time since they'd been outside on the balcony. She shook her head silently, knowing she looked desperately freaked. Not caring much.

"How he felt about you. It was a balm to him. You were a gift he never expected."

Gwen, too. With the…with the platitudes. Rain's mind was racing and her throat was constricting. She had cried too much already. She was moving into shocked silence. Into that kind of personality whose feelings were all capped, sealed, boxed and stored because if they were let out, they'd destroy you and lots of other people around you. Her mind was racing with this new self that was trying to take over the more open, raw person she knew in herself. Rain shook her head some more, trying to get her voice back. Not okay. Not yet. "I didn't get enough of him," Rain whispered, alone now in the world. "It's not fair."

Gwen put her little purse on the balcony wall between them decisively. "What do you want, Rain?" she demanded, turning squarely to her. "What are you after?"

Rain shook her head again. "What do you want from *me*?" she blurted back. "What's that supposed to *mean*, 'What do I want…?'" Rain waved her arms toward the wake. "I know what I *don't* want!" She looked across 20th Street to where Karl had been talking on his cell. He was standing, holding onto a bar of the park fence, staring at the open phone in his hand.

Rain turned her back on him again and looked at Gwen. "I want my own show," she said. "I want to make a living as an artist. I want to be left alone to paint, but I want to know somebody wants them when I'm done. I want painting and thinking about painting to fill my life. Not just be a little hobby. I want to find the right set of tracks for me and then just GO on them. I want to already be wrapped up in a project for better or for worse, not trying to *find* anything anymore."

"Alright then," Gwen smiled broadly at her. "That's what I wanted to know."

"What?" Rain said, frustrated, not understanding how Gwen could fail to hear the plaintive drone in everything she had just said. "That doesn't mean anything. Dad's gone."

"Yes, but don't you know what he wanted for you?"

"No, I don't. What?" Rain jabbed her fingers at the concrete balcony wall she was leaning against.

"He wanted you to want things, to have a sense of your own purpose, no matter what it was." Gwen took up her little purse, undid it and snapped it shut again, placing its small handle over her wrist. An ending gesture. Like she had sorted out something tricky and was thoroughly done with it.

GREEN

Of asphodel, that greeny flower,
I come, my sweet,
to sing to you!
My heart rouses
thinking to bring you news
of something
that concerns you
and concerns many men. Look at
what passes for the new.
You will not find it there but in
despised poems.
It is difficult
to get the news from poems
yet men die miserably every day
for lack
of what is found there.

—WILLIAM CARLOS WILLIAMS

N aïvete, inexperience,
eco-sensitivity, cash,
freshness, healthy growth,
sickliness, envy,
countryside fields and woods. Go.

Green Earth, or Terre Verde, is among the oldest pigments known. An earth pigment or clay like Umber, it varies widely depending on the supplier. Some pigments change dramatically with the addition of titanium from a deep earthy green to a sky blue or bright yellow. Malachite, while not perhaps caveman era, also goes back quite far in use, being a simple product of copper. Verdigris is also derived from copper but it is more of a blue green. The copper and arsenic pigments have better tinting strength and staying power than the earths which can brown over the years. The Impressionists accused the Dutch masters of being obsessed with browns, but some conservators theorize that it is the discoloration of brighter, original hues over the centuries that is responsible for their earthy palette.

The train ride from Grand Central took about an hour. By giant rent-a-van, however, the journey took at least two. Add to that the hour and a half it took Rain to inch over to lower-left-Soho, or NoCa (North of Canal), or HoTuHo (Holland Tunnel Hollow)—or whatever the real-estate developers were trying to name it at that moment—where she emptied her whole studio with both Quinn and Stan and one of their more hearty girlfriends, all putting in serious elbow grease in exchange for venti lattes and muffins.

Rain endured their ribbing about her fabulous studio, since its imminent destruction only allowed it to go so far.

"You'll have us up to the country?" Stan asked, all lock-jawed and playful.

"I really have no idea what I'll find up there..." Rain said.

"Dee da deer da deer da deer da dee..." Stan sang. The opening bars of the banjo duel from *Deliverance*.

"That seriously has me freaked out now," Rain laughed, climbing in to the high, trucker-style driver's seat.

Quinn looked up at Rain with a little tweak of sadness on his face. "Call sometime," he said.

"Come on!" Rain howled. "You're making me feel like I'm moving away or something," she laughed. Her friends didn't join in.

The girlfriend shuffled away and Stan said, "See ya Rainy," and chucked her on the knee.

Quinn came in closer. He was like a brother to Rain. She had known Quinn since middle school and she had always, always had a huge crush on him. Each new girlfriend he retained was like a fresh heartbreak for her, even though the one time he had tried to kiss her she had laughed at him and punched him in the shoulder.

"You need anything..." Quinn said. Half sentences were like code between them. 'You call me' was the rest of it.

Rain scanned the directions to the Highland Morrow paint factory she had gotten off their Website, since she'd read in the Escapes section in the *Times* that their yearly open-house tour was on the last day of August. That was how Rain discovered that the cabin was right next door to it. The directions were nearly identical. Though one was on Mahican Brook Road and the other on Old Post Road, they were evidently mere steps away from each other.

The buzz of the big van engine still rang inside her as Rain locked it up out front of a rather anonymous looking structure that MapQuest seemed to believe was her "cabin."

Already fifteen minutes late, Rain dashed directly down the little dirt road toward the factory she'd passed at the poky little intersection.

She had called ahead to reserve a spot in the tour, so she trotted down and bustled noisily through the front door to the factory, where she was greeted by a man in a paper cap who asked her name like this was Studio 54 in high 1976.

"Rain Madlin, I think…" Rain said uncertainly. The man looked up at her quizzically. "It's either under Madlin or Morton. I forget which one I used," she added apologetically.

"Madlin," the man said. "Go ahead on in. They've started in the conference room."

The building wasn't as big as the term factory might suggest. Its large inner space had high ceilings and at the back a large, loft office behind paned glass walls above a spiral staircase. The conference room, the shades pulled low, overflowed with visitors, and the only place to stand was right in front, near to the man speaking.

James Morrow himself. Though tall and masculine, there was something of the injured creature about him. He carried a mood of barely discernible irritation as he projected images onto a screen.

He had one of those old-fashioned overhead projectors that involved a heavy light box with a magnifying redirectioner on a crane above it projecting onto a screen. Rain's math professors had used these contraptions in high school, their cracking, wax-stick pencils tick-tick-ticking on the film as they wrote out problems.

Instead, Morrow slapped transparencies on the lightbox, one after another. Great, thunderous, Renaissance paintings, shown in closer and closer shots, down to abstracted paint strokes, bits of crude, tiny particles suspended in various media, oils, sizes.

"So how did he, did VAN EYCK, or REMBRANDT, or TITIAN translate the brilliant color we see out there in the world and capture it for all eternity on the face of a stretched canvas?"

Rain was in the doorway's threshold to the side of the screen and had to crane her neck over to see what was being projected.

Morrow flipped off the last transparency and refocused the crane. His own hands projected onto the screen. They gingerly fingered cuttings of bright green leaves of grass and a handful of flowers.

"The chemical—the *al*chemical processes that makes a leaf so brilliantly green will not outlast the plant's lifespan."

Morrow took the bright, green blade of grass and rubbed it until it darkened to a watery grey.

"The absorption and reflection of light on those particulates—that delicate combination—is the key to every shade, every value, every tone, every hue in the spectrum. And that structure is the result of a constant pulsing chain of reactions through the plant's veins. Gone when the plant no longer lives. Pluck a flower," he moved to some carefully dried roses, "and it will fade and crumble in an instant of art's lifetime." Morrow pulverized it. "We value permanence and stability in pigments. Those without these qualities we call fugitive."

Morrow moved past Rain, excusing himself as he reached behind her for the light switch. He stopped awkwardly as he met her eye and then turned back toward the rest of the room.

"We'll be…" he said and his voice wavered suddenly, "we'll be heading into the uh…other room." He pushed past Rain and led the group into the large center room of the factory amidst the mixing, the boxing and the tubing.

Morrow yanked out trays of crumbled rose madder, roots drying in a huge, box-like kiln. The trays were rough-hewn and shaped like morgue shelves.

Taking a chalky, brilliant-yellow ball from a box, he tossed it to Rain. Morrow looked at her more acutely as she scrambled to catch it, his brow furrowing. The group chuckled nervously.

"Urine of cows fed only on mango leaves," he said.

Rain, unperturbed, turned it over and weighed it in her hand, an easy, bouncing assessment. Morrow snatched it back and turned away.

"Color is a product of life's layers. A cheek. The high tone of blood coursing beneath the fatty tissue, yellowing and rounding the tone. The infinite shades of melanin stretched over that and a final layer—a sheen of oil perhaps? Or the ash of the unwashed? A dusting of mineral powder?"

Morrow did not look at Rain while he spoke. It was as though he were afraid to look at her. He continued to walk, quickly, and sort through materials and vials and canisters. The factory amazed Rain. She could hear gasps coming from the others.

"Particles that capture such subtlety, that bounce the light back to us in such infinite variety and with such fine distinction—they're worth everything to the artist. The colorman will go anywhere to achieve those little bits of grime if they'll reduce into the desired powders." He saved the best for last. "The finest lapis lazuli, roots of far-flung flora, rare beetles, even mummies—which make the beautiful purplish brown we call *caput mortuum*." Morrow held up a tin box and opened it. "It was prized to the point of fakery in the eighteenth century, but then again they were using it for medicine as well as pigment. He dipped a finger in and wiped it along a white card on the table. Some visitors recoiled. Others leaned forward. Rain was intrigued by the rich, purply streak. It could just have been the hype, but it was mysteriously beautiful, the smear of color seeming to suck light toward it, even bending the white of the card toward its deep purple glow.

"And before anyone asks," Morrow added crankily, "yes: modern labs can synthetically reproduce many of these," he paused, "…colors. These earthly tones and plenty not of this earth. Not interesting to me, however. And not very interesting to most artists who want to capture the plentiful magic of the world around them through the myriad lenses they have available to them. Chemical hues might resemble the original thing quite uncannily," he paused and shot a glance toward Rain. "Quite uncannily," he said it again. "But when used, when pushed and pulled and combined with other hues, their inferiority becomes obvious. They are simply not the original thing…" he paused again. "Not the same thing at all no matter how uncannily…"

Morrow trailed off and continued along to the other side of the room.

Rain dashed behind him. Absurdly, it felt as though he were running from her.

"Uh, excuse me," Rain said, finally catching up to him. "How do you fake a mummy?" Nervous laughter bubbled from a few people in the group.

"Bitumen," Morrow said, not looking at her. "Uh, wrappings, herbs and a dead body from the poorhouse or an alley some-where. Bitumen is the key: it's a kind of tar. Hydrocarbons from a distillation of petroleum in the case of the real mummies from Egypt. At one point, the real ones were mostly gone," he explained. "This was during the eighteenth century, when there was a nice trade in mummies. People couldn't get enough of them."

Awkward murmurs from the group interrupted his digression. "It produces that stunningly translucent rich brown," Morrow said to them as if this would make them all understand.

"One more thing," Rain said, before he could move on, "you said 'alchemical' earlier. What is that exactly?"

"What do you think it is?" Morrow asked back abruptly.

"I guess I thought it was false chemistry."

"Ah, yes, an attempt to create gold?" He averted his gaze.

"A sort of magic?" Rain offered.

Morrow still avoided looking at her. He pinched his nose with his fingers impatiently. It was a gesture similar to one of Karl's.

Morrow strayed from her while answering. "Alchemy is simply the application of fundamental processes that underlie all chemical principles. Heat…" Morrow indicated the kiln, Bunsen burners, ovens and forges, "…pressure, hydration…" He led them into an enormous, vault-like room. A greenhouse of sorts filled with a grid work of pools. "And time," he said.

They looked at the pools. A couple of workers slowly stirred and poked at them.

"What are these?" Rain asked. Morrow's gruffness inspired some kind of eager honor student within her.

"They're…it's stand oil. Oils and fats that will become the bases for the pigments. The stabilizers…" Morrow interrupted himself, pinching his brow again. He appeared to be wilting. "I'm sorry, but I'm going to have to leave you here. I'm…"

Morrow left the small tour group standing in this enormous greenhouse. Rain watched him go and then walked along the aisles. The pools were dense and slick surfaced, and appeared as a series of small, populated ponds. The workers moved slowly around the shallow pools, stirring and poking delicately.

An assistant took questions from the group, which slowly dispersed. Rain slipped away, wandering through rooms they had already toured.

Eventually, she found herself before a spiral staircase under the high, window-paned offices. She could see James Morrow standing on the landing, still and quiet, his back to her.

"Excuse me?" she called up to him.

James turned and saw Rain below him.

"I'm sorry to bother you, Mr. Morrow," Rain said. "I just wanted to thank you for the tour. I'm moving into the little cabin on the edge of the woods there."

"Yes, of course," James said, without smiling. "John Morton's cabin."

Rain couldn't speak for a beat. "My father," she said when she finally found her voice again.

Morrow looked at her directly for the first time. "I'm so sorry for your loss," he said genuinely.

"You knew him?"

"Not well. Not…I'm terribly sorry. I have to…"

Morrow retreated into his office, leaving Rain alone.

Morrow watched Rain out of his office window as she tromped across the small lawn toward the dirt road. He reached out without looking and took up the portrait of the young woman on his desk, held it in one hand and rubbed his thumb along the glass all the while keeping his eyes trained on Rain's back as she hiked up the road toward the cabin.

As Rain approached the cabin along the dirt road, its dark-stained, board-and-batten and broad, mossy roofline nearly disappeared into the woods, despite its striking modern lines. The cabin stared blandly back at Rain, as unfamiliar and unapproachable as when she had first pulled up in front of it.

She could make out the outline of a small door bizarrely cut into a wider garage-style lifting doorway.

The heavy cap of the low roofline and the odd door didn't reveal what this place might have been—a storage shed or possibly a power station's outbuilding. But when she unlocked and then raised the larger door up, tucking it seamlessly into its slot between the roof and ceiling—the cabin opened up in a welcoming, broad gesture. She entered and slid pocket panels of screening across the opening, turning the upper part of the cabin into one, big, screened porch.

The opened space was like a proscenium, a bed and bath alcove to the left and a small efficiency-style, Pullman kitchen to the right. The rest of the interior lay a few steps down from the entrance. The ceiling angled toward enormous windows looking out into the woods. More windows extended around the right side of the house, bringing in generous light. One expanse of wall was painted a silvery graphite, with one small painting humbly hung in the center. Sheets covered the furniture; cabinets were thrown open and empty. Despite work to be done, the cabin was far from the abandoned shed Rain had expected.

A wall divided the bedroom from the living room, but only an empty bookshelf and an inset ceiling track gave privacy from the kitchen. In the small living area, two long tables lay side by side. Tucked together, they might have been her father's desk. The broad but diffuse light from the woods cast ornamental shadows over the draped forms. Distracted by the grand space and clever design in the cabin, Rain abruptly yanked the sheets from the tables, sending whorls of dust into the air and revealing beautiful pieces crafted in pine and loaded with a dozen or so cardboard boxes.

Having settled in, Rain used the tables to organize the papers she'd unearthed. Rain's laptop and printer lay on the other table along with her camera and some extra lenses. Cleaning supplies and bundled linens lay about. A huge boxy couch in mustard-orange tweed sat in front of the great glass windows. Some mismatched wooden chairs and a few smaller tables and lamps were scattered about.

Rain slit open the boxes, trying to makes sense of their contents, doling them into emptied boxes marked "Columbia U. Library," "Keep" and "Trash." Letters and some of the photographs were going into the library box. Only a very few photos landed in the keep box.

It seemed whole eras of her father's life had been locked up in here, thankfully kept dry and dark in the sealed boxes. Rain found herself disturbed by the fact that her father's passing in some ways felt alright, and that this sudden equanimity seemed to outweigh her grief. Flipping through pictures she hadn't seen before, she expected—and eventually began *trying*—to feel sorrow and the kind of railing-at-heaven sense of unfairness that she was feeling at the wake. But instead, she saw a life fully lived. A life that had been fun and filled with success and meaning and fully experienced at every moment—along with, of course, the prolific and thorough renderings of those times in her father's books and letters, even in articles and lectures. But it didn't seem right to feel such easy admiration and a sense of liberation now: it was too early for that, wasn't it?

Rain hopped back up the stage steps and pushed aside one of the screen doors. The patio was broad and welcoming with the garage doors up. Tarps covered well-preserved wrought iron furniture. A fire-pit and chimney stood, detached, at the patio's edge. Though years of weather had blown and iced and rained into it, Rain could still detect ash at the base of the hearth. As she took a stretch and a deep breath of country air, Rain turned and took in the view toward the beautiful old brick-faced factory building down the dirt road. Highland Morrow and its strange and haunted chief. It was near enough to add a picturesque sense of company, but far enough to feel apart.

On her way back in, she noticed another black tarp against the house. A sculpture maybe? She lifted a corner. Powder-blue enamel. Chrome. A wheel. It was the Vespa she'd seen in her father's pictures. Faded, pale blue and cream. Flat tires. Dirty. But no rust.

All at once, Rain felt a terrible mix of excitement and anguish. She sat down at the end of the porch looking at the Vespa through tears of a pure, Christmas-morning, greedy joy mingled oddly with a bitter feeling that she'd missed out on something. Even before she had gone to boarding school when she was fourteen, her father had moved them through several different apartments in the city, always casting off excess belongings. Though she had never acknowledged it, their impermanent transience had untethered her. Whatever longing for a more stable family life she might have harbored, this was not for the daughter of John Ray Morton. They were supposed to be quite above such conventional desires. But this house, though merely her father's storage facility, carried vast chunks of his past and hers, too.

Giving in to the tears, Rain tried to sort out this strange cocktail of feelings. We treat grief so delicately, not wanting to disturb the wasp's nest that it is. Others approach us gingerly and even when we "give in" to it, we're somehow throwing ourselves upon only a single aspect. The lonely howl. But in reality, grief is messy and boisterous, crowded with the accordion shaped collapse of time that a life's end creates. All of her father's life and her time with him seemed suddenly to carry equal weight, so that what she got from him in her daily life no longer outweighed the past. "The Past," which John Ray Morton very literally and literarily always put down as "merely a construct of the mind," as if events once passed weren't real anymore, as if we could choose to empty them of significance and only apply onto them that which our clearest thinking and most logical brain could concoct.

Rain could still feel that familiar sense of being cast adrift. But the house, this Vespa, the heaps of photographs in the boxes and just being locked to a piece of the earth made her feel ruddered and thrillingly in control. She still couldn't shake off that inappropriate Christmas feeling, like she had been given a gift she'd never even hoped to wish for. She felt resentful and angry at the one person she'd give anything to see again. How could she be unearthing anger now? When he was alive, she had felt nothing but gratitude toward him.

This realization threw her into a new eruption of tears. Out of which she immediately let out a self-conscious laugh, realizing that if anyone walked up the road and saw her, sitting there patting a dirty old moped and gasping with these hiccupping sobs, they would probably think she was having a seizure or arguing with some unseen adversary through a locked door. She was in conversation with herself, and Rain felt for the first time in years that she was waking up, that she was feeling her own emotions. That there was a Rain Morton Madlin, not just daughter-of, wife-of.

She shook her head at herself, wiping the tears from her face with her tee-shirt. What the hell kind of backwards person was she? She never conceived of herself as anything lesser or overly connected to her dad or to Karl, but a huge smile spread across her face as she stood savoring the realization that she was at HER cabin with HER stuff.

Back in the cabin, Rain fell heavily onto the couch and pulled a box of pictures she'd been sorting through toward her with her foot.

John with various vintage celebrities, John at the cabin looking tanned and windblown, John with friends, John fishing, John sailing, John hiking, John with those same friends. The woman in some of the pictures was dark haired and clear eyed and had a familiar look about her.

Rain flipped the photo. "Alice, 1975" was written on the back.

Rain tossed it back into the box and grabbed her old leather rucksack. She stuffed it with her camera, a water bottle and a small sketchbook, grabbed her iPod out of its dock and plugged into it, shoving it into the bag, which she swung onto her back.

Straight off the porch and past the Vespa, Rain didn't bother to close up the cabin behind her. She took to the narrow wooded trail as if she were bicycling, churning her gait from her first steps like she was riding through the woods.

Her iPod blasted the pace, the rhythm pumping through her head as she pounded through the forest, hitting one spectacular view of the Hudson valley after another. Bull Hill here, Storm King over a bend in the river there, the train tracks of the Hudson Line chugging past Little Stony Point and into the tunnel under Breakneck Ridge.

Rain stood, watching a train scream past, watching the river keeping its steady flow behind it. Tears streamed down her cheeks and she abruptly took off again along the trail.

Vanderkill didn't have much of a town center. No traffic lights, not even a stop sign along Route 9D, the road iterating the river's curves coursing through the highlands. It did, however, have its own post office and one small gas station with antique pumps that rolled the numbers inside little windows, slot-machine style. And it had Vanderkill Market, a tiny coffee and take-out shop, sparsely stocked with sundries but which drew an impressive breakfast crowd. Rain pulled up in front on the shiny, newly refurbished Vespa and parked it between a silver Hummer and a matching silver Prius. The front windows were crowded with flyers for music, theater and art events in the area. It was morning, so the place was heavy with baked goods and gourmet bits and pieces, cellophane wrappers twinkling under the perpetually lit Christmas lights. Customers gathered and hitched themselves up to the front window-sill bar to catch up and sort through their mail.

As Rain ordered her coffee, the woman behind the counter noticed her paint-stained hands. "You new at the factory?"

"Excuse me?"

"Sorry. I'm Chassie, own the place." She was tall with choppy, blonde hair and thick hands. "Couldn't help but notice paint on your hands. You new over at Highland Morrow?"

"The paints? No, I'm... I paint. Messily... I'm in the little cabin right next to it, though."

Chassie said, "Right there and you're a painter?" She shook her head and took her time fitting the little cardboard belt onto the cup.

"Well, nobody buys them," Rain said awkwardly.

"Yet!" Chassie slammed the cup down in front of Rain and pointed up to the left. "No modesty allowed in here. I've got a sign up..." She did. MODESTY-FREE ZONE it said right alongside the one that said, UNACCOMPANIED CHILDREN WILL BE SOLD.

Chassie stopped pretending to serve her and asked, "You take the tour?"

"First day here, actually. I just pulled into town and went straight to the factory."

"Smart girl," Chassie said. "You're lucky actually. He's been cutting back the tours. Used to be once a season, then once a year. Now you never know."

Chassie pounded the empty cup in front of Rain for emphasis. "Speak of the devils! Here's Alvaro and Anne."

Rain shook hands. "Oh, Alvaro from Highland Morrow."

"And this is Anne," Alvaro said. "My wife, Anne Donohue."

"Nice to meet you. I'm Rain. Rain Morton Madlin."

"Rain-rain Morton Madlin, Alvaro and A-anne," Chassie chanted the names like a children's rhyme.

"Just…too much, isn't it?" Rain smiled with embarrassment.

"She loves to give people crap about names!" Anne said. She was pretty and pale with snow-white coloring, dark hair and bright lipstick. Her manner was enthusiastic and down to earth at the same time. Like she either didn't know how pretty she was, or she'd had to get used to making people feel at ease about it. She leaned in, meeting Rain's eyes. "We were at a party last week and she finds this woman Cat and this other lady Kitty and she just has to drag them together and do a whole Uma-Oprah thing on them." Anne smiled sidelong at Chassie. "And it was just as not funny that time."

"It was funny!" Chassie insisted. "You should hear what people do with my name!"

"We love you, Chassie, darling," Anne said. And then to Rain, "Did I hear you're a painter?"

Rain, feeling a bit cornered, said, "I don't really have a gallery yet, but I've got some bites and I'm working really hard on getting my first show." Rain looked self-consciously at the empty paper cup Chassie was holding, wondering why she was telling them this. It was both more certain and less certain than she was making it sound. It had been so long, college probably, since she'd had to meet new people and explain herself with external facts: major, dorm, hometown. And now, here, though some things were clear already, city transplant, for example, there were these other externals that could be told or skipped: job, marital status, financial situation, famous father. Rain knew how people reacted to this last, and never particularly enjoyed the kind of fawning even the most reasonably sophisticated people would then throw her way. It was such an awkward dance—anything genuine from them amounted to a lot of outsized praise that Rain then had to heft graciously on his behalf, the few cagier ones often shooting looks at her the rest of the time, which let on their own mix of feelings about celebrity and status, our American hierarchy, or maybe it was that they didn't give a damn. She hated the whole rigmarole, which was why she had taken Karl's name. But her own name still popped to her lips unbidden, even after so many years.

Chassie finally poured a cup for Rain. "First cup's on the house," she said, shooing her aside to take Alvaro's order.

"That's fantastic!" Anne was saying.

"Do you…?" Rain asked, stopping herself.

Rain walked with Alvaro and Anne over to the fixings counter where they added their various milks and sugars and packets of sweeteners.

"I mean do you make…?" Somehow the question seemed too intimate. Are you an artist. In Rain's personal lexicon it was kind of like *are you in the game?* Or *do you think you're important* or something equally judgmental and inappropriately statussy.

"No, no," Anne laughed. "I am hopelessly non-artistic, no." She laughed and batted Alvaro's arm. "Alvaro's a musician and that's about all the art our lives can take."

The man was beautiful. Rain had noticed him at the factory. Pretty almost. And everything about him, the way he moved and held himself—it all broadcasted his devotion to his wife. He seemed like the kind of find a woman of very specific tastes would land upon. Uncommonly attractive, yet uniquely devoted.

Alvaro gave his wife a warm glance and a touch on her arm. "Anne is a big shot in the city," he said playfully.

"Stop!" Anne said, looking pleased.

"Anne runs all the marketing for a group of very large department stores. That's all I'm gonna say."

"Wow," said Rain. "That's impressive."

"I just love to shop," Anne whispered conspiratorially. "I'd love to see your paintings sometime, though."

"Oh, I…" Rain wasn't sure why she felt so nervous suddenly. This woman was just like the princesses in the cartoons she had loved as a little girl. Warm, generous, gorgeous and sisterly in a fairy-tale way. Rain never had good luck with women friends. Her college roommate was hugely introverted and while it worked smoothly for them as roommates, she never actually thought of Marie as a friend. Marie was the one who had been so intimidated by her father. Her best friends were Stan and Quinn. Straight guys who were more brothers to her than boyfriend material.

Rain wasn't one of those women other women didn't like, but she just didn't know how to go about girl talk. In a way, Gwen was her closest woman friend, but there was a firm, safe distance between them that kept her from the full-out, giggly closeness that she saw depicted in movies and on TV.

But this Anne made Rain feel buoyed and hopeful. "Yeah, let's do that! Thanks!" she called to Chassie at the counter, raising her coffee up high.

Autumn was just beginning to touch the Hudson Valley. The season marked the region's ridiculous, gilded-lily, high point. Too perfect, too beautiful, too thoroughly scene-set. The historic villages filled with tourists who strolled down the middle of busy little side streets with their heads leisurely swiveling as if what they were seeing were set up for show. And you couldn't really blame them. The beautifully maintained little cottages with American flags sailing out front. The prolific bunchings of cornstalks, haystacks and other charming country fall-dom. And the highland mountains rising picturesquely above, deepening as the season progressed into those reds and golds and looming straight above the mighty Hudson, all made the place postcard ready.

When the leaves were in full glory, however, the colors were outrageous and almost mocking. Each tree a further degree of impossible fire from the last. Aglow with white gold through neon orange to cherry red, along with remaining bits of glowing bright green, all set in the most obvious layering to show off their depth and complement and deepen each other.

Rain was out discovering trails through the highlands every day for hours at a time, making photographs. She told herself it was just a hobby, a blowing off of steam. She was drawn toward those landscapes, framing shots by climbing around to get the perfect view, then tilting down, catching the tracks low next to the river, shooting montages with dozens of photos focused on one view.

The colors called to her. The light and shape of the landscape teased and tempted her.

But Rain's studio was filling up with her scrubby abstracts. There were days, as she was working, patiently building up her odd, nest-like constructions that she wondered what she was doing there and whether she would be living there just a season. Days when she let her mind push ahead into winter and spring in the little house, the fresh air of the country washing her inside and out. Inside her secret mind, she saw herself gardening herbs and making soap, maybe even having babies here, but then she would brush all that away as sentimentality. No, it was hard enough, this path she had set herself on. And again she pictured the show at Shuldenfrei, wondered at what new phase of life it would launch her into. Thought about how different she would feel once she was a real artist.

In the meantime, she formed her days around house projects, studio time, walks and a little cooking, only very occasionally panged by the realization that she was happier alone and orphaned than she had ever been in her life.

Rain felt like she was hiding in some strange little cul-de-sac of life. Off to the side, all on her own, and free.

One late morning, Rain was in sweats, checking email on her laptop.

"Finally," she muttered.

The email was from Karl. No subject. It read (in caps):

MAIL NOT BEING FORWARDED. NEED STATEMENT FROM BROKER. K.

Rain was frozen. Actually surprised. That was it?

The next email was from James Morrow—subject line "Re: Thank You for the Tour" and read:

Dear Rain Morton,

Thank you for your note. I appreciate your kind words. I did know your father, though I had not seen him for many years. I've left a small token of welcome at your doorstep. I've been ill and have forgotten all my manners. Please accept, forgive and allow me to grovel a bit.

Yours most sincerely, James Morrow

Rain rose, coffee mug in hand, and went to the front door of the cabin.

Emerging into the fine, early-fall morning, dry and bright, Rain sat on the front stoop of the cabin, rubbing her face. She took in the view, each day bringing a fresh crop of impossible color to the woods. She looked around and spotted the box squatting right next to her. It was worn looking but polished, about the size of a bread box. Rain ran her hand along its smooth surfaces, regarding it casually, like you might a friendly cat if you're not particularly a cat person. As she woke up a little, she put the coffee mug down and fingered the box's old-fashioned latch. Inside were sparkling bottles and tubes, all adorned with hand-pressed Highland Morrow labels.

Rain gasped, and quietly said, "James Morrow..."

Her hands moved around inside the box, touching and lifting bottles and mysterious looking tools from their velvet-lined slots. Her fingers found a small, letter-pressed card that read: *FOR THE PAINTER. LET IT RAIN. MAY THIS SUPPLY LAST UNTIL I FINISH A MORE WORTHY SET.* And was signed with quill and ink, *JAMES*.

Dear James Morrow,

I'm flabbergasted! I can't thank you enough for this incredible artifact! I feel like I've come into the possession of a work of art in and of itself, though surely it is undeserved.

I thank you for your generosity and hope that I might one day give you a painting worthy of such a self-contained perfection as this.

Yours, Rain Morton

Rain was slouching in one of the old ratty couches at the Market, working on her computer, making a composite out of some of the photographs she had been taking, when Chassie flopped down into the couch next to her.

"So, you're a photographer," she said.

"Nah," Rain said. "Just reference."

"So you paint landscapes?" Chassie asked.

"More abstract, I guess," Rain said as Chassie tried to peer over her shoulder. "I really just do this other stuff as a hobby. To relax, I guess."

"Maybe that ought to tell you something," said Chassie.

A pair of low-slung Levis swiveled into view. "What would you know about it," the woman wearing them said, accusingly.

"It's from *What Color Is Your Parachute?*," Chassie answered sincerely. "I'm reading it for Hunter. By the way, Rain, this is Marisol? Marisol: Straight-Girl."

"Nice to meet you," Rain extended a hand to Marisol, who took it in a surprisingly floppy little handshake. Marisol smiled apologetically.

"Hunter's my brother," Chassie told Rain.

"Hopeless playboy goof. Not even a real brother," Marisol was smiling and nudging Chassie with her torso.

"Real as far as I care," said Chassie. "I adopted him after my Dad died. Grew up with him. He's my family."

Marisol perked up. "Yeah, maybe Straight Girl'd like him." She flashed her perfect teeth and leaned past Chassie to grab the *Post* from the coffee table.

"Married, I think," said Chassie, looking at Rain and making a face.

Rain was watching their little show, amused, and only then realized they had moved the game onto her. "Yup, married," she said a little weakly.

"Not married very much though. I think," said Chassie. Marisol laughed at this, shifted her butt into the couch next to Chassie and snapped open the paper. Rain was trying to keep her expression light and amused looking. "I kid!" Chassie said.

"Omigod, she's going to start avoiding this place. I kid, I joke!" she said, slapping Rain's leg. Chassie rose. "Gotta go grind some beans, now." She put a hand on Rain's shoulder as she passed behind her and said, "Sorry. Run my mouth for my own amusement and crap slips out. Don't hate me."

"You're hard to keep up with!" Rain said, wondering how she could possibly be so easy to read.

"Good, I like that." Chassie laughed and went behind the counter. "And you are required at dinner tomorrow!"

Rain smiled and nodded and then turned back to where Chassie had gone. "Excuse me?"

"You heard me!" Chassie said.

Marisol tore part of the front page of the paper off and began writing on it. Her very long, manicured fingernails caused her to wrap her fingers around the pen childishly, where they glinted and clicked as she wrote a phone number, an address and "8:00 Saturday—BE THERE."

Morrow's house was on the opposite side of the factory and though small, it enjoyed a seasonal view of the Hudson from the back porch and upper-rear windows. During summer, the greenery was too thick to see anything but an occasional tiny glimpse of river. But during the long, gray winters, the water shone up at the house encouragingly.

James had maintained the little house carefully if not imaginatively over the decades of his widowerhood. Honeysuckle and jasmine grew up over the porch and enclosed the house in their fragrant embrace. Morrow cut the vines back in the winter, dried them and burned them, carefully and slowly, into drawing charcoal. Their stubs still hung possessively around the entrance in a brown, twiggy halo during the cold months. The lawn was mowed, the leaves raked and Morrow retained the interior cleaning services of one Roselle Jenkins whose work was efficient and thorough.

What Mrs. Jenkins found when she stepped in through the split Dutch doors every Monday was a place that felt like a display to her. She did find dust and the odd stray evidence of life in the house, but her impression was always that the occupants spent little time there. Life appeared to take place only in three or four distinct corners of the building, and the rest of it never changed in the slightest detail. A chair by a window in the living room, for example. The arms were worn, the books and newspapers in stacks by the lamp changed each time Mrs. Jenkins came, but the chair next to it gathered dust undisturbed. A couple of books, a pair of women's reading glasses and even a water glass were set carefully on a small table. It was a sad little tableau and once Mrs. Jenkins came to understand it, she refreshed the water in the glass every time she cleaned, thinking that Mr. Morrow was keeping an offering to his departed wife there.

The kitchen, distinctly dated by its appliances and the little curtains over shelves in place of proper cabinets, was another place of limited life. The refrigerator, one of those curved impenetrable tombs from the 1940s, held a few wrapped, unmarked packages. Beer, cheese and a few sausages. It was cavernous and empty, no cheery sauces or jars or anything friendly. The metal grill shelves rang hollowly when Mrs. Jenkins defrosted the freezer every couple of months to keep its little internal metal box from taking over the small space. Behind the curtains on the shelves sat strange tin boxes of crackers, teas and unrecognizable jars of imported condiments that Mrs. Jenkins found slightly menacing.

Not that Mrs. Jenkins made those sorts of judgments, no. It took quite a high degree of oddity to impress Mrs. Jenkins after all those years of cleaning houses. Years of tissues and magazines and electronic doohickeys, stashes of booze and empty bottles in odd places, pills upon pills, medical equipment, straps and contraptions and dirty underpants, nothing seemed all that surprising to her anymore. But it was more a matter of breezing past the implications of people's private spheres, rather than actually accepting any of what she saw.

Mostly Mrs. Jenkins tried to feel about those things the way she'd like some theoretical housekeeper in her own life to feel. Nothing. Really nothing. Just a kind of slipping by.

It must have been forty years that Mrs. Jenkins had been walking into people's houses without their being present. So that feeling she used to get when she was first cleaning houses on her own was familiar—but had so long ago been banished by her practical nature and sleeves-rolled-up work ethic—and so it surprised her that she felt an ear-ringing hollowness at Mr. Morrow's. She guessed it must have been the doubled layer of residents missing, Mrs. Morrow having been gone many years before she began working for Mr. Morrow. It was a rather outsized shock, however, to Mrs. Jenkins, when she had first learned that Mrs. Morrow had been dead so long.

She had been cleaning Morrow's house for almost a year by then. The Morrows were never around and her contact with them was limited to the envelope she found waiting for her on the kitchen table every week and the very occasional phone call from Mr. Morrow asking to change the date or cancel a week. He had always paid her for the weeks he cancelled and was very generous at the holidays. But, considering herself the kind of person who understood things, it was very disconcerting to her to realize that she had not made any conclusions about the very particular strangeness of the Morrow house.

It was in the most casual of conversations with Donna at the grocery store that she learned about it. Why they had been talking about the Morrows, Mrs. Jenkins couldn't remember, but she did remember how cavalierly Donna corrected her about Mrs. Morrow being dead as she slid bacon and orange juice and ground beef and cans of beans over the sensor's beep and straight into the shushing plastic bags. How her gasp and clapped hand over her heart were greeted by one of Donna's quirky, sidelong looks. And how Donna wondered aloud why a death from almost twenty-five years before should touch Mrs. Jenkins so deeply. Somehow Donna's finding her shock curious made Mrs. Jenkins feel the need to downplay the more serious amazement she felt to discover that Mrs. Morrow had been so long gone. So she put her hand back down, worked her wallet open and composed her face into a more appropriate expression.

Shutting her wallet with a decisive little snap, Mrs. Jenkins had thanked Donna and had declined to ask any more questions when the checker had made leading remarks about there having been intriguing circumstances. She had made sure to leave Donna with an expression of casual merriment. But the next Monday when she had entered the Morrow house, Mrs. Jenkins had felt distinctly haunted.

She had entered tentatively, not with the clatter she usually employed to flush out the silence of locked, waiting houses. The chair that Mrs. Jenkins only now understood as Mrs. Morrow's seemed to bare itself to her, with the lady's glasses atop the books she must have been reading. They were a hardcover of a Norman Mailer book and two paperbacks with bent back covers, *Zen and the Art of Motorcycle Maintenance* and something called *Danville's Mission*. She had dusted these books over and over for months without ever noting that they never changed. Tentatively, she picked one up and looked at the back cover. *Danville's Mission* by John Ray Morton. Pulitzer Prize for 1971, with its black-and-white author photo of a young, delicate-featured man looking off into the light and distance. The casual ease of his expression was contrasted neatly by the tight, white shirt and thin, dark tie. He looked sun kissed and blithe. His hair was combed neatly, except for a piece that blew handsomely across his laughing face. Mrs. Jenkins put the book back in its place, the author's face back down against the book beneath it and delicately returned Mrs. Morrow's reading glasses atop it. She felt oddly devastated. She needed to get her work done and get to three more houses that day. But just this once. Just in order to shake out the juju she was feeling, Mrs. Jenkins decided to take a quick look around. And she knew just where she wanted to look.

Mrs. Jenkins went directly to the door leading to the third floor of the house. The floor Mr. Morrow had told her she needn't bother with. He had never expressly forbidden her access to it, but he had employed her to do the first two floors of the house only, and in her efficiency and experience, Mrs. Jenkins had never had the leisure to explore. Nor, of course, had she the idea that there would be anything unusual to see.

Behind the door, Mrs. Jenkins was surprised to find a wide entryway and a broad set of stairs. No tiny attic stairwell, but a fresh, broad access way. The steps were mostly stacked with boxes and bags and odd piles of books and papers, but there was a clear pathway on the right-hand side all the way up. Mrs. Jenkins glanced up and saw that there was ample natural light flooding the room, though its walls and ceilings were unfinished, dark-stained wood. As she mounted the stairs and more and more of the attic space came into view, she could see that it was not a storage space nor a finished rumpus room, but a vast formal display. Cases on pedestals, glass-fronted shelves full of objects, an easel with a huge painting of a landscape that looked familiar. She stopped. Turned to leave. Stopped again. Went quickly up into the space to get a closer look.

A series of shadow boxes along the hallway revealed their collections of what looked like garbage to Mrs. Jenkins. Garbage displayed in cases and press boxes. A decades-old toothbrush with its squared shape and red gummy pick, squeezed-out tubes of various ointments, used makeup compacts, brushes and hair clips. And what must have been matted hair, gathered from a brush or drain. Other displays held beads and earrings, hung carefully against the background with t-pins. Further into the space Mrs. Jenkins could see huge Riker boxes, the press boxes her father-in-law had used to display his butterfly collections, but these were broad and tall as a human being. Wrinkled violently against the glass were women's garments of all sorts, Mrs. Jenkins didn't know, she didn't see, because as soon as her gaze fell upon them in the angled winter light from the high windows, she stopped, gasped out loud, turned and pranced as fast as her aging body would allow her back down the stairs and out of the door. Breathing heavily, Mrs. Jenkins shut the door tightly, testing the handle twice and then, shaking her head with sympathy for poor Mr. Morrow, obviously driven witless by this loss, she went about cleaning the saner first two floors of this lonely and unhappy house.

Rain moved back and forth between her printer and the wall, sheet after sheet emerging with portions of the image she was creating. She taped them into a huge grid on the wall next to one of her blank canvasses, stood back and looked, backed up and considered, then reapproached and repositioned a sheet carefully. The composite brought certain elements of the landscape loudly to the fore and the grid she had created, off-kilter as it was, gave a disorienting, vertiginous feeling.

Her music was blasting, she was sipping a beer from the bottle as she worked, and the waning light of the day was escaping slowly out the windows and through the huge open doors of the cabin.

Rain stepped back up the stairs to the kitchen table where she had left the as-yet untouched box of paints. She ran her hands over the glossy wood again. Finally she set down her bottle, opened the box and pulled out a tube. Stroked it with her thumb. Took out another. Then she put them all back and closed the box.

"You planning to frame it?"

Rain jumped, made a save on her tipping beer bottle and turned to find James Morrow standing at the threshold of her cabin. "What?" she gasped, pressing her hand to her collarbone in a ridiculously old-movie gesture she hadn't even realized was in her.

"I'm sorry," Morrow said as he stepped back away from the doorway. "I'm sorry to startle you."

"No, no," Rain said. "I didn't catch what you said." She ran over and hit the power button on the stereo. The sudden silence was engulfing. "Thank you," she said. "Thank you SO much for this…this amazing…"

"Well you can't take it with you."

"I'm sorry?"

"The paints. You have to use them."

"I thought…" Rain faltered, looking down at the box.

"I mean they're *for* you," he said. "However, you are going to have to actually squeeze the paint out of them."

"Oh, I… They're just too beautiful. I can't imagine messing them up. It's like a jewelry box."

"I suspected as much from your note. That's why I came by. Don't let it be a sarcophagus—you're supposed to *use* it."

James went into the kitchen and opened the box, sliding a palette she hadn't noticed out from the lid. Then he grabbed out two tubes: a Burnt Umber and the large tube of white.

She watched him helplessly. "It's just too nice."

He squeezed large dollops from both tubes on the polished wooden palette.

Rain laughed, "No!! Oh, my God!"

Morrow dipped his fingers into the paints, rubbed his hands together and proceeded to grab all of the tubes, bottles and brushes in the box.

Rain turned away while he was doing this. Widening her eyes as though she were witnessing somebody running a combine over a Louis Vuitton trunk.

"It's nothing," Morrow said casually. "It's meaningless. It's an incomplete thing without you messing it up."

Rain turned back around as Morrow wiped his hands on the little chamois tucked neatly in its own slot.

"Uh. Thank you?" she said.

Morrow dispensed linseed oil, mineral spirits and turpentine into small metal cups he'd clipped onto the palette, grabbed the palette knife and two or three brushes and plunged them into the paints.

"There," he said, "use it."

Between chastened and sarcastic, Rain said, "Sure will. Thank you for that."

Morrow tossed the chamois on the box and turned to leave rather abruptly. He turned back in the doorway and said, "I want to see that on canvas next time I come by." With that, he stepped out into the now fully dark evening and disappeared back down the road toward the factory.

Morrow's manner was such a mix of gruff kindness and something else, she thought. Like hopelessness with humor. Dark knowingness. Rain was very comfortable with curmudgeons though, so he didn't scare her. Just interested her. She was unsure why he was being so nice to her. Perhaps he had admired her father.

Suddenly alone again, Rain looked across the living area to the composite she'd taped on the wall and the large canvas leaning there.

With a shake of her head, she turned away and put one of her small sanded blocks of wood onto the table alongside the palette. Onto this she sketched out a classic, representational landscape. A miniature of the large composite she'd just worked out.

She had never used Highland Morrow paint before, though she had seen it in art supply stores. It was very expensive and Rain had always thought that the prices reflected the cachet rather than the actual paints. She used high-grade oils from Britain and France, occasionally switching a brand, but mostly sticking to a kind of formula of this tube from this mark and this tube from another. She liked the greener Umber made by Sennelier and the browner Raw Sienna from Winsor & Newton. These are among the finest oils available, and certainly not cheap, but Highland Morrow were like the rougher-looking, one-off jewelry pieces on the main floor of Barney's as compared to the finest samples from Tiffany's. They were for people who needed not only to get things no one else could afford, but that no one else even knew about. Or so Rain thought.

As she dealt colors around the palette, she could feel by the weight of the tubes that these paints were invariably dense. They felt like platinum in the hand, like asteroids, heavier than they should be. And as the colors snaked their way out onto the pale neutral face of the palette, they asserted themselves individually in their diverse personalities. The Ultramarine hummed into deep and rich low mound, the Yellow Ochre sluiced out hard and straight, the Viridian and the Burnt Sienna made juicy, layered mountains.

When Rain started mixing the paints, she saw how they brought out new qualities in each other rather than ever muting or cutting the other. She found herself lost in the mixing, bringing this and that color to fullness with the Titanium White and to another kind of more transparent lightness with the zinc. Many of the paints had a jewel-like transparency along with intense tinting strength. It took very little of any one color to bend the one she was mixing. By the time Rain looked up again, she had mixed all the wild variety of fall-leaf tones; the brights and dims of shadow and gold of that particular fall glow; the heavy blue of the bright, fall sky along with the golds and grays and purples of the Hudson River clouds; and the subtle steel of the train tracks lit by those skies. She had enough that she could have tackled the big canvas, but she just set to work on some small wood blocks she had prepared, painting with great globs of color in a loose and brushy style. She discovered the confidence and pleasure in finding the tone and stroke that would speak what she saw. Nothing at stake, nothing to prove, this "realist" painting, made up from a mix of images she had collected. It felt like the first thing she had ever painted. This luscious feeling of discovery, of bravery—as she took areas past ugly stages into sudden beauty and evocation—was surprising and what it did most of all was make time disappear completely. Rain forgot to eat; she felt no fatigue, and it was only the faint blue growing brighter in the view out the window, and the sound of birds starting to warble, that woke her out of her trance and made her stumble across the proscenium to fall into her bed with the most beautiful kind of exhaustion she had felt since she couldn't remember when.

Rain navigated the Vespa up a steep, hair-pinning, paved road to an early Robber-Baron-era castle on top of a ridge. From her jacket pocket she pulled out and checked again the directions to be sure she was in the right place. There was a glow from inside one of the downstairs rooms, but the building, however impressive, looked mostly abandoned. As she pulled off her helmet and tucked it into the seat compartment of the bike, the heavy, front door flew open and Chassie came loping out toward her holding a martini glass.

"Rain-Rain!" she hooted. "Fashionably on time!"

"Chassie!" Rain said, hugging her warmly. Chassie had on a black-velvet version of the big, washed-denim shirt that was her uniform, along with the usual, black, unstructured pants and clogs. She was so down to earth and normal seeming, that her circumstances must have been inherited generations back. She encouraged enthusiasm and honesty. "This place is incredible!" Rain gushed.

"Isn't it great?" Chassie agreed. "You come right inside, now. You need to meet the chef."

Chassie led Rain into the enormous foyer. The place was artfully lit and tastefully minimalist in decor. Beyond the structure, however, there was nothing terribly show-offy about the place—simply huge expanses of space and sweeping stairwells. There were a few very good paintings and antiques around, but nothing looked too recently upholstered or painted, and the newer items, though not tasteless, were distinctly down market. A treadmill, rower and an exercise bike sat in one corner of the living room.

Chassie, following Rain's gaze, said, "We don't heat the whole place anymore, so we tend to live in it like a big apartment." Arriving in the spacious kitchen, Chassie introduced a well-maintained woman in her upper-certain years who appeared to be directing the cooking. "Violetta, this is the Rain Morton-Morton that I was telling you about."

"Madlin," Rain said, reaching out to Violetta. "Morton Madlin."

Violetta wiped her hands on a cloth hanging from her apron. "Very pleased," she said in a light accent. "What will you have?"

she asked, indicating a very well-stocked bar on one side of the kitchen. "Chassie, you get for her," she commanded in a motherly tone.

"What's pouring?" Rain asked genially.

"Pisco Sours!" Chassie said heading over to the bar. "I'm a drink divvy. I can tell what you'd like, I guarantee it. Have a seat." Chassie indicated a row of small black barstools at an island in the middle of the kitchen. Violetta directed the help to lay out some appetizers.

Marisol came in from a back door of the kitchen with a martini glass drained of something pink. Her hair was still wet, but her makeup was perfect and she was wearing a vintage Pucci pantsuit with swirls and eddies of color lurching all over it. Little pointy, bright-orange pumps peeked out underneath the flowing cuffs.

Chassie received a big smooch over by the bar. "You look absolutely FAMOUS my dear," Chassie told her.

"Thank you, love," Marisol said. "Just came in for a refill, then it's hair."

"Did I tell you?" Chassie said to Marisol and Violetta, "Rain-Rain is a painter." She topped off the sour with bitters and a dollop of foam from the shaker.

"I…" Rain stopped herself from apologizing and took the drink from Chassie.

"I adore art," Violetta said, assuming an expression that probably intended great enthusiasm, but looked terribly bored nonetheless. Beautifully flaccid facial muscles failing to engage. "It's so *creative*," she sighed. "Do you know our mysterious James Morrow then?"

"No, yeah. The tour was great," Rain said. "He seems really interesting, very…interesting."

"What do you mean, *interesting*?" Chassie prodded.

"Well, he brought me…uh, gave me some paints…and I… and then…" she stammered.

Marisol raised an eyebrow and threw out her hip. "You mean the man himself?"

"Well, yeah," Rain said. "Is that unusual?"

"He only comes out for the tours, stays pretty much to himself otherwise…" Chassie replied knowingly. "Small town."

"He's really sick I think, huh?" Marisol offered.

"Dying, I heard," Violetta said, leaning in conspiratorially.

"Did you know the wife?" Chassie asked her.

"No, never met her," Violetta said. "But can you imagine?"

Chassie looked at Rain and explained, "James had a wife who died. Train."

"Tragedy," said Violetta. "And that's just the beginning of the story."

"Never was the same," said Chassie, shaking her head.

"You, don't know, my dear," said Violetta, pinching Chassie's cheek. "You were in diapers."

"And you were in the city," Chassie said. "Everybody knows the Morrow story, or some version of it, but few know the man…"

"Enough of this morbid sad shit," said Marisol, taking her freshened cocktail from Chassie. "I gotta dry my hair."

The doorbell rang. "Oh, that'll be Marco! Darling boy!" Violetta said, removing the apron she was wearing to reveal a quite decent figure in a stylish wrap dress and big beads.

Chassie reentered the kitchen pulling Anne behind her with Alvaro following close behind. "Not yet, Violetta!" she called out cheerfully.

Violetta twinkled a look at Rain, a hard fold that could either have been real exasperation or just a wink. Rain smiled at her.

Anne sat down next to Rain at the kitchen bar and Chassie lowered the lights. It felt like a restaurant kitchen after closing.

"Good to see you," Anne said, and kissed Rain breezily on the cheek. "How've you been settling in?" Anne took her gin and tonic from Chassie with a mouthed thanks.

"Good. Fine, I guess," Rain said. "I've been enjoying it more than I expected. Lots of hiking. I thought I'd be in the city more, but I seem to be spending all my time here."

"Oh, my Lord, if I could do that!" Anne stopped herself and laughed, "Actually, no, I'm lying. I couldn't live without the city. Love it there. Love my stores." She took a sip of her drink. "But I have to tell you, that first mouthful of country air when I get off the train every night? It's the best thing I've ever tasted in my life." Anne leaned back and ran her hands through her hair. It fell back around her face in abundant freshness and she shook her head lightly. "Love the city. Love the country. Lovin' life!" She offered up her glass for a clink with Rain.

Rain took another sip of the limey, sweet-and-sour drink Chassie had made for her. It was exotic, kind of Mojito-like, but felt foreign on her tongue.

The doorbell rang again. David and Melia. Rain was trying to remember names as the room began to fill up, but finally just looked for Anne when it was time to head into the dining room. Her sour had been magically kept full regardless of what she thought was rather constant sipping, but everyone left their cocktails in the kitchen when they retired to the enormous dining hall, so with one last gulp, she put the thing down and found her way to a seat near Anne.

"Right here, honey," Anne was saying, holding onto a chair next to hers. The dining room was right out of central casting. The table was filled with plates and silver and cutlery and linens and fully lit candelabras. Tangles of berried vines snaked around the center of the table; they were decorated with what appeared to be nests holding huge stalks of artichokes, giant, red and white turnips and some kind of pocked vegetable Rain couldn't identify. It all had a Peter Greenaway feel, odd, but utterly opulent.

"Violetta, all Violetta," was all Chassie would say as she brushed off all of her guests' gasps and compliments. Chassie poured wines all around, reds and whites. The first course was already served at each guest's place. A white gazpacho with a large cube of lightly charred bread at the center and a rough sprinkling of fresh chive.

Rain had attended her share of lavish meals in her life. She used to go with her father and Gwen to penthouses and back rooms of restaurants in the city, but there was something so purely enjoyable about this meal and the generosity with which it was offered. Chassie was pleased by pleasing her guests, and even the self-absorbed Marisol seemed to be enjoying herself.

Just as Violetta's uniformed help were clearing the first course plates, a commotion in the kitchen grabbed Chassie's attention and a huge smile split her face. "HUNTER!" she cried, jumping up.

Just then, through the kitchen's swinging doors came a young man with dark-cocoa skin, small sprightly dreads and light green eyes. He lit up, matching Chassie's smile and the two of them snapped into a tremendous bear hug, the door smacking Hunter from behind, but not budging them a bit.

"Hunt," she murmured, fixing on his eyes and holding on to his arms.

"Chase," he echoed.

Chassie turned around. "Everybody? You remember my brother, Hunter?"

Alvaro came around the table and slapped him on the back and Anne stood to kiss him. Hunter's face was still wide open with greeting when he encountered Rain awkwardly still in her seat. "Very nice to meet *you*," Hunter said sweetly as he went on to embrace and shake hands with everyone at the table. "But I've interrupted!" Hunter bellowed. His place had been set and he joined right in as the main course came from the kitchen and made its rounds.

"So Rain. You're painting," Anne said finally when the din had died down a bit.

"Yes. Most of the time. Though I'm a ways off from making a living off it," she said.

Anne looked over at Alvaro, who was engrossed with talking to Hunter. "Well, you don't know unless you try. He could quit, but he'd rather keep the day job until his music can support him instead of me." Anne gave Rain a sidelong wry smile. "Well, that, and his sick-puppy attachment to Morrow."

"Morrow seems to have everybody intrigued around here," Rain said, giving Anne a slightly quizzical look. One that invited information, but allowed her to take a pass on gossiping if she wanted.

Anne nodded and smiled. "Morrow intrigues people. I can't say I know any more about him than anybody else. Alvaro's probably closest, and yet he said it's sometimes like taking care of a wild animal, a circus lion. It all looks mellow and calm and almost boring, but you have to remember to keep this intense respect and do everything it needs before it needs it."

"A lion?"

"Oh, no. He never gets worked up. It's more this sense of what's behind him. You're getting this second hand from me, and I think Alvaro's a little too much in awe of him for some reason."

"Maybe the lion's drugged," she said laughing, "or neutered."

Anne laughed. "Well, evidently the yoga teacher wouldn't agree."

"Ah-ha!" Rain said. "Never too old."

"I don't know, he seems pretty well-preserved, don't you think?"

"I guess," Rain said. "Though I've never done the whole daddy-boyfriend thing."

"No. Ick," Anne chortled. They looked again over at Alvaro, who Rain realized must be a bit younger than Anne. They were similar looking in a way—thick black hair on pale skin, fine features and thick lips—though her features added up to snow-white Irish, his to Euro-South-American.

"So what do you do the rest of the time?" Anne asked. "When you're not painting."

"Nothing all that interesting," Rain said. "Worked in a gallery for a while, temped a little, do a little graphic design."

"What brought you up here?"

"Well," Rain laughed. She thought about all of the disclosure required to answer such a simple question.

"That's alright," Anne said, giving her another of her wry smiles. "Nah, stay mysterious, that's okay…"

"No!" Rain exclaimed. "No mystery at all. My husband is an art history professor, and he got a fellowship in London this semester. I'd just inherited this cabin up here so we rented out our place in the city for the fall and I came up to do some painting."

"Nice!" Anne said. "Wow, it makes this place seem like an art colony. So often people come here either because they've just had babies or are just about to!"

"Oh, God," Rain said. "I always say I'm on the five-year plan with all of that, and if you ask me next year, I'll tell you I'll think about it in five years…"

Anne laughed and looked down at her plate. "What about you?" Rain asked, but someone said something to Anne from across the table and she seemed not to have heard her, so Rain dropped it.

Hunter was telling a story about being in Bangladesh. He had just gotten back from there, and he very soberly described the street scenes, the intense poverty and disease and then more glowingly he talked about the fantastic, quirky and generous musicians he stayed with and the project he'd been involved in there.

Dessert was served along with port in the music room. Chassie built a fire in the enormous fireplace. Candlelight was the room's only other illumination. It cast the most romantic light on all of the faces. Even Violetta looked like the twenty-year-old she clearly paid a great deal to resemble.

"I adore art," she said, sidling up to Anne and Rain. "I want to meet this Morrow, and I think we have a dinner, nah?"

Anne said, "That sounds great." She looked at Rain.

"I will take care of everything," Violetta said. "The Halloween, nah?"

Rain nodded, unsure of what she meant. "Yeah, that sounds great."

"Okay, it's good," Violetta said and she almost pursed her lips.

As she walked over to sit with Marco, Anne said, "She's a character. I'm surprised she doesn't know Morrow already."

"I couldn't figure out if she worked for Chassie at first," Rain said quietly to Anne.

"Oh, no," Anne said. "She could probably buy and sell Chassie ten times over. She was a big model in the sixties, I think. Started a little makeup line in the seventies, which was bought out. She'd be a caterer if she could bear to earn money, but she just throws these huge events at other people's houses.

Won't do local politics or charities. Just fun. She's a little," Anne rolled her eyes, "you know, eccentric. But sweet."

"She doesn't have parties at her house?"

"Nope. I'm not even sure where she lives right now. Some penthouse in the city, and a rented place up here, I think. Got places all over. Stays with people a lot. Hotels. She's a lot of fun."

The music was a pleasant loose noodling on the keys by Alvaro while Hunter accompanied with resonant chords and moody rhythms on his steel guitar. They all watched, transfixed, as the two played a lazy, glowing, unending set.

Riding home on the Vespa down and up dirt roads and Route 9D's dark stretches, Rain comforted herself with the thought that the only person she could kill driving this thing drunk was herself. She hummed and droned out *vroom-vroom* noises to herself as she rode down the long mountainside and along the smaller roads back to her little house. And despite the fact that she was feeling no pain that night, she resolved to buy herself something against the impending cold.

The next morning, a phone message broadcasted through the house, waking her up. It was Chassie, congratulating her on her Halloween plans. "Don't worry, though," she said, not very reassuringly. "It'll only be Violetta, Marco, Anne and Alvaro, me, Marisol and Hunter *and* your special guest, Mr. James 'Reclusive' Morrow. We're counting on you!"

Rain lunged for the phone. "Chassie? Chassie?" but Chassie had already hung up.

YELLOW

Yellow, yellow, yellow, yellow!
It is not a color.
It is summer!
It is the wind on a willow,
the lap of waves, the shadow
under a bush, a bird, a bluebird,
three herons, a dead hawk
rotting on a pole—

—WILLIAM CARLOS WILLIAMS

Y er Yella. Coward.
Bile, piss, puss, disease.
So too sunshine, flowers, lemons and warmth.
Bananas, bread and eggs.

The sweetness of melons, tomatoes, peppers, corn and the sizzling skins of roasted fowl.

Yellow used to be protected by law. Not any pigment in particular, but yellowness. The dairy lobby forced margarines to be sold lard-white with a tiny spot of yellow dye inside for the buyer to knead into it, so as not to infringe upon the yellowness of the real thing. So important to them and to the consumer was the yellow of that fat.

It was a Tuesday in late fall. Like any other Tuesday, he supposed. Just another Tuesday. Morrow rose early as always. As every day of his adult life, he lay in bed for a moment in the dark considering the broken rectangles of pale light fighting their way around the pitch black of his shuttered windows and remembered.

But this morning he felt shaken. He had been shoved out of his routine. It used to be he would lay there and remember, think of the woman he lost so many years before, and, like a mantra, tell himself how he could have changed things, kept her from leaving, kept her love.

This morning, Morrow lay in bed thinking about her once again. But her youthful face was more alive in his mind now.

Alive and right down the road. He felt wide awake and confused, zinged up with hope and heartbeat and energy, an energy that rose up around the crumbling feeling of his illness, buoying up whatever was left of him in a foamy, numbing sea.

Clinging to his routines as if to a life raft, Morrow dressed, took his tea and went over to unlock the factory doors. But this morning, rather than getting to his paperwork, Morrow returned to his house. He was haunting his own house now, standing there feeling like it was the wrong time of day, the wrong Tuesday. Something was terribly wrong. Everything about the way he had made it through his days before was wrong. He needed to remake it. To fix what had broken.

Suddenly he saw it. It was all clear to him. He could stop fighting it, just embrace what felt right to do. He had no other plans, no kind of trajectory before. It was like he was waiting for her to come and give him this purpose. His imminent death, something to arrange for and work toward. That it could matter and might be felt.

Morrow took the stairs two at a time, a ringing in every muscle and bone in his body propelling him upward toward his project. He felt healed. This Tuesday, today, would begin it. He'd figured it out.

The day came and went, Morrow began to feel the familiar achy fatigue returning to him, so he took stock of his progress. The attic room he'd been working in was empty now. All of the Riker boxes were emptied and stacked neatly by the door, boxes and bags were heaped by the stairs.

Photographs, letters, a journal and a few small paintings were stacked next to the Riker boxes and these were the only items that remained when James carried out the bags and boxes filled with the rest of her belongings. These items that made her his.

The proof of their shared experience. These he hauled across the lawn in the dark toward the glow from the now silent factory. Inside, on the main floor, James shook out the plastic bags and shoe boxes onto the vast clean metal counters.

Now he brought pliers, cutters and hammers into play, prying stones from metal fittings, resins apart from wire, pulling bristles out of wooden brushes, cutting bone buttons from jackets and shirts, cutting away elastic from skirts and separating shoe leather from soles. Some for the incinerator, others to an acid bath, stones in the crusher and metals to the forge.

Nights and nights of this activity, distilling objects down, most for the incinerator to make lamp black, some materials ashed all the way to a translucent white. James' house began to empty and one night he even hauled a chair across the lawn toward the factory.

Throughout all this, he worked with a light sense of irony playing on his consciousness. In so carefully preserving his memories, he had been locking in rage and despair, but in destroying them, he honored them.

Hiking on the trails around Mahican Brook Road, Rain had started to get used to the solitude, the utter peace of uninterrupted nature so that one day, hearing a noise from behind her through the thump from her iPod, she jumped, her body apparently convinced she'd be facing down a rabid raccoon or a mountain lion or something. She looked over her shoulder and pulled an earbud out, finding neither of those things. But then, suddenly, from out of the woods came three emergency workers and one other hiker hauling gear and a large, orange, human-carrying pallet.

"Watch out!" One of the paramedics hooted.

"Oh, jeez!" Rain exclaimed. "Can I help?"

"Thanks, we got it," the paramedic said. "He'll be fine. Just a leg."

Rain stepped off the trail and let the group pass. The hiker was pretty beat up. His friend was pale and roughed up, though still up and walking.

When they had passed her, the second paramedic turned and called back to Rain, "Hey, be careful up there!"

"Yeah! One trip a day, huh?" The paramedics chuckled.

Back on her trail again, Rain was not watching where she was going, clicking through tracks on her iPod, when she nearly tripped over a mountain bike propped up against a tree.

She tugged one of the wires back out from her ear.

"Hello?" she called.

A loud cracking sounded above her head, and she flinched and peered up into the branches to find a brown-skinned, green-eyed young man perched there. Hunter, from Chassie's party. He was dressed in hiking pants and an ill-fitting, hand-knit wool sweater.

Stepping aside, Rain said, "Oh, I'm sorry."

"No!" Hunter exclaimed. "Hey wait."

He jumped down gracefully from the tree. "Hunter, from Chassie's. You're Rain, right?"

Rain was flustered. He was so beautiful. "Right," she began. "Your playing, it was so…" Hunter grabbed her hand and shook it, his hand so big and soft and warm that Rain blurted giddily, "Yeah, nice to see you. Again, I guess."

"Chassie told me about you," said Hunter.

"She seems to be the source," Rain said.

"Oh, yes, of all things," Hunter said laughing. "She's my girl. Which way you headed?"

Rain pointed on down the trail.

"Uh-huh. Have you seen the waterfall?" he asked.

"What waterfall?"

"Oh, yeah," Hunter said, full of charm and pluck. "Okay. I've got some things to show you, I think." He took up his bike and began pushing it along the trail.

Rain looked around. "Oh, I've got to…" she trailed off.

"You've got to see it," Hunter said enthusiastically. "Come on, you're going to love this."

Hunter ditched his bike at the gated mouth of a smaller trail and Rain followed him as he danced his way delicately, goat-like, down the narrow winding path.

Rain could hear the falls even before she saw the shallow winding creek. As the trail leveled off next to the water, the dramatic falls came gradually into view.

About forty feet high and almost as wide, with boulders dividing and redirecting their flow, the falls had a pretty wading pool at their base. Hunter pulled off his sweater and marched into the pool, walking right in with his hiking sandals and pants and all. It was knee deep.

"Come on in, it's fantastic!"

"It's October!" Rain exclaimed.

"It's an Indian summer! Enjoy the global warming! Come on, you got those quick dry pants: put 'em to use!"

Rain muttered softly to herself, "What'chyou talking about my pants." Taking off her boots and socks, she rolled her pants up and dropped her backpack. As she picked her way in, the water felt so cold it gripped her ankles hard, her feet reading every stone along the bottom of the shallow pool.

Watching her struggle along, Hunter gave Rain a friendly little splash as she took another step toward him, and the surprise of it made her lose her step. But just as she started to go down, Hunter caught her valiantly. The proximity took them both off-guard and there was a dangerous moment of connection, his green eyes lit-up and close. He held her for a moment longer that he should have.

Rain said, "I'm, uhm…" She stood, getting better footing and unconsciously pressing her left thumb to her wedding ring.

"I saw that," Hunter said graciously, nodding at her ring. "No worries." Hunter took her right hand in his and helped her back to shore. "We'll bring you sandals next time."

Out of the water, Hunter threw himself down at the side of the falls and ripped into his backpack where he retrieved some apples, a hunk of cheese and a thermos of hot tea.

"Tea," he said. "The real thing. Lapsang Souchong—it's like whisky, you gotta try it."

Rain put her boots back on and joined Hunter on his patch of soft ground. She took her camera out of her pack and photographed Hunter's hands, the apples and cheese, the pouring tea and cascading waterfall behind. Hunter was a willing and easy subject. Didn't get uncomfortable. Just let her photograph him.

Rain took the thermos top when Hunter passed it to her. She tasted it. Liquid smoke, toast and burning fires, barley and oak barrels.

"Mmmm," she said, nodding. "So did you grow up here?"

"My parents were the caretakers at the castle. I grew up playing over there all my life. Chassie and me were just like brother and sister. Had no idea we were any different from them."

Rain passed the thermos top back to him. "And you're different from them?" she asked.

"According to some," Hunter said, smiling wryly at her. "As I'll just assume you know…" Then he gave her a crooked smile and said, "Not me and Chassie, though. She was no-nonsense. I think we had more to do with forming each others' personalities than anything else."

"Pesky outside world…" Rain said.

Hunter resumed cutting apples and handed a slice to Rain on his Opinel knife. "That and cash," he said.

"Irritating," Rain said. She took the apple and some cheese from him.

"The old man left me an inheritance, though. Chassie set that up, I'm pretty sure," Hunter said. "So I travel. Play music."

"Your parents still here?"

"Well, my dad passed just before the old man, but Mom's doing alright. Getting on for sure. She stays at the retirement community down in the village. Loves it. Got the Mah Jhong ladies all sewn up. And what about you? What brings you up here?"

"My dad had a little house. Left it to me."

"Did he die recently?"

"Couple months ago."

"Oh, I'm sorry."

"Yeah."

"Where's the place?"

"It's the little cabin on the edge of the Highland Morrow grounds."

"I know that place. John Morton, the writer, used to live there."

"Yeah, that's my father."

"Oh!"

"Yeah."

"I like his stuff, man. He was good at what he did. I am truly sorry."

"Yeah."

"Weird for you having him be so famous?"

"It's not as weird as you'd think," Rain said. "I was Daddy's girl, so he was just famous for *me*, you know?"

"You famous, too?"

"Oh, no," Rain laughed. "No, totally incognito."

"Artist?"

"Trying."

"Right. You just are."

"Not much of a résumé behind me," Rain said, sheepishly.

"Well, it's the doing it, right?" Hunter said. "Look at you: you can't even have a picnic without thinking that way."

Rain turned her camera in her hands. "I'm sorry," she said.

Hunter laughed. "You're the real thing," he told her, shaking his head.

"Whatever that means," Rain said, and they both laughed, allowing their eyes to meet under the beams of sunlight working their way through the branches in the waterfall's cove.

The cabin was looking more like a house, the inside more like a working studio. Paintings were stacked up along the walls. Opened boxes of paints, supports, mediums, cans of turp and mineral spirits and old coffee cans stuffed with brushes covered the surfaces of the two large tables. The couch was filled up with stacks of books and magazines. Running her fingers lightly over a half-dozen small paintings lined up on the table, Rain picked one up. It was loosely rendered and rich, depicting the river and the railroad tracks from a high vantage point. She looked up at the large canvas she had set up next to the landscape composite on the wall. It was covered with her scrubby black markings now. Carefully placing the small landscape down into ripped muslin cloth, Rain wrapped it and pushed it into her backpack.

She arrived at the factory to find Alvaro there working late. He greeted her warmly and directed her right back to Morrow's office. Rain wound her way through the factory floor, past a warren of rooms and shelves of beautiful junk and finally found the stairwell to Morrow's office. Peering up, she could see that Morrow's desk was empty, so she climbed the stairs thinking she'd just leave it there for him. But she surprised him at another table where he was hunched down working over a tray.

Morrow jumped. "Holy…!"

"Oh! I'm so sorry! I just wanted…! Oh, I'm so…"

Rain glimpsed a tuft of fur, wet and red in the tray James was working over, but he quickly covered it with a metal lid.

Morrow said, "It's good to see you. I'm glad you, uh…" He looked around.

"Please forgive me," Rain said, recovering. "I just wanted to bring you a little token of thanks."

Rain held out her painting still wrapped in muslin.

"No," Morrow said. "No, you shouldn't have…I'm honored. It's a…I'm just honored."

Morrow moved so slowly toward her that Rain lurched at him, proffering her gift. As he unwrapped the painting, his smile faded.

Rain couldn't help but notice his distress. "I hope you… I hope you don't hate it."

"No, please," Morrow began, as if waking up again. He hung the painting on the wall and stepped back to view it.

"I know it isn't very good, but…"

Morrow said, "No."

"…I just thought I'd give you a little token of thanks while I…"

"No," Morrow said.

"…worked on something more appropriate to say thanks…"

"No. No. Rain. No. I love the painting. I'm sorry I'm so…" He took a chair and pointed to one for her. "I'm so…" He pinched his nose again. He sat there silently, his glance rising to a framed photograph on his desk again and again. Rain didn't sit, she watched him. He wiped his eyes, wiped them again. Coughed.

In the silence, James looked up to find Rain's face streaked with tears, her eyes shining and reddened.

"I'm so sorry!" James said, looking even more devastated.

Rain was embarrassed. "No," she said, trying to puff out a casual laugh. "I think because my Dad...you know."

James cleared his throat and rubbed his face, like he was trying to wipe something away. He breathed deeply. Rain took his cue and wiped her face too. They smiled at each other with a small polite relief.

"I'm so sorry, Rain Morton. I'm moved. That's all."

"No, no, no. I'm sorry. I'm not sure what's come over me. Uhm," Rain said, feeling ridiculous now. "I came to say I'm having an open studio—a Halloween dinner—for a couple of people at my cabin next week. And I was hoping you would be willing to come."

Morrow broke into a small rare grin and said, "That's very kind. Yes, I will."

As she walked back up the dirt road to her house, Morrow's emotion lingered with her. She tried to make sense of her tears. Was she missing her father who was close in age to Morrow? Someone Morrow knew from the old days? But there was something else, something elusive. By the time she got back home, however, she had convinced herself it was just the awkwardness of crying right in front of him, this odd character she barely knew.

Home. For the first time she actually felt like she might be home. Something in the history this place held for her, the abundance of the wooded trails. And even the unfamiliar feeling of belonging she got on the dirt road.

Though she used a digital camera, Rain still cocked a vestigial film advance lever. It was the appendix of cameras. It certainly had no use, but Rain felt that since it couldn't hurt, why take the risk of removing it? Thumbing it between shots forced her to shift her hold on a view, forced a fresh angle and new way into a scene for each shot.

There was something of the specter in the way James entered her house; he was silent in his step, waiting patiently until decorum forced him to speak.

"This is beautiful," he said just as Rain registered his presence.

"Better than the art, I think," Rain said, on auto-self-deprecate. She gave herself an inner forehead slap and hoped James hadn't heard her. Her nerves felt like they were leaking out from every pore.

Before he crossed the threshold, Violetta sidled over to James from the kitchen where she had been directing the cooking. "Ah, no, I adore art," she said, offering James a glass.

"Do you remember Violetta?" Rain asked. She stayed on the lower level and watched the two of them up at the doorway. They were truly peers, his aging accelerated by illness and hers, impeded artificially, balancing out the unfair advantage older men have over their female counterparts.

"No, darling, no," Violetta said.

James took the glass from her. "You look familiar," he said, awkward but polite. He reached for her hand and lifted her fingers slightly short of the kiss that Violetta seemed to expect.

"We've never met," she smiled coyly at him. "I arrange this to meet you."

"I see..." James said warily, but without missing Violetta's playfulness. He let go of her hand and raised his eyebrows over toward Rain.

"I finish," Violetta said with a sudden enthusiasm. "You chat, uh?"

Violetta turned back to the kitchen, only one helper accompanying her tonight. Morrow walked down the steps to the main room to join Rain and handed her the rumpled paper bag he was clutching. Inside were clumpy oil paint sticks. They were thick, like sidewalk chalk, but rough and very heavy. Dark, brilliant, intense blue.

"Lapis?" she asked, though she already knew.

James nodded.

"These are incredibly valuable," Rain said with a crooked smile.

"And concentrated, yes," he admitted. "But I happen to know somebody who makes them. I brought them to you because they're pre-worn and you can't get too precious about them. They'll look the same whether you keep them locked up or use them," he continued, half playful, half gruff. "So you may as well use them."

"Thank you," Rain said. "They're beautiful."

Violetta approached them with a plate of fig and crumbled goat cheese on tiny toasts. "You talk art now, and I make art in the kitchen," she joked.

Rain shrugged off Violetta's giddiness and led James to the window facing the high wall where she had hung her paintings.

They looked distressingly themed to her this night. Too appropriate a backdrop for an All Hallows Eve. *Decorative* was the word that occurred to her, the devastating insult spat back and forth between realists and abstract artists. Realists charged abstractionists with making mere objects, design elements for a space lacking any content. Abstract painters, on the other hand, disdained pretty pictures as pointless and antiquated regurgitations of our most conventional minds.

Straddling the two warring camps could cause an artist to volley opposing insults at herself and to confront her own worst self-assessment.

Morrow nodded. "So, do you think your work is changing?"

Rain looked down at her shoes. James hadn't seen her work before, only the small piece she'd given to him. Knowing she was more or less ready to bring them down to Ben Schuldenfrei in the city, she had thought she should be brave enough to let people see them tonight. This, however, wasn't the kind of reaction that she was looking for. "Well," Rain said slowly. "I think I've finally completed something. Maybe I hurried to do it before it was gone."

James appeared to consider this. Rain was familiar with flat and unenthusiastic responses like "interesting," "different," and "tell me about these," but James seemed to know what he was seeing. "I think you can't help but do what you have to do," he commented vaguely.

"You sound like my stepmother. 'Art is a disease!' she always says," Rain laughed. "Yeah, thanks."

"More of a mixed blessing," James said, without smiling. "A gift with a stiff price-tag."

"You don't like them," Rain said with a lightness she hoped would conceal her disappointment.

"I never said that. I wouldn't say that. They're accomplished." James took a sip of his wine. "I'm afraid I'm afflicted with my own disease."

Rain frowned, expecting to hear about his illness.

"No, no," James said. "No, I am cursed with an inability to flatter. You shouldn't listen to me at all. I am just one viewer, really, it's meaningless."

"Now I'm intrigued," Rain said furrowing her brow. "Now you're going to have to tell me what you think!"

"Well," James cleared his throat, "for example, I don't think that was meant for that canvas." He pointed to the large abstract that she had previously planned as a landscape.

"You saw that the other day?" Rain asked.

"I saw the work you brought me. This is different. From another time perhaps?"

Rain was self-conscious. "I know, I know," she agreed. "It's work I started when I was in the city. But I have a chance for a show, and I have to play that out, don't I?"

"I think the cart has to follow the horse," Morrow said. "What you need to do is keep the horse happy. Give it what it needs. The career is the cart. The healthier the horse, the better carts she can pull. Things hop on," he paused. "How far can I drag out this metaphor?"

Rain laughed uneasily, trying to appear light hearted about the whole endeavor. "Well, if I am just finishing up a haul here, I can't just dump it all off by the side of the road, can I?"

Morrow gave an enigmatic shrug which left Rain a bit deflated.

"Maybe it's…"

"What?" Rain asked, as if she were preparing to take her punishment.

"I might simply have a prejudice toward purer, unmuddied…"

"Oh!" Rain laughed. "Oh, the colors! Yes, I would imagine you wouldn't like the way I work so much. It's just a layering, a piling on. You can see hints of the original color if you look close."

"I wouldn't mention it if I hadn't seen, hadn't seen…"

"What, the little painting I gave you?"

"You have a rare understanding of color, of those colors," James said solemnly.

"Oh," Rain laughed a little more genuinely this time, trying to slough off his gravity. "Well, thanks."

"That sensitivity can't be taught. It's a rare talent." With that, James turned on his heel and abruptly marched back up toward the kitchen to offer help.

Rain stared at the paintings. These constructions. They may have started to get a little too skillful by the last one. Like a charicature of what began as an emotion. She couldn't tell if it was good or bad that her hand couldn't help learning a deftness with her technique. Did that deftness lessen the work, or did it enhance it? It was part of the dirty trick of personal discovery in art. Artists who kept to a singular subject and style risked losing freshness, losing their own thrill of discovery. But artists who switched media, styles and voices risked not ever developing an individual voice. Showing off skill either way can become mannered, tricked-up. Cubism? Yes, I can do that. Drips? Yup. Photo-realist ketchup bottles? Yes, that too. Sooner or later it devolved into wow-factor. It wasn't lack of talent: it was just that those hoop jumps began to say less and less until one's art became ultimately pedestrian. There was no comparing imitators to Picasso, Pollock or Goings. But staying in too narrow a style, even a style of one's own invention, risked becoming that same kind of inauthentic, unfelt labor. Of course, the most slap-dash Rothko would be gratefully received today, but artists work in an uncertain world. Art historians might find moments of self-assurance in artists' letters and journals; however, these same moments appear to be foolish ravings in the case of an unknown artist. When is a painting finished? When are you on the right track? Does your work speak to anyone? You don't know, and you can't.

Hooting and howling outside pulled Rain out of her reverie. The rest had arrived.

Violetta was directing her helper in the final touches, and the cocktails had loosened up the company. Violetta's newest boy, a day-trader named Mark, boomed with laughter and back-slapping ease. He had collected Hunter and Marisol, the most handsome people at the party, and had them over by the iPod dock navigating around Rain's collection. Alvaro chatted with Morrow near the windows and Anne approached Rain at the bar table. She set her hip against the table near Rain, leaned in and looked toward her husband.

"I've never seen that man this far out of his safety zone," she said quietly to Rain.

"Who, Alvaro?" Rain asked.

"No, Morrow," Anne replied, sipping her wine. "He's a puzzle, that man. Alvaro thinks he's fascinating—damaged or something. His wife dying, maybe."

"He does seem to go back and forth. Really friendly and interesting. Then suddenly shut down."

"Alvaro likes to save broken birds," Anne said with a fond shake of her head.

"Violetta hadn't met him before?" Rain asked.

"No, and she's been dying to. Maybe she's considering trying one out a little closer to her own age," Anne said, glancing over at Brad or Todd or whatever his name was. "Too bad James is already taken."

"He's got a girlfriend?" Rain asked, grinning and turning her back to the room.

"Remember? The yoga teacher?" Anne said, turning too. She opened another bottle of wine while Rain organized glasses.

"Oh, the yoga teacher," Rain said.

"He hired her to do OT with the staff. Kind of a feng shui of holding your body while you work so you don't strain yourself," she explained.

Rain shook her head. "How do you know everything that goes on around here?" she asked.

Anne laughed. "Well that one wasn't very hard. I've got an inside man…"

Rain laughed with her.

It was unseasonably warm. The air had a softness warm enough to bring the aromas of the fallen leaves, so Rain had left the screen doors pulled across the front of the cabin, the big door tucked up into the roof.

"Bon appétit!" Violetta cried cheerfully, and everyone eagerly gathered at their carefully assigned place. Another aspect of Violetta's art was guest arrangement. Rain had witnessed it before anyone arrived—she had worked the seating chart of nine carefully, in the manner of an architect considering undergirding structures. She assessed the various personalities, creating the right mix. A few of her cardinal rules: separate couples, alternate men and women where possible. It was eye opening to Rain. Though she'd witnessed Gwen's quite accomplished entertaining, her approach had always been far more casual. Rain suspected this high-level calculation might be something that had gone on with Gwen, too, perhaps just a tad less conspicuously. Violetta clearly enjoyed every part of the process. She'd been at Rain's since early in the day, arranging vegetables to be chopped in pretty heaps like a cooking show, even carefully removing from sight stickers, bands and plastic bags to hide the mundane.

First course was local artisanal cheese and morel tart. The individually plated tarts had rough, turned edges and steamed lightly around a nest of wilted baby watercress and toasted pine nuts. The crusts were browned to a perfect gold, a depth of color ranging from the darkest crunchy edges to the lightest doughy depths, and the mushrooms settled into a dense, black, brown and white tangle inside.

Chassie had the unique ability to corral a proper dinner party conversation. Through the hum of chatter, it was Chassie's booming voice that unified the table saying, "Well that's that, you see? This generation doesn't believe in calling the world out on its bad behavior. Instead we blame ourselves for having a sour outlook and medicate our disappointment away. Soon there will be no more eccentrics in the world, eh, James?" She raised her glass to James.

"No," Anne protested, uncharacteristically against the flow of conversation. "I don't believe that," she said, shaking her head firmly and briefly silencing the table.

"I think," she continued, "that people struggle more than you'd suspect, coming to terms with their disappointments in life. I think we don't let on what a struggle that often is."

"That's where Chassie's point about eccentrics comes in, though," Mark said. "Artists as a matter of fact," he looked encouragingly at Rain and at Alvaro and Hunter.

"Right?" he asked. "You can't create when you're zoned out and in a happy place, right?"

"Nothing happens when it's truly dark," Hunter countered. "All that romanticizing? We like our artists to burn bright and flame out?" Hunter wiped his mouth with his napkin and tossed it back into his lap. "Nah," he said. "Musicians are only productive in a state of managing their weaknesses. I'd imagine it's the same for artists." He let his eyes flash to Rain as he said this. Rain felt a zing through her veins as their eyes met. She tried to cover for it by sticking her wine glass up to her mouth, but then forgot what it was there for. Hid a smile behind it.

"Tell me," Violetta said to James. "Do you take mood and meaning in consideration when you are producing a line?"

James appeared to consider this for a moment, looking down at his plate and pushing the food around with his fork. Then he raised his gaze to meet Violetta's eye. "You mean MY mood?" he asked lightly. He looked over at Alvaro. "I don't know, do I?"

"No, no," Violetta said. "I mean the mood of color!"

"Colors have no moods," James said flatly, looking back down at his plate.

"Surely you are familiar with color meanings and studies…"

"Studies!" James said dismissively.

Violetta plowed onward, either not catching James cuts, or not permitting them. "Studies to show that pink is elevate the mood. Red is fire up the energy. Green is depressant and yellow is stimulating, I think, bile or the liver?" She surveyed the table as though appealing for back-up.

"Yellow," James said. "Yellow. What is yellow? There are sour yellows and creamy yellows, sickly yellows and sunny yellows."

"Golden," Violetta perservered earnestly. "A nice, golden yellow."

"Sure," James said. "A tone, a single note or maybe even a chord can be said to be sad or wistful or maniacal. But once you put it into a context, it is simply there to serve the whole. Even in color-field work, where a single color is the main player, the color is still in context. The lighting, the frame, where and how it is hung, it all works as a system for better or for worse. Ideally for some purpose, I suppose…"

Just then, as the awkwardness began to settle in to a distinct feeling of unease, Rain heard the crunch of wheels on gravel. Rain thought it might be a good time to interrupt where this conversation appeared to be going, the strangeness and contrarian moods the guests seem to be indulging. Thinking it might be another of Violetta's staff arriving, Rain rose and looked at Violetta.

Door-slamming and muttered-curses wafted too loudly through the open front of the cabin. A sudden banging at the screen doors made Rain straighten and exclaim in amazement, "Karl!"

Karl ripped the screen on the lower panel with his suitcase and continued to shove against the sliding door like it was stuck. "Could you get this?" he shouted.

Rain realized she had made no move to help him and, recovering, put down the plates she'd picked up and rushed up to the entry level to help slide open the door.

"What are you doing here?" Rain asked as he banged again against the door jamb struggling with his luggage over the threshold.

"What does it look like?" Karl snapped. "Trying to get my damn bags through the door."

By the time Rain had controlled her surprise enough to look around, everyone had gotten their coats and were gathering up bags, stacking plates and saying their good-byes.

Chassie and Marisol stood in the doorway and gave Rain upbeat farewells. They embraced her, keeping a very purposeful cheer to their manners, despite Karl's loud ablutions in the kitchen.

Anne gripped Rain in too tight a hug, indicating clearly she knew this wasn't a good surprise, wordlessly conveying her support. Rain averted her gaze from her friend's face, the connection between the two of them wouldn't allow it, far too much might be revealed there. As she and Alvaro headed toward their car, Anne turned and called out, "Call me!," catching Rain's eyes. So much sympathy and understanding flashed from her that Rain just turned away without answering.

Karl was griping while hunting around for something to eat. Violetta's catering assistant was quickly washing dishes and packaging leftovers. Tugging up the sleeves of her long, leather gloves,

Violetta said. "She will stay until she is finish, you must keep the dishes, darling."

"Oh, my goodness!" Rain said. "That's too much!"

"No," Violetta said, putting her hand over Rain's. "We have more nights like this one, eh?" As she air kissed Rain on both cheeks and back for a third, she let her eye stray over to Karl for an instant. "Hunter? You need driving?" she asked.

Karl hadn't made any effort to speak to any of the guests and was almost grunting as he poked around in the plastic dishes inside the fridge.

"Nah, thanks, Violetta, the girls are waiting for me." Hunter didn't seem to be in any hurry as he carried his untouched guitar along with some glasses up to the kitchenette. He gave Karl a cursory hello and placed the glasses by the sink and his guitar case on the floor. Turning to Rain, who was standing awkwardly in the doorway as her guests paraded out, Hunter boldly took her hand and kissed it and then her cheek. "The work is great," he said. "You keep that up, okay?"

Rain looked at him, a little confused. He glanced over at her paintings and nodded slightly. She was trying to work her mind around Karl only feet away from her and this Hunter with this scent, this redolence that hovered around him and that left her breathless. "Okay," she said, trying to bite off her regret. "Okay, you have a safe trip." Rain felt a growing pang of sadness roll through her, her gut betraying her mind.

She closed the door thinking everyone had left and asked the catering assistant if she could help. She insisted that Rain should leave it to her. Rain felt oddly almost afraid of Karl. Guilty for what she was thinking. Turning around toward the studio, Rain was surprised to see James strolling casually over to the couch and sitting down with his freshened glass of port.

It was all too exhausting: Karl's surprise, his moodiness, this James. She was not sure why he had stayed, but she found she was glad for it. Rain stepped back down to the living-room to James.

Quietly, she said, "Well, I'm glad *some*body could stay!"

"The port's too good," Morrow said, eyeing his glass critically. "Violetta knows her spirits."

Karl emerged from the bathroom and crossed to the kitchen. He didn't acknowledge the woman there, but called to Rain, "What is this stuff? What kind of…"

Rain came back up and set a plate, silverware and a glass for him.

She located the neatly stored leftovers in the fridge and set them next to the place setting at the kitchen table. She poured wine into a clean glass and, without looking at him, asked, "So, what happened?"

"What happened?" Karl repeated, looking at the table Rain had set and the containers of food as if he had no idea what they were for. "The thing has to end sometime. Nobody said it was permanent."

"I just thought you'd said you were staying past New Year's," Rain explained and she stepped slowly away from the table, having stopped short of actually serving him.

Karl started ripping the tops off the containers. "What, do I need permission to come here? Is that what this is?"

Rain turned away from him and went back down to sit in a low chair next to the couch. She and James watched Karl standing in the kitchen shoveling food out onto the plate noisily and shakily, as if this were the first time he'd actually had to serve himself. He managed to make this most mundane of tasks dramatic and filled the space with a blunt energy.

"I knew this man who lived in the Hudson Valley in the seventies," Morrow said to Rain, but loud enough to project toward the kitchen. "Amazing fellow."

Morrow kept his tone casual, but clearly included Karl. "Completely blind. More than legally blind. The man couldn't see the slightest glimmer of light. He was my supplier for a certain root that's very tricky to find."

Karl didn't look up or indicate he could hear, but James continued, watching Karl as he spoke. "Extraordinary stuff," he said. "The highest grade of it is dusty and ragged in its raw state. This man could sniff out the good stuff. He was genius at it."

Karl banged the plates around on the table, shoving them aside and hunting around for a napkin, finally settling on a paper towel.

"Imagine that," Morrow continued. "A blind man, my best supplier of the finest grade madder root whose only purpose he'll never ever have the ability to appreciate. "

"Sad," Rain said, watching Karl, too.

"What's that?" Morrow asked her.

"It strikes me as sad," Rain said, finally looking over at James.

Morrow sipped his port. "Somehow he never struck me that way. He seemed profound. Generous in a spiritual sort of way. He valued those roots for what they gave him. A good and pleasant living. And you know the most extraordinary thing…?"

Karl finally sat at the kitchen table on the upper level, even though the larger table was still in the center of the space with chairs all around it.

"What's that?" Rain asked James.

"This man had the most beautiful wife," Morrow said. He looked back over toward Karl, who was exerting all his energy eating now, breathing heavily through his mouth as he chewed.

"You can't imagine. She was stunning. Ice-blue eyes, subtle glow to her skin, white-blond hair. Not the slenderest girl in the world, but that only added to her beauty. Like a rose," he added, "a figure from classical painting."

"That's a waste," Karl finally contributed, his mouth full. "Fat girl?"

"No," James said. "It just used to strike me that however pleasant she may have been to touch, her visual impact was unsurpassed. And I always wondered whether he knew."

"Well," Rain said, "what's beauty for, anyway? Or for whom?"

"For her own pleasure, surely?" Morrow replied, looking at Rain again. "Most men stop seeing their wives after a time, don't you think?"

The catering assistant finished and took her coat from Rain's bed, pulling up the zipper and strapping a messenger bag over her head. She gave a little wave and slipped silently out the door.

Morrow finished his port and put his hand out over it palm down when Rain reached for the bottle.

"I should be going," he said.

Rain stood with him. "Thanks for staying," she told him.

Morrow looked down and hesitated, took a breath as if he wanted to tell her something. Rain looked at him curiously. But then the moment passed, and Morrow was putting on his jacket.

"I have a short trip home," he said dryly.

As Morrow passed him, Karl muttered, "Nice to meet you," without looking up at him.

At the door, Morrow stopped, looking out toward the darkened factory. Quietly and without looking at her, he said, "If you need anything..." to Rain, and then walked away into the darkness.

Rain stood on the threshold, watching him go.

Walking slowly back down into the studio, she sat in the sofa, facing her paintings. She stared at them, almost surprised to find them still there—hard evidence of the time she and Karl had been apart.

Karl finished his dinner, wiped his mouth and threw the paper towel back down on the plate. "This place is posh, huh?" he said. "Didn't expect it to be so nice."

"Thanks," she said. She looked around the room feeling how awkward it was to have a home without him. He had been gone less than three months, but it already felt like he was a piece of history.

As he approached her, Rain subtly recoiled and, surprising them both, Karl noticed this. He slid to the far end of the couch, his back to her paintings. He hadn't looked at them yet, or if he had, he'd said nothing about them.

He sat and picked at his pants. "Look," Karl said, "look," like this was difficult for him. "I think I haven't been so great lately."

Rain still felt guilty about how disappointed she was to see him darkening her doorway that evening, and she self-consciously tried to open herself to him, opening her folded arms, her whole body projecting her feelings.

"Right," Rain said, not having expected honesty from him.

Karl said, "I had…it was…in England…"

And all at once Karl was sobbing. Rain watched him with a mixture of shock and utter lack of feeling.

Karl cried and blubbered and wiped his face with his sleeves. His face was red and puffy. She had never seen him actually cry before. She had never even seen him vulnerable. "What is this?" she asked, honestly confused. "Is this about us?"

"NO!" Karl sobbed and then caught himself. "Yes…well, sort of. I'm so sorry, Rain!"

Rain grabbed a napkin from the side table and handed it to him. He reached out to her, but she pulled her hand away and sat back again gazing at him.

He mopped up his face and blew his nose.

"This isn't about me at all, is it?" she asked.

Karl began crying afresh. "Oh, my God. I'm in so much pain, I think I'm going to die!"

Finally it hit her. She had really thought this could have been about them. A little bit. But the emotion didn't fit. It was sad, but nothing like this. And all at once, like Tetris, click-click-click-click-click, it all fell into a solid brick wall of fact.

"You had a girlfriend!" Rain announced slowly but confidently.

Karl grunted, like he'd been shot. "Oh, my GOD!" he snorted and coughed.

Of course. The day she came home early and he was naked in the bed. The elevator, the phone calls, the having to go out to endless meetings leading up to the trip. Suddenly not wanting her to go to England. The emaciated, nasty, British Turner Prize chick.

Rain said calmly, "Uh-huh, and now you've come crying to me about it." She shook her head and looked at their clearly reflected images in the enormous window. The old glass warbled the image of the brightly lit room behind them. They were silhouetted little heads poking above the big block of darkness that was the heavy couch. They were stowaways in a cartoon boat. Or children in a huge tub.

Rain felt a surge of anger roll through her. "You were such a dick to me. Practically the whole time we were married. MARRIED!" She shook her head. "Why did I ever marry you?"

Karl sniffled, "We were…"

Rain interrupted him. "No, don't bother. Really, I do know what it's like to be this hurt," she said, looking back at him now. "I do. I honestly never knew you had girlfriends, but it might have helped all those times I was suffering."

"Not girl*friendsss*!" Karl insisted, offended.

"So this one was the only one?" Rain asked.

"No!" Karl cried and then quickly corrected himself. "Yes, I mean." He crumpled again. "Oh, my God! She ripped my heart out!" He was crying again and reached for a used cocktail napkin himself this time.

"Alright," Rain said impatiently, as if she could stop his tears by the sheer intensity of not caring. "I mean, it just astonishes me that for such a long time I let you hurt me and hurt me."

"I didn't do this to *you*!" Karl insisted. "I stayed with you, I came back, I'm here now!" As though his presence was all that was required.

"No," Rain said. "No you're not."

"Those people are still at the loft!" he whined. Could it be that the grain of feeling she thought had guided him to her for comfort in his moment of great pain was just about the apartment?

Rain stood unsteadily. She glimpsed her reflection in the plate glass behind Karl's head: a grown woman now, the port going to her head. The bathtub image reminded her of that slidey feeling you got when you stood up out of a warm tub and regular gravity had you again as the bubbles slowly slid down your skin toward your still-submerged feet. There was a pull to just sit back down into the remaining warmth, but you knew only further pruniness and rapid cooling awaited you there. The more bracing scrub of the towel and jammies and bed would make the cold and depressing gravity of stepping out worth it in the end.

"Do you think I care where you go live? At Daddy's funeral?" she said, stepping out of the tub now, pacing away from him. "When I couldn't even find you?" Rain started clearing bottles and stray silverware from the table. "It all makes sense now." She climbed the steps to the kitchen and slammed a glass down onto the countertop. "How occasionally you'd just be so mean. You were probably late to go see her or wanted to call or something."

Karl remained an inert lump on the couch. "Rain," he pleaded. "I'm broken. I'm in little pieces right now. Please!"

"Seriously though, that *Penelope?*" He folded a little deeper with the mention of her name. Rain stared at him, hoping he would say no-not-her. Though why it made any difference, she wasn't sure. But it did make a difference. That woman irritated her. She was intimidating and beneath Rain at the same time. Exactly the wrong woman to have broken open her marriage. Precisely the woman Rain would like to have scratched from her husband's acquaintance, let alone the center of his piggish little heart. "That one, huh?" she said. "Had to be her?"

"She's cruel," Karl moaned, his face inside his two hands now.

"Oh, yeah, I'll bet," Rain said. "You obviously don't like the nice ones."

"Rain, I…" Karl began, his eyes softened toward her. She knew he was going to start in with something worshipful. She was inside him in some ways. Five years of being together, three of being married, and you know how the other person thinks. You know what they're going to say just by the expression on their face.

"Don't!" Rain interrupted him. "Really, really don't even think about doing that right now. It's disgusting and creepy right now to even think of you and me. You are sitting here broken into little pieces over that person and I'm feeling all sorts of anger and nausea and, yes, even jealousy, but I think it's all FALSE. It's false, and I don't think you even deserve the kind of jealousy I'm feeling, which has a lot more to do with hating her as a person than anything to do with you, Karl. No, but because she is a nasty, self-centered, angry, bitch and your being suckered by that, makes me see what I believe was always in the core of you, which is an empty, shallow, little pit of need."

She was cleaning up full-throttle now. "That's right," she said, talking as if to herself. "I wish you had let this slip earlier, Karl. Really. I wish I'd known. It would have spared me so much hassle. You haven't wounded me, not that you seem to care about that. You hurt me slowly and steadily over such a long time that I built up a huge Karl-shaped callous in my heart that I hadn't even realized was there." She looked up at him suddenly. "Did you drive here?"

"I have a rental car," Karl said into his lap, not appearing to grasp the significance of the question.

"Good," Rain said, taking a reprieve from the cleaning. "Karl," she said. "I know I've said a lot of things tonight."

"I deserve it," Karl said abjectly.

"Well, I couldn't care less how you feel about it. I don't want to talk to you anymore. I'm finished. I don't want to talk to you ever again."

Karl looked up, a little shocked maybe. "People," he said, "people work through…"

"First, 'people'," Rain said. "Not me. Next, this thing with this woman is just an excuse. You were wrong for me. You've been bad for me. I quit graduate school for you. I skipped countless trips with my Dad to be with you and now he's gone…"

"You want to blame that on me, too?" Karl asked, rallying briefly.

"No. Just makes it all the more obvious what a bad decision that was. So I'm making a good decision now."

Rain slid open the screen door and pushed Karl's suitcases out from against the wall with her foot.

Karl looked up at her from the couch. "Rain, please! Where am I supposed to go?"

"Away," Rain said. "Just away. From here."

"You can't," Karl protested.

Rain said. "I can. And I am."

"Am I nothing to you? Now that you have your house and your inheritance, you don't need me anymore?" Karl's face was twisted now, his despair turning to righteous indignation.

"I'm not going to argue," Rain said. "I'm not going to let you make this my fault." She stood her ground at the door.

Karl rose slowly from the couch. "I guess I thought we meant something to each other."

"What I thought you might have been meant something to what I am now. But you aren't and now I realize you never were."

Karl laughed bitterly. "That makes no sense."

"I don't care what you understand," Rain said. "Could you leave, please?"

He strode toward her, but she stepped back from the doorway as he neared her. She looked away from him as he struggled his luggage out the door. As he left, Rain pulled shut the garage doors against the night and stood listening to doors slamming, the engine starting up and the crunch of gravel as the car pulled away down the road. Her relief grew with that distance, but she couldn't shake that teetering feeling. Her little house suddenly felt echoey and frightening. Her body tingled and her mind raced. The wine from dinner and the port and all the confusion and emotion left her a shambles. When she couldn't hear the car anymore, she threw open the smaller door and looked out.

The decision started in her stomach. She didn't give it time to reach her head before she was out the door and on the Vespa in the warm night.

It was late, too late for trick-or-treaters. None had knocked during the party, though Violetta had left bags of candy in a cauldron by the door. The guests had assured Rain that this was normal. Any local kids were trundled into the next village with its Main Street and tight gridwork of houses. She passed a group of partially costumed, marauding teenagers, furtively tossing eggs. Rain swerved toward one of them menacingly. They dispersed and howled and whacked each other as she sped away.

Although she had not gotten completely comfortable riding the Vespa at night, she performed this ride on automatic, barely aware of what she was doing. She was inside her head, examining her reaction to Karl's affair. A part of her felt for him, which was disturbing. Felt sorry for him, that is. Really sympathized with all that grief and heartbreak. Was the remainder only ego? Was it just a matter of pride that made her kick him out with so little hesitation?

It struck her then as a revelation. However she thought she might have reacted in that kind of situation, even if she had been able to imagine it in her deeper self, even if she knew, it was nothing like how it actually played out. Betrayal struck at her at a primitive level, and there was nothing she could have done to rise above it at that moment. She had felt like a child presented with options for immediate gratification versus future possibilities of abstract goods for others. Yeah, she knew what the grownups wanted her to say, but hell…

It was too overpowering, too much having held it together while the things she depended on in her life collapsed. And too much her turn now.

The lights were still ablaze within the castle as she pulled up and jammed the kickstand down on the Vespa. She marched to the front door, a few strides ahead of her self-awareness. Hunter answered.

Rain pulled at his arm, nervously averting her gaze from him. He came into the fragrant night with her, slowly closing the heavy wooden door behind him.

Though her face was downturned, she was broadcasting her feelings to him clearly with her silence, her hand lingering on his arm, the slight tremble there. Hunter said nothing. He just slowly wrapped her in his arms as if they had already been lovers, holding her still and close a long time before whispering, "I have to leave tomorrow for Jaipur."

Rain was warm and buried in his chest, her face tucked in by his arm. "I know," she whispered. Looking up at him she said quietly, "That's perfect." And she kissed him, bringing her lips to his like magnets. Kissing him filled her, welled up inside her, crowding out all the emptiness, filling every corner and crevasse of her. She could feel it in her fingers, in her hips, along her breasts, down on the soles of her feet. With Karl it had always felt like he was drinking up, drawing something from her. But with Hunter, she felt she fed a hunger she never knew was there. His soft, warm lips and perfect, gentle-firm kissing gathered her whole body and mind up into him. She had to rise up to her toes to reach him, but as their kissing got more intense, each of them taking small steps into more daring, more heat, more openness to the other, suddenly Hunter picked her up in his strong arms and hoisted her onto the waist-high stone wall at the entryway. Rain opened her knees and drew him closer to her and kept on kissing him, neither of them in a hurry, just enjoying this give and take, this communication of everything they'd both been feeling since the first time they had seen each other. It was a conversation. A *yes, I said, yes, me too, yes, I did too*. A giving, an offering up, a grateful taking, like discovering they had something very rare in common and then having more and more and more confirmation of it. Rain had this confident feeling of knowing him, of a kind of trust that was built out of having no expectations of him. She could feel the unhurried pleasure he was taking in kissing her and it told her that even though he would be satisfied if nothing else were to come of that evening, he just *had* to kiss her, kiss her for no other reason than the kissing. And somehow, this almost involuntary compulsion, combined with his exquisite self-control, made Rain's head swim with desire for him. When they eased up, laying their brows against each other, catching their breath, she felt him giving her the lead, but eagerly following her wherever she wanted to take them. It felt like they had been out in the doorway for hours, and when the lights switched off inside, they both let out a small laugh at the same time.

Finally, Rain said, "You stay in the barn?"

"Mm-hmm," Hunter replied, low and quiet.

"Can we go there?" Rain asked, matching that low tone.

Hunter wrapped his arms around her waist again, lifting her up off the stone wall and letting her body slide slowly down his until her feet gently touched the ground. He was holding her tight enough to press on her breathing, but it was a delicious kind of pressure, just at the edge of too much. Every way he touched her seemed to tell her things, affirm volumes of hopes and secret wishes. As he let her go, he ran his hands down her arms and took one of her hands. It was warm and dry and she felt her small hand fitting into his large one like it was where it always belonged.

They began walking side by side and Rain said, "I think…" and then she laughed. It seemed absurd all of the sudden, she didn't want it to come off the wrong way.

"What is it?" Hunter asked.

It felt like they had to resort to spoken language now that they were not pressed up against each other. Sad, fallible talk.

"I don't want you to take this the wrong way," Rain said, looking up at him quickly, "but your leaving tomorrow makes me feel," she paused, "reckless."

They continued walking together, unhurried, but steadily. "I get it," Hunter said thoughtfully, "and I trust you," he added quietly.

As they walked on silently, Rain realized that she had just told Hunter she was glad he was leaving and that he had just witnessed her husband's return. His trust surprised her. It somehow made him vulnerable, though he had struck her as so much the playboy. The connection she felt and his claim of vulnerability were unexpected, but she still felt that the end marker on their being together was a good thing. It created this opportunity to let their feelings roam freely, carelessly. It both locked them to the present and liberated them.

Once inside the dark studio, then to the four-poster bed, the night became a blur of love and loss of self. A tangle of bodies, his dark skin and her pale skin blending into perfect caramel. Rain lost track of limbs, eyes, lips, time, colors, meaning, space. Their movements felt purposeless. It was an instinctual dance, just expression and pleasure, no taking turns, no work, just a gathering and gathering and gathering each other, no peak to end things, just being lost in the mountain range of peak after peak, rolling cozily down into one valley after another, drifting off as they both finally succumbed to a dazed exhaustion.

It was still dark when Rain awakened in Hunter's bed. She looked around his studio, the barn that Chassie fixed up as an apartment to hold some of his things and bring him back from time to time. The full moon beamed brightly through the paned windows. They were under a thick down comforter, Hunter facing away from her, his broad brown shoulders an angular promontory. "Perfect," Rain whispered, and kissed him lightly right at the tip of his shoulder. She dressed quietly, found a pen on a desk and pulled an envelope from a waste paper basket below. *Have a great trip, thank you for the healing. ~R.,* Rain wrote and left her note on the bed.

The skies were lightening and a chill had descended over the valley as Rain pulled her collar in tight and sped home, realizing she hadn't worn her helmet. She took it slow on the empty roads all the way back, passing shaving-creamed mailboxes, eggs pitched on the roadway and silly-stringed bushes. Thankfully, there was no such damage to her little house, being on such a secluded dirt road. But inside, it still had a stale post-party feel.

Pulling her jeans off, Rain climbed right into her chilly bed with a great sigh and a cozy shudder, thinking maybe she would survive all this after all.

ORANGE

I am not a painter, I am a poet.
Why? I think I would rather be
a painter, but I am not....
...One day I am thinking of
a color: orange. I write a line
about orange. Pretty soon it was a
whole page of words, not lines.
Then another page. There should be
so much more, not of orange, of
words, of how terrible orange is
and life. Days go by. It is even in
prose, I am a real poet. My poem
is finished and I haven't mentioned
orange yet. It's twelve poems, I call
it ORANGES....

—FRANK O'HARA

Fall leaves and pumpkins. Work zone. Browns and clays, desert earth. Ceratine, a bad fake tan and the usual alert level these days.

Though orange is a large and important part of the spectrum, and the key to most flesh tones, rarely does it figure solitarily on the palette. Orange darkened is a good chocolate brown, rich and deep. Lighter, it is creamy-pale flesh, pushed this way to yellowish, that way to a greenish undertone. Mixing a decent flesh tone usually begins with the orangey brown of Burnt Sienna, opened out by Titanium White, lightly for darker skin tones, more thickly for the lighter ones. The reddish undertone is more conspicuous at this stage, and a warm yellow needs to come in and soften that. Depending on the tone of skin you're looking to match, some version of orange needs to bring it to life. A crimson mixed with cool-lemon yellow yields a bright reflective area; any of the Cadmiums, even a straight-from-the-tube Cadmium Orange, gives deeper shadows their warmth. Human skin has been called almost every color, from white to yellow to red to brown to black, but unless you're drinking colloidal silver, it actually leans some way toward orange. Orange: everything that is not blue. Blue's complement.

Morrow crushed, distilled and incorporated remnants of the matter he'd gathered, from ashes to crushed bits, to scrapings of soot left from flames, to poundings of gold and powdered stones. It was important that a pigment stayed true and intense, that it retained its luminosity and hue and not damage pigments next to it or mixed into it. He tested, adjusted and retested this quality repeatedly with washes on small cards. James was working on this project now with Alvaro's overtime help. Morrow relied on Alvaro's availability, and his unique ability to be present and helpful, yet somehow invisible and non-judging. The two transformed the sundry materials he had gathered into pigments, dyes and lakes, incorporating them into the various supports, glues, and gessoes he had created. They filled tubes and bottles and boxes. The project was nearly finished.

The portable speakers resting on the passenger side seat were cranked all the way up. Rain drove a rental van alongside the railroad tracks and river views on her way in to the city.

Karl hadn't seen or said anything about the paintings she'd hung for the dinner party. He had been so involved in his own drama that he had overlooked them entirely. But at least the timing of his collapse had not been too disruptive to her project—she'd been able to finish them. Twelve canvasses, all large, fully rendered. And she was fairly certain she wouldn't have had it in her to complete them had he come while she was still working on them.

Still, her mind reran the same thoughts like an animal licking its wounds. She wondered why she had married him; she felt the anger at his betrayal; she questioned her own emotion—whether she was angry only because she was so deeply insulted by his wanting someone else, or whether this really was heartbreak.

Rain was too angry at him to be sad, too insulted to be sorry and too disgusted to know whether she was just relieved to be rid of him. After all, his affair had given her the perfect out. Had she just waited around for him to give her this free pass? No amount of impatient bad treatment could have released her from him, as long as he kept to the letter of their vows. She had always thought she was stuck with his unkindness and stingy affections. But shouldn't she have left him earlier? Shouldn't she have fought him, demanded better treatment, threatened divorce?

As she drove, Rain realized she was passing cars right and left, weaving around the Westchester traffic like an emergency vehicle. Approaching the little Henry Hudson Bridge at Manhattan's northern tip, Rain consciously slowed down and reigned in her driving, not wanting to cut short this second chance, this wide-open vista of whatever was going to be the rest of her life.

The van rolled along the Henry Hudson Parkway as it sloped down under the George Washington bridge and slid along the river, chasing joggers along the quay, passing little moored sailboats, yachts and fishing boats.

But the wound licking persisted. Why had she been such a stooge in her marriage? Why had she let him treat her rudely and never balked at it? Why had she enabled his tantrums and selfishness? She hadn't wanted to work it out with him. She hadn't wanted it to work. She had made an effort in the beginning, fighting with him, much to her uncomfortable surprise. Being wrecked by little arguments as much as big ones and being shocked to find him cozy and happy after having vented all of his frustrations on her. As their marriage went on and he seemed to get happier and happier, Rain now realized that she had wanted out, but that she wanted it to end decisively and blamelessly.

She didn't put him into bed with someone else though. That was his own doing.

It was him. His fault. She wouldn't have wanted out if he hadn't been so difficult. She would have continued on that way forever if he hadn't rent it open as he did, letting her walk away so easily.

Still, she couldn't help it. It made her giddy—this freedom, this secret exit off the long straight highway she thought was her life.

A parking spot right in front of Shuldenfrei on Greene and Canal could only be a good omen. Most of the big-name galleries had already defected up to Chelsea, and the back blocks of Soho were crammed with chain boutiques—sleek furniture stores, fine gardening supplies, faux hippie frocks, and high-end bed-and-bath shops filled with 600-count Egyptian cotton, organic lavender and calendula oils. Ben Shuldenfrei had inherited his father's Soho gallery and had kept it in the same white-washed space during the decade he'd run it.

The gallery sitter was the usual skinny young thing, coiffed and dressed like a caricature of the women she saw coming in to buy art. She studiously ignored Rain who stood right in front of her at the high front desk.

The girl deliberately continued to stuff envelopes while Rain shuffled and cleared her throat. Just as Rain began to seriously consider reaching over and snatching an envelope out of her hands, the girl looked up, eyes only reluctantly following her chin's lift and said, "How can I help you?" in a polished apathy.

Rain plastered on an equally insincere smile. "Right. Is Ben around?"

"I'll see," the girl said. She actually stuffed another envelope before getting up slowly, and adjusted her very tight skirt as she minced back to Ben's office.

She returned. "Mr. Shuldenfrei will see you now," she chimed.

Rain swiveled past her, muttering, "Mr. Shuldenfrei…"

Heading into his office, she cried, "Ben! Great to see you!"

Ben had always been a little grouchy and odd—overly direct perhaps, unadorned in the way he delivered his opinions. But Rain felt they shared a sensibility. She felt unintimidated by him, despite his being a mover in the art world.

He seemed to wince as she entered his office.

"I've got them," Rain told him jovially.

"Rain, I…" Ben said.

"They're right out front in a rental van."

"You can…" Ben began again. "Yeah, yeah. Bring 'em in to the viewing room. Give me a minute, okay? I'll meet you in there."

As Rain headed back to the van, the girl at the desk averted her gaze. Rain didn't bother to make her help. Soon enough for that.

"Gee!" Rain heard the familiar hoot coming from down the sidewalk. It was Quinn. She had left a message for him as she took off in the morning, hoping he'd come down and help her unload. "Gee, kid!" he hooted. He was on one of those tiny aluminum stick scooters, hat tipped back revealing his lengthening forehead, the thick strap of his satchel digging into his blazer.

"Quinn!" Rain yelled back. He flicked his scooter closed and popped it into his messenger bag, hugging her around one of her canvasses.

"This is huge Rain. Let me get that." Quinn took three paintings into the gallery.

One by one, they unwrapped the canvasses, all twelve of them, and leaned them around the back room. The vestibule to the inner office was decorated as a sparse, well-lit living-room with Eameses, a Le Corbusier coffee table, one Noguchi lamp in the corner and plenty of wall space. Once the paintings were inside the back office, Quinn gave Rain a chuck to her shoulder and said, "I'll wait out there."

She could hear Ben before he got into the room "…because if they can't wait for the Jenkinses, then Cincinnati's gonna end up with it. And Michael, tell Steph if she doesn't get that ad on my desk by three o'clock, I can't use it. She is not doing this to me again." Ben barked instructions to his directors who followed him with pads and scribbled as he spoke. "Hold it," he said, parading into the back room. "I'll be back with you in five." The directors retreated silently. Rain was suddenly aware that his usual curmudgeonliness with her had been flattened to a strained politeness. "Yes, Rain," he blurted.

He looked at her canvasses, turning his back to her. Rain regarded them nervously. She dared a glance at Ben, but he didn't really look like he was seeing the paintings. He was snapping his phone with one finger—a nervous tick she hadn't noticed in him before.

Finally Rain ventured, "Sooo… They're in the same vein as the ones you saw in the summer…and liked…and wanted to show… Remember?"

"Yeah, they're…" Ben said. "They're very accomplished, Rain. Great work."

Rain wasn't sure where this kind of feigned enthusiasm was coming from. Politeness wasn't Ben's usual card.

"You remember we talked about this," Rain said, slowly creeping up on the idea things were not going well.

"Yeah, Rain. I do remember that, but I'm afraid…" Ben said, keeping his back to her. Again, not the Ben she knew.

Suddenly it was clear. Very suddenly. And her face flushed bright with that vertiginous, teetering feeling she got when the worst kind of news hit her. Worse than Karl's revelation. Far worse. How she could have been this stupid? How could have gone through with this farce? She had been set up and had underestimated her husband's cruelty and quick work.

Her self-pity threatening to turn to anger, Rain asked, "He called you already?"

"He came on Friday, Rain," Ben said, putting a hand up to his brow. "Late. Didn't have anywhere to stay, I think was what he said." Ben gave her a wry look.

Rain was aghast. "He went straight to you to take this from me?"

"Rain, I'm in a really bad position here," Ben said, turning away again to avoid her gaze.

Rain's face was hot and her throat was closing, but her rage was more than the humiliation crashing down on her.

She walked over and plunked down into the black Eames. "That's just…it's low! I think it's low."

"This is very awkward for me, Rain. Karl and I go way back. Where was he supposed to stay? The renters have another week at his apartment. Uh, I mean—your apartment…whatever." Ben shook his head and turned away again. "I had no idea you were planning on coming in today."

"We said after the beginning of November, remember? You even said a Tuesday. You said just come in and bring them…"

"You know Rain, I was willing to help you out. I like these pictures. I have no doubt you'll do very well with them. It's just that I feel…I feel…"

"Did he give you an ultimatum?"

"He didn't…" Ben said, pressing his palms against his temples. "I'm not going to… I can't… I just can't."

"You know, I never thought of you as the loyal type, Ben."

"Yeah, well, thanks," Ben said. "I think."

Rain got up and began stacking her canvases. This was more than just a matter of showing up and getting a humiliating rejection. This was carting your children with you on that rejection holiday. They were not easy to move. They were not gracefully going to disappear when you needed them to. They were needy and beginning to make their boisterous and inconvenient presence known. They were embarrassing you and your humiliation was burning into them.

"Rain," Ben said, standing limply by the Noguchi like a crooked lamp himself. "Rain, it's not that I don't think they're good. You've got to understand. Come on, you work with Gwen, you know how it is! It's not a rejection. It's just that I probably wouldn't have been showing them in the first place, right?!"

This casual toss landed like a grenade in Rain's brain. She plugged it. Reinserted its key. She knew it would go off, anyway, but she had to block it for just as long as it took to carefully remove every single one of these canvasses.

"I didn't think you... I'm surprised. That's all." Rain barely managed to push out something coherent.

"Didn't think I what? We're still early in the process with each other. You have to find the right fit for you, Rain. You know that. It's about so much more than the quality of the work. I think there are lots of galleries that could make something of John Ray Morton's daughter. That sort of thing could be very interesting to some people."

Rain had never purposefully benefitted from her surname. Literary stars' kids seldom merit entrée to the hot clubs or events or swag, anyway. But somehow, watching the present generation of offspring-to-the-stars run their media circuses created in her a crushing dread of appearing to be anything similar. Some of them, coming from show families, she knew were playing out their own true callings. They were in the can't-help-it category, but the ones who made empty media presence out of their names, they were the ones Rain focused on and dreaded.

At a moment like this, she felt like a fraud. Even though she had liked her work. She had thought it would do well in a gallery. This gallery. "I worked really hard on these. Focussed on them for this."

Ben took hold of his mouth with his large hand. "Mmmm. Maybe…"

"What?"

"Look I don't want to say anything Rain. I just know we're not a fit right now. Someone else would be able to take much better…"

"But what were you going to say," Rain said her question quietly, like she was begging.

Ben sighed, shrugged, walked over to Rain and put his big warm hand on her shoulder. "They look like you painted them for a show. And maybe…maybe your head was going in a different direction. And…and I feel a little bit responsible."

A little bit! Rain wanted to disappear on the spot. Didn't want to do the niceties of hugging and saying goodbye, of being offered help getting the work back out of the gallery, of being reassured that she'll do "great with them" somewhere else. So she just grabbed two of the paintings and walked out without saying a word.

Quinn was still in the gallery. When she walked past him dangling a painting in each hand, Quinn turned and beamed at her. He quickly caught on to what had just happened and trotted into the viewing room to collect more, quietly excusing himself to Ben as if he were the housekeeper.

Rain sat in the driver's seat while Quinn brought the rest of the pictures out, draped them in their plastic sheeting and filed them into the back. She was dry-eyed but in shock.

"Lock it up," Quinn ordered. "The van'll be fine here. You come with me."

Rain did as she was told and Quinn held her arm as they turned the corner and ducked into the Lucky Strike on Broome.

It was only two o'clock, but Quinn ordered two scotches and sat quietly with her while they waited for them. When the drinks arrived, Quinn raised his glass and gurgled in a decent, if exaggerated, brogue, "To the stoooarms brrrutilizin' the cooooasts!"

Rain threw hers back and Quinn ordered another round.

Rain gasped as she weakly attempted and then finally managed to say, "This is such a cliché."

"Clichés are there for a reason," Quinn said, raising up his glass and gesturing encouragingly to Rain with his elbow. "It's spot-hitting is what it is. A scotch in the afternoon would never be this tasty without a good ass-whipping to warm you up for it."

Tears literally flew forward out of Rain's eyes as she laughed and cried at the same time. When she regained her breath she said, "This was so goddamn embarrassing! It's going to be a good laugh for a lot of people!"

"What people?" Quinn asked, mock-looking around. "Besides, do you think this was the first time some dick gallery fuck has screwed someone?" Quinn nodded knowingly. "Promises," he laughed ruefully. "Nothing is actually real until it's a memory!" He put down his glass.

"But why am I such a naïve asshole?"

"That's the best kind of asshole to be," Quinn said.

Rain's voice was still squeaky and constricted and her breathing was still all wrong. "I...Karl and I...I think it has to do with me kicking Karl out."

Quinn didn't look up at her, just nodded slowly. "You think it's over for good?"

Rain laughed again and coughed. "If it wasn't before, I'd think this would clinch it."

"Then good riddance," Quinn declared. "You're better off."

"I know you never liked him," Rain said, not particularly defensive.

"Not an easy guy to love," Quinn said. "A little tightly wound I think. He struck me as a little bit… How can I put this…he seemed kind of alien to me. I got the feeling he didn't particularly enjoy me or Stan or anybody but you."

"He knew better than to say that to me. Though I can't say I have any perspective at all at this point." Rain took a sip off the top of the new shot glass. She shook her head. "I feel really, really stupid. Ben just basically said he never would have shown me in the first place. Like this thing with Karl actually released him from the obligation, rather than the other way around."

"Let me tell you something Rain," Quinn said. "I've witnessed some hair-raising nastiness in the art world and I'm not gonna say that wasn't a bad one, but the good things are always a result of dumb luck and perseverance. You're gonna get flattened again and again and the only difference between a hobbyist and a real artist is that the real artist is just too dumb to get discouraged."

"Cliché?" Rain said, raising her glass.

"Cliché," Quinn echoed, clinking glasses with her cheerily. "Another one?"

"No! No," Rain protested. "I've got to get that van back. I shouldn't have had two."

Quinn looked thoughtful. His car-free city life had never involved such calculations. Then he brightened. "One more, then we grab you a coffee and a movie to sober up. I don't have to be back at work this afternoon."

"I'll *do* it," Rain said, imitating Stan in a way that made Quinn laugh.

"Hey, hey, hey," Quinn teased, "you know what Stan would say about all this…"

"Hm," Rain said, with an expectant smile.

"*Rain, Rain, go away,*" he recited gravely and they both laughed. "*Come again some OTHER day!*"

Croton's rail yard was long and wide and stretched far north of the commuter parking lot and switching station. Rain drove in past the yellow and blue MTA pickups, dark green dumpsters and brown trailer sheds along the access road that ran between the rail cars and the river. Far past this was Croton's Municipal Garage with its mini-Alps of salt and gravel and its fleet of plows. At the end of the drive lay a few parking spots, two or three picnic tables and a boat launch where the access road sank gently below the water level and into the marsh flats. The water glittered with hot pink and dark blue reflections of the reddening Hudson sky. About a half hour south of Vanderkill, Croton's river front combined down-to-earth functional rail beds with an open public park and a little yacht club with its restaurant.

Driving away from the city, Rain had begun to feel the weight of her own head. She wasn't drunk anymore, just exhausted and beginning to feel everything from which those scotches had given her reprieve. Tired, vulnerable and sick, she drew the van to a halt just shy of the water at the launch. One other car was parked there, but it looked empty and Rain suspected it was a commuter avoiding the parking fees in the stadium-sized parking lot at the station. She put the van into park, shut the engine down and lowered her head down on the thin, oversized steering wheel.

The moment when Ben had turned back to face her started playing in her mind. The moment she recognized the meaning in his expression. It pressed in on her throat and face, coming unbidden and unstoppable. Rain pulled out her phone and hit the speed dial for Gwen.

"Haloo-aloo?" Gwen answered cheerily. Rain had gotten Gwen the cellphone for Christmas the previous year, despite Gwen's objections that she would never learn how to use it. It was too newfangled and she had no interest in being reachable.

But she had adored the thing from the start and now knew more tricks with it than Rain did.

"Ra-ain. Is that you?" Gwen asked.

Rain's voice didn't work. She listened.

"Rain?"

"Yeah." Rain managed to push out the word.

"I think I've got a bad connection, honey. Can you hear me?"

"Yes," Rain said.

"Is everything alright, dear?"

"Not really," Rain's voice was all wrong. She was not sure why she was trying so hard not to cry, just that she might not ever stop. It might not ever be okay again. It was stupid. She didn't even really care about Ben Shuldenfrei anyway. It was probably the wrong place for her. Probably the wrong style of work. If it had gone well, if she had gotten the show, wouldn't she have been stuck with a style she had lost faith in?

"Rain, what's happened? Are you okay?"

"I'm fine," Rain replied. She cleared her throat again and again, realizing that the attempt was futile. Just a tightness that wouldn't go away. She swallowed hard. "Ben Shuldenfrei took a pass."

"I see," Gwen said.

Rain waited.

"I don't think he really wanted to give me a show in the first place," she continued. Gwen said nothing. "I kicked Karl out."

"I thought he was gone," Gwen said.

"He came back," Rain said, "and then he left."

After a silence, Gwen sighed. Clearly. Good connection after all. "Well, that's a good thing I suppose."

"I think I was really stupid," Rain choked, then erupted into a sob.

"Rain, sweetheart," Gwen said, "in my experience there's only one way to get smart. And that is to be stupid sometimes."

"I should have known," Rain managed through her tears. "Ben was just offering it for Karl…"

"Look Rain, he's only trying to run a gallery. You can't be nice in this business. Artists' feelings cannot be a factor in these decisions. Critics and their good graces on the other hand…"

"But I should have known that. Why did I go in there?"

"Looking for punishment? I assure you I couldn't tell you, dear," Gwen said. "Listen, you don't need Karl Madlin. He's not as powerful as he thinks he is. He has some friends and soon enough it won't be that interesting to block you anymore. What you need is to escape his influence. Do your own work. Then you'll find a place."

"I'm not influenced."

"Oh. Okay, alright. I think you were. You can't expect to be free of someone's hold on you in just a couple of days."

"But he's been gone since August."

"Karl's insidious. A sneak. The hooks he put in you will take years to work free."

"You don't sound very sympathetic," Rain said quietly. "I'm not sure why I called."

"I think you've always known how I felt about him."

"I guess I wanted to talk to Dad."

"Yes, well, so do I, dear."

Silence.

"Okay, bye," Rain choked out and snapped her phone shut. The whole world felt empty and shut off. Her father would have made her feel better. He would have made everything right again.

Rain watched the river turn purple under the tones of the spectacular deepening sky. Blending fields of crazy hues gestured dramatically across the horizon and stretched upward. Rain left the van to see it better. She had a clear view of the water, but the tracks lay in endless lines and crossings in the foreground. Rain opened the back of the van and took the box cutter out from the tool crate. Pulling one of the canvasses toward her, she slashed the plastic from it, yanked it free and held the piece up against the sky.

It was formulaic and facile. It was predictable and pompous. Deceitful and dead. It was just plain bad, and it was sticking to her like fly paper.

Rain gripped the stretcher bar and plunged her box cutter straight into the canvas. Past its gooey facade and into the weave. It stuck a little, the still-drying inner layers of paint hanging on to the blade and pushing the canvas inward. Yanking the blade out again, Rain hauled off and slashed the canvas straight through from left to right. A surprising waft of pleasure darted through her. She did it again. And then again and again and again. Ribbons of slashed canvas flapped and caught the fading light.

Rain frisbeed that one onto the ground and retrieved another one.

The stabbing and slashing, she knew, might look violent or angry, and while she was quite enjoying the self-absorbed drama, it was also a liberation she sought. Each stab was a release. Each slash unburdened barriers she hadn't realized she'd constructed. She went at it efficiently, methodically and passionately.

When she had destroyed the last one, Rain pulled the shreds from their stretcher bars just as if she were pulling leftovers from nearly spent Thanksgiving turkeys. Just…busy. Doing a job.

The exertion calmed her. She kicked around bits of canvas, grinding them into the dirt under her shoes. It was getting dark now, the light show of the Hudson River sunset spent. Rain took in the empty rail yard, the commuter trains still coming and going on the tracks further in toward the water.

The glow of the lamplight and hovering darkness made her self-conscious again. Rain kicked the mess she had made into a heap and bundled it into one of the dumpsters. She loaded the stretcher bars and larger pieces of plastic back into the van, retracted the box cutter and tossed it after them.

No one cares if you're not an artist, she thought. There are things in the world worthy of pain and self-sacrifice for which it is worth working past obstacles: curing disease, saving the environment, nurturing minds and bodies and spirits of needy children. But to be this distraught over a pass from a gallery? Doesn't even rank.

Rain started up the van and rolled quietly back to the entrance. The chain-link gates were shut. A thick steel chain was strung between poles and an oversized padlock secured them. Coils of barbed wire topped the fence. They seemed rather pointless seeing that she would need to get the van over, too.

Whatever gut feeling of release she had enjoyed during her fit was gone now, replaced by the certainty that she was just a stupid stupid girl. She felt dwarfed by everything outside her own stupid life, and she felt something she hadn't allowed herself in a long time: shame.

It all collapsed on her at once. The hollowness of her marriage. The emptiness in the wake of her father's loss. The sputtering, non-existent career. The waste of years on making art that was of no interest to anyone, that was useless, misguided and fraudulent. Her own personal just general distastefulness.

Her motherlessness.

Rain had stored most of her art supplies. Paints, brushes and solvents were packed in boxes. Photo compositions were pulled down and boxed away with them. Two empty boxes of hair dye and a pair of scissors lay next to the sink in the kitchen.

The high graphite wall where she had hung her work was barren. On it now, was only the small painting that had been there when she'd arrived, a pretty, loosely painted landscape signed A.M.

The place was stripped and dressed as a conventional little home, just with no one living in it. Empty tables, open space, the big mustard-colored couch gaping without the stacks of books and magazines. A case of good scotch sat on one of the tables. One bottle was opened and about four fingers down.

Someone knocked at the door, closed now against the growing cold.

After a long pause, a slight stirring disturbed the rumpled bed.

Another knock.

No further movement.

When Rain caught the first glance at her hair in the bathroom mirror she let out a laugh. A kind of "oops!" Rain's hair had gone from thick and long with shaggy bangs brushing her eyelashes, to a shorn pixie shag. Naturally a dark chestnut brown, it was dyed all the way to white-white, with touches of neon blue at the tips. She did remember doing it. Remembered her satisfaction at its brightness and oddness. On the toilet, Rain put her face in her hands and her elbows on her knees and rested there, letting everything that led up to the haircut sink in. When she had first came back to the house, her odyssey to New York City felt as if she had returned to the house to assess its betrayal of her, and to reassert an ownership she had never really felt in the first place. Homer's Penelope was the very ideal of fidelity and undying marital faith, but in her own version of the epic poem,

Rain was Odysseus' men, dragged along through something they never asked for, Karl's Odysseus casting them through all kinds of hell to get to a woman who was a tease tempting everyone for her own entertainment. Let them play out their own drama. Rain was jumping ship.

As loud as this haircut was, Rain hadn't done it for anybody else's reaction. It was simply that her hair was bothersome. It needed to go. She needed a change that she could register for herself. She was still slightly drunk when she awoke at two that afternoon, but she was well aware of how people overreact to hair.

In her teens, Rain had cut her own hair now and then. Once to the scalp. She had liked it choppy and odd like that and she'd colored her face with beams of orange and green eyeshadow and worn huge earrings that she felt complemented the 'do. Once on an airplane, a woman had asked her what had made her do it. That was curious to Rain, since the woman hadn't known her. Just seeing a choppy buzz on a young girl seemed to require an explanation. Rain didn't mean it as any kind of statement. She wasn't trying to provoke, just to please herself. Maybe that was provocative enough? She told the woman it was just hair. It keeps growing.

Cutting her hair this time wasn't without emotion or defiance or even self-mutilatory urges urges, but like before it really wasn't for anybody else's benefit. If she wanted to let the truth of it out, it was something inside her that reacted against the normal consumer culture. The getting a regular job, the having regular belongings, a regular relationship and a regular routine. The hair would prevent her from being hired anywhere too regular. It was strange to her, when she allowed this thought in, that she had so little trust in herself that she felt she needed to brand herself to avoid this fate. These thoughts made her want another drink, however, so she figured she'd better get one piece of business out of the way before reentering her comfortable haze.

Yanking a big knit cap down over her ears, Rain held a second wooden chest she had found outside her door in both hands in front of her rather formally like something she didn't want to disturb. She walked down her road without a coat in the forty-degree chill, grateful for the hat.

Though Alvaro wasn't around, the other employees knew Rain by now and she walked right in to find James in the oil room.

"Rain!" Morrow said with a rare smile. "I came by to drop… well, to drop that off." He glanced up at her big hat.

"Thanks," Rain said, shifting her head down self-consciously. "Yeah, that's why I'm here."

James brought Rain to a counter over by a window that looked out over the marshes stretching to the Hudson. Rain placed the box, this one larger than the first one he had given her, up on the counter and gave it a tiny shove toward him.

"I can't accept this, James," Rain said. "I really appreciate your belief in me, but I can't."

Morrow stared at her.

She didn't return the gaze. "I'm not a painter," Rain said carefully. "I'm not painting…anymore."

"That's," Morrow said, "that's not true."

"I wanted to give this back so that somebody who'll use it can have it," Rain said. "Not me."

"But it has to be you," James said quietly.

She looked up at him, confused. "No," she said. "No, you don't understand. I'm not going to do it anymore. I give up." Rain realized she was hearing the edges of desperation in her own voice, but she couldn't stop it.

"I'm afraid this is no good to anyone else. It's for you, Rain," he said. "I made it for you."

Rain cupped her hand to her forehead, rubbing her temple under the itchy hat, just trying to hide her face.

"Look," Rain began, her voice betraying her again. She coughed to cover it. "I found out there was no show, and it confirmed what I think you were trying to tell me the other night." She gave him a fake smile. "Yep, you were right. Weak stuff. Uninteresting. And now I've got to figure out something else to do with my life." Her voice cracked. She didn't have a plan. Nothing.

"Stop," Morrow said quietly.

Rain began crying openly. She didn't care whom she was talking to, where she was; she just went on as if to herself. "I don't know what to do anymore. Dad's gone. Gwen doesn't care. I'm alone…"

Suddenly Morrow shouted, "Stop! Stop it now!"

They looked at each other, both equally horrified. She, surprised and baffled. He, surprised and distraught. Then he turned abruptly and left.

Rain staggered back to the cabin alone, freezing in the November chill. She poured a huge tumbler of scotch and climbed into bed. Put the iPod on and drank herself to sleep.

It must have been the end of November. Rain was fairly certain that it had been almost a month by then of existing on booze and soups and cans of beans. She considered the nearly bare branches outside with detachment. There was no pressure to render them, to see them as anything but a static symbol for the approaching winter. There was no need to judge the depth of light and shadow, to learn from the cools and warms or see how the oranges of the few remaining leaves combined warm yellows, reds, even dusty greens and purples. That blackish brown of the branches, really an amalgam of silver on steel blue with chill, yellow highlights was nothing she needed to grasp.

She could just be.

And let them be.

She could just live without this. Maybe she would, after all. Get some kind of job where you go and you do something and then you walk out of there and weren't doing it any more for a whole evening and night and morning. Entire weekends of nothing you have to do.

The small black-and-white television got bad reception, but Rain had been watching it night and day ever since she got it in one of the boxes Karl sent. She ran long wires with sheets of tin foil along the antennae to achieve a rough, grainy picture. Once, back in the city, she had defiantly cut the cord on the thing, having forgotten to unplug it first. She must have jumped two feet in the air at the resulting pop. A fat, black, electrical-tape bandage bound the cord now. She had left it behind on purpose. But Karl was methodically shipping to her everything she'd owned at the apartment, every shred she'd ever brought, bought or been given.

So the broken TV asserted its ugly pull on her. She especially enjoyed watching the most base reality shows she could find. There weren't too many, since she was relying on what she could tune in on network TV alone. But she liked watching the ones where people wallowed in their worst selves, building themselves up on teetery self-righteousness, being torn down to child-like tears and tantrums and then rallying again for something she suspected they didn't even believe in themselves. It was fascinating. Especially the shows with teenagers and young adults. Their lectures and little fights sounded like sharpened echoes of whatever they must have grown up around. You could feel the shadows of screaming parents in their practiced head-bobs and devastatingly dismissive body language. Surely they were unaware of the hardened selves they were portraying. They appeared so ruthless. So self-assured. But of course self-doubt didn't read on television. Just the way it could inadvertently concede defeat in the middle of a fight, rather than indicate the opportunity for—or the process of—growth that it actually was. But if you could never be seen actually learning anything, and if you had to be televised around the clock, there was not going to *be* an after, was there?

The clock was meaningless to her. The days were light or dark in random order. Rain had unplugged the landline and turned off her cell, but mail still came along with the stoic postman. She had occasional face-offs with him over Karl's boxes or fat envelopes from lawyers wanting signatures. For all his blankness, his knock was an earth-shattering banging at the door. He had become her alarm clock. Rain waited for his shock or even some kind of judgment since she had been a cave-dweller now for weeks. The hair at least. The blue tips fading and the roots growing in. But no reaction came. This guy—young really, kind of hip—kept a preternatural detachment. Before her self-confinement, Rain had tried to greet him with a few words when she had to sign for something or when he caught her outside on his rounds. She always got the impression that he had absolutely no interest in speaking to her. She was starting to take it a little personally until it occurred to her that he went to every house in Vanderkill Township. Every house. Shut-ins must have been nothing to him. He'd surely already witnessed squinted eyes, funky bed-head and morning breath at two p.m.; that, and the acrid stink of chicken broth and daytime television wafting out through doorways.

Time was like a ski rope, Rain decided. You could either grip onto it and be carried forward or just let go and watch it slip by, bringing whatever it drags along past you. Then you can grab on again if like, and just keep moving along with the pointlessness of its never-ending cycling. Not being a skier, the climb of the mountain to make the run thing was not part of the metaphor for her. So it worked. It's how time felt at the moment. She watched time's sequences scroll by like TV.

Drinking helped. The month became a slidey blur that was just ow-kay to her scotch-soaked self. Having inherited her father's iron veins when it came to alcohol, Rain could keep up a fairly steady buzz without resorting to a hangover. But it was in a particularly ow-kay state that Rain found Chassie in her doorway one evening rather early. The sun had started to disappear at four-thirty, so it seemed night enough to Rain. It was only with the regular-sounding knock at her door that Rain realized she was drunk. She literally had to tip her torso at the stairs and force her legs to churn the steps until she swung open the door and found a familiar face there.

"Oh!" Rain exclaimed, with a small laugh designed to show just how "ow-kay" everything was. The introduction of this familiar, yet unexpected, element into her house suddenly made Rain feel very very drunk. When before it was, you know, just a teensy buzz.

"Come in!" Rain said, with what she realized immediately was an overdramatic swing of her arm. She turned her head away to avoid putting a swimmy gaze on Chassie and stepped back.

Chassie entered slowly. "Hey," she said, laughing low. "hey there cowgirl. Nice 'do."

"Thnkyoo-p," Rain said in a little clip, trying to rein in the horses of her drunkenness; she wasn't sure why. It was just embarrassing to be drunk all by yourself in your stupid little house and not even painting at all.

Chassie headed on in. "Place looks…uhm…kinda empty," she remarked. "What's goin' on, what-cha smokin'?"

"Smokin' some smokey shit," Rain muttered casually, following Chassie down into the living-room. She picked up a bottle of the Lagavulin and tilted its bottom toward Chassie.

"Holy mackerel, that's the real deal, innit?"

"Mmmm-hm, straight?" Rain asked, poking the bottle toward her guest.

"Whew," Chassie said. "Some ice maybe?"

Rain was relieved to see Chassie bounce up the steps back to the kitchen to help herself. Rain slumped into the couch. Hit the TV button off with her foot.

Chassie joined her with a splash of scotch in a lowball glass filled with ice. Rain tucked her tumbler out of sight around the side of the couch.

"So what's going on?" Chassie asked. "You've disappeared!"

"Yeah," Rain said, rubbing her hand around her tousled rough hair. "Yeah, I'm…I have no excuses," Rain said finally, looking at Chassie and readjusting her posture.

"Just worried about you a little," Chassie said, taking a smell of her glass. "Hunter keeps calling me, blah, blah Rain, blah blah. He can't get in touch with you. Nobody's seen you."

"I…"

"Is everything okay?"

"I don't know," Rain said. "I hope I didn't…I didn't mean to, uh…I guess I thought since he was leaving it would be alright to, uh…"

"No no!" Chassie said, getting her drift. "You know, I mean, TMI and all. Don't want to be all in your business. Just so you know, my very independent brother would totally kill me for coming here and checking up on you. But I don't really operate that way. He's wanting to be in touch with you. I don't see you anymore, so here I am."

"Oh…em…gee…" Rain sniggered sarcastically, but she looked down, picking at her pajamas.

"You are not okay," Chassie declared finally, lowering her glass.

"I will be," Rain said. "Just woodshedding."

"I thought that involved actually bringing along your instrument," Chassie said, looking around at the empty space and taking a sip of the scotch. She coughed. "Seems like your instrument's been put away."

Rain felt her head swimming again and kept her gaze down in her lap so that Chassie wouldn't realize how drunk she really was. It was making her feel pathetic and she was starting to resent it. Not the booze, but the intrusion. Chassie's bright light shining on her. Everything had been nice and dim before Chassie walked in here. But now it was glaring and humiliating.

Chassie leaned forward and put her glass down on the table in front of them.

"I mean, don't get me wrong," she said. "I don't know you that well, but I thought I got to know you a little and… Well, it just doesn't seem like you wanna live like this. Who would?"

"TMI…" Rain mused. "*Ten Merry Indians? Terribly Muddy Input? Terrific Managerial Involvement?*" She tried laughing at her own hilarity. Didn't really manage it.

"Yeah," Chassie said. "*Too Much Information.* Okay. I hear you. I just want you to know that I love my brother. Love him to death, but he's not worth throwing everything in your life away for."

"Oh!" Rain gasped, looking up finally, a little burst of adrenaline clearing her head a little. "Oh, ha ha!" she laughed. "No! Hunter? No…"

"This isn't about Hunter?" Chassie asked, smiling with embarrassment.

"*This*," Rain said, gesturing all around her like she was scratching turntables "is all an *illu-usion*!" She laughed again. "No, really. I'm fine. The Hunter thing was good. So good. It was just what I needed, the one good thing in a big stretch of lameness, patheticism, randomania… Don't you like it?" Rain gestured at Chassie's orphaned glass on the table.

"Too strong for me!" Chassie winced. "I need mixers, for God's sake!"

"Fresh out," Rain said, allowing herself to look at Chassie calmly now.

Rain thought she'd handled the rest of the visit well. She knew it didn't last too much longer. She white-lied about spending some time in the city, told what she had hoped was a slightly exaggerated version of recent events, playing up the self-pity in order to appear to be coping.

Chassie said something about seeing her sometime, that she should come get some coffee, give Hunter a call if she felt like it. Rain was pretty sure she didn't pass out on the couch before Chassie was actually out the door. But she didn't have a very sharp image of her leaving either.

This definitely could have been a dream. Had it begun in a dream and then melted into regular? She was lurching through rooms, clubs and smoky back offices. Places turned one into another in that distinctly impossible but acceptable dream-like way. She was sick and trying to find a place to lie down. A place to be alone. But everywhere she went, people were crowding her, taking up couches and beds and extra chairs. She searched for a bathroom and lurched through hollow, institutional locker rooms, tiled vistas of porcelain commodes of all sorts, but they were all occupied or overflowing, stuffed with paper or gushing over. Then she was in the cabin, on the floor by the couch, and then lurching up the steps and out into the chill dawn, turning and tripping down toward the trail-head by the back of the house. She was still drunk, sick and confused. Half in the dream, she must have awakened herself from having to be sick. Coming to a teetery halt in the middle of the path Rain barely made it to the side by a tree before vomiting. Two large birds overhead screamed and squawked at her accusingly as she emptied out her gut into the leaves.

Her heaving breaths and the leaves drenched in her sick gave off a languid blue steam in the soft glow of the dawn. Rain turned and leaned her back against the tree, feeling the chill start to break through her hot skin.

The birds screamed and threatened overhead and she wondered if she was still in the dream.

But as Rain turned to walk back to the cabin, she spotted an odd shape in the path. A tiny square of something almost white. She stooped to pick it up. Canvas. A tiny postage stamp-sized piece of canvas with dense markings of paint on one side—a piece from her destroyed paintings. She felt the swelling of amazement, looked up to the still shrieking birds. It must have stuck to her shoe, blown onto the van and released when she brought it back here to unload the stretcher bars before returning it. No miracles for her today. She half-ran back to the cabin, shut the doors tightly and locked herself in, falling back asleep on top of her bed as the sun finally started to burn off the dawn's haze.

Rain was not supposed to be painting. There were days that just slipped by without her notice, and there were days she leaned on hard to blow through. Like running a wind-up toy in the direction of its action, forcing it to blitz through its little routine too fast, occasionally slipping forward out of its gears so you have to back up a click in order to resume pushing it too hard. She spent one whole day over a pack of cards, doling out various solitaires one after another with a kind of amazement. Am I still doing this? Oh, man, yeah. Am I throwing away an entire day, a whole day into the garbage can? How many more hours, can I bear it?

In this same sloth, Rain entered the world of online info-porn. Blogs, news-feeds, celebrity gossip, a past-time in which she'd never really indulged before, having lived in the luddite paradise of vintage New York pursuits—art, the bona-fide paper *New York Times*, plays and performance art with real, actual human-beings-in-the-flesh performing. But the twin dervishes of television and the Web have exactly the numbing, time-sucking effect she was looking for. Surfing while watching TV seemed to be the perfect combination, like cookies and milk.

Somehow, she realized later, she needed to tear herself down completely before she could rebuild.

Rain would not remember how she came across her first subject. Probably one of those celebrity carrion sites, the ones that spewed some new distraction every ten minutes. Since all of it rolled past her fairly loosely, she never was able to trace back why she found herself in a particular corner of the cyber-world. But her obsession became a county sheriff's site in Colorado where their daily siezures of felons, other offenders, and "transit holds" were posted in large clean digital files. At first, Rain told herself she was just collecting, just two clicks, right-click, select, didn't mean anything. But soon she started to draw them. She didn't collect just any mugshots. They were always women, always fairly young and never the guarded or the mirthful. Only those who looked somewhat raw. Who appeared fully aware of what was happening to them. These were brightly lit, direct face shots without any protection. Sometimes there were red eyes, runny mascara, and puffed noses. But Rain wasn't interested in the criminal caricature. Mostly they were DUIs, with some petty theft, the occasional drug possession and domestic battery. Most of the "transit holds" were longer-term criminals, and seemed more comfortable and less laid bare in their mugshots. She was surprised to find more than a few quite cheery faces among these troubled people, and it made her imagine a photographer trying to lighten his days by saying or doing something to provoke the incongruous grins. Something to belie and mask regret, desperation and fear.

She collected these images liberally since they were only posted for five days after their "alleged" incident. At times she would find the same face reappearing. This was an entirely different level of interesting to her, since, inevitably, they looked worse, emptied of their last traces of hope in the second or even third shot. Whittling down her haul to a few more interesting faces, she then drew some of those. Finally, one night, without fanfare, she pulled out the first paint box James had given her, and, working very quickly, she painted one of them in the same manner she had done all those self-portraits she'd hidden from Karl in the city. She had developed the habit long ago of penciling the date and title on the back of her work. On these mugshots she scrawled "self-portrait" along with a number and date. She told herself it was just because she hadn't noted the subject's name, but she liked what the title connoted. Renaissance artists would sometimes insert self-portraits into tableaux, where they stood in for a disciple or a king, and Rain had always appreciated that cheekiness. This full reversal, this using anonymous women in trouble as models for herself turned that tradition on its head in a pleasing kind of way.

They were her, after all. Circumstances had them living in Colorado and dealing with young kids, a violent ex-boyfriend, money troubles or just plain boredom. So what force kept her here, in this charming little cabin so near New York City, fighting with herself over making art or not making art under the influence of self-imposed jail-time and bottles of scotch. What forced these expectations on her? She hadn't chosen her father, but she had tried to follow him. He had been called a "shaper of culture," a "prince of letters," "influential and inimitable." He never put pressure on her to be an artist or to shape her experience into art. Yet her life was steeped in it. The way doctors' kids, firefighters' kids and cops' kids grew up feeling that kind of responsibility toward the world, having watched it rule their parents' lives. It became difficult to justify turning away from one's inheritance.

The faces she was sketching put her in mind of the Mona Lisa, eventually—the vague, indecipherable expression she looked for in the mugshots having that similar quality of multiplicity. Even the most raw of her subjects showed a kind of combination of awe and confusion when they weren't just completely giving themselves to the camera, totally present, totally exposed. They weren't Mona Lisa smiles: they were Leonardo all-and-nothings. It was that level of fascination that kept Rain at them one after another. The Mona Lisa, however, was what gave Rain the idea to incorporate the landscapes she'd been gathering behind the figures. Precipitous views down steep mountain-sides, river and train tracks running behind the subjects. Once she'd sketched them out, they appealed to her immediately. The women's eyes always glinted with the same two strips of sharp reflection—ceiling fluorescent fixtures behind the photographer. The glints were subtle and delivered a sense of interior space. Rain gave them careful treatment in each portrait and the result was an intriguing feeling of the subject being outside looking in.

Rain sketched out a plan for a larger work with a full-length figure and a still life of petty crime accoutrements in the composition. Imagined ones, fictions—she wasn't particularly interested in the details of each person's real experience. Only in the stark emotion splayed on their faces. She snapped a number of shots of herself from the neck down in poses from classical antiquity to use for reference—strange little gestures of the hand, pointer touched to thumb, raised palm.

It occurred to her that Thanksgiving was coming up, or had it passed? Though she had been ignoring news programs, the TV ads and some of the specials she surfed past were starting to show signs of holiday hysteria. By this time, Rain had been away from the world for almost a month. She was starting to get used to this hermetic life, this oddball rhythm, this time alone with herself.

Someone knocked at the door. Not the postman's familiar crashing, but a normal knock. She was lying awake, so it was probably past two, but when she peered out the bedroom window wondering if Chassie had come back, and if she could hide from her, Rain was shocked to see Gwen at her doorstep.

"Just a minute," Rain croaked, coughed and yelled again, "… just a minute!"

She threw on a pair of jeans and the first sweater she could lay a hand on. The place was a chaotic mess. Not exactly trashed, but maybe too well lived in. Luckily, she'd done a couple of weeks worth of dishes the day before, but she hadn't put any of the recent drawings or paintings away, nor the sundry supplies she'd only half unpacked and spread around the living-room tables. And she'd taped drawings all over the glass of the big window and laid them on the floor, everywhere.

When she opened the door, Gwen sighed heavily. She held two large shopping bags and turned to call to the driver in the black town car. "Six o'clock, Sergei," she said, and he nodded and started back down the road.

Rain couldn't figure out if she was moved, touched, annoyed or horrified by her stepmother's visit, only that she couldn't manage to get a word out. She was just relieved not to be drunk this time.

"Well?" Gwen said, looking at her up and down without verbal comment, but her eyes lingered on the hair. "I turned down my nephew and his awful wife, hired that car and I'm here." She held out the two shopping bags to Rain. "So, let's eat," she said.

Rain took the bags from Gwen and looked at them. One was filled with take-out food containers, the other with bottles: wine and seltzer.

"Thanksgiving," Rain said finally. "Oh." And she stepped aside and let Gwen enter.

As Gwen crossed the threshold, Rain ran ahead of her down the living-room steps, set the bags down and quickly brushed aside the pencil portraits she had laid out in a careful grid on the table. She stacked them and tossed them on the sideboard alongside the dozen or so small oil sketches drying there.

Gwen walked down the steps, slowly looking around the place and took hold of one of the old wooden school chairs at the table.

She sighed and looked at Rain wearily. "Do you want to shower while I set the table?"

When Rain emerged again from behind the bedroom curtain, she saw the table set prettily for two, a candle burning and wine poured. Gwen was looking through the portraits.

"Gwen," Rain said, feeling sheepish for some reason. "Gwen."

Gwen looked at her. "Hmm. It's still blue," she said, shaking her head with a smile.

Rain ran her fingers through her hair. She liked the way it had grown in with the dark brown roots giving dimension to the white. She might do without the blue tips now, though. They had faded to a bit of a robin's egg, rather than the original chemical blue she'd painted on there.

"Alright, now," Gwen said. "Come on, let's eat."

The food was to Gwen's standards, elegant without being fussy. Wild rice with currants and walnuts, pomegranate-glazed roast turkey, sweet potato galette with pecans and brûlé maple crust, a relatively plain stuffing and tiny pumpkin pie tartlets for dessert. Rain hadn't realized how tired she'd become of canned food. She felt longings filling up that had been gurgling along empty for weeks. Gushing praises on the meal, on Gwen's coming to see her, the wine, all of it, Rain could hear a clumsy desperation in her own voice.

"Stop," Gwen said, as always, impossible to thank or praise. "Stop, I can't stand it when you grovel!"

"I'm not groveling," Rain retorted, bruised. Gwen's sharpness seemed to jump from somewhere else. "It's Thanksgiving, after all," Rain said. "I'm just giving some thanks…"

Gwen chuckled and then looked out the great glass window at the gathering darkness. "Days seem shorter up here," she said.

"The city, too, Gwen. You just don't notice it there," Rain said.

"Why did you turn off your phones? What's going on up here? You had me worried." She gave one of her conclusive sniffs.

"I just…" Rain was embarrassed. Somehow in front of Gwen, depression seemed self-indulgent.

"You've been working," Gwen said, glancing at the sideboard with a lift of her chin. She was giving Rain an out on the tougher topic.

"Oh," she said dismissively. "I don't know what those are, really."

"They're what you have to do," Gwen said. "They're all women." Gwen was confident as always in her assessment. Then she asked, "Are you looking for somebody?"

"What?" Rain asked.

"Seems you're looking for a missing face."

"Oh, those," Rain said. "I found them on the Internet. Mugshots."

"Guilty women's faces," Gwen said. Another knowing sniff escaped. She held out her wine glass for Rain to refill.

The candle appeared to be glowing brighter now as the light dwindled around them.

"Your father never spoke to you about your mother," Gwen said. "It's marked you."

"I'm fine," Rain said, annoyed. An old refrain between the two of them. Gwen would insist she had crippling pathos. Rain would deny it. "Lots of people have broken oddball families. It's not that unusual."

"You don't even know your own history," Gwen said. "And you need to. This work you're doing. It's good." This was rare coming from Gwen, and Rain was almost alarmed. Gwen never handed out unequivocal praise. Most especially not about art. Her highest compliment was typically back-handed, like *not bad.*

"But you can't hole up like a hermit for the rest of your life. You need to live," Gwen said. "You need to function."

Rain felt her cheeks getting hot. Having her pain acknowledged both thrilled and shamed her. What she was feeling was real. She wasn't just lazy and self-indulgent. At the same time, she couldn't bear the unfamiliar flattery.

"I'm functioning. I wasn't even painting for a while. This is a step forward," Rain insisted. "I'm doing much better now."

"You were conceived here, Rain. Did you know that?" Gwen asked.

"Sort of," Rain said, taken aback for some reason. "I guess."

"Your parents never married."

"What? No." Rain said, confused. "What do you mean they weren't married?" It wasn't that it mattered to her, but she was unsure where all this was going.

"John planned on telling you about her, sometime," Gwen said. "I think the longer he didn't talk to you about her, the more difficult it seemed."

"Wait," Rain said, moving back slightly in her chair. "Why are you telling me this now? What's this about?"

"John never liked to talk about her, even though I tried to get him to. He meant to. He always said he would, eventually, and then one day he's gone and you lose two parents at the same time."

"It doesn't matter, Gwen," Rain said shaking her head, but not looking at her. "I just didn't have a mother, that's all. It's not a big deal."

"It is," Gwen said. "Believe me, I know it is. Look at Robert and Barbara. Both my own children, both live in California." Gwen's children were almost old enough to be Rain's parents themselves. Gwen always joked that they were trying to be as far away from her as possible, but she never made any attempt to blend her families. Just let people be.

"I was a terrible mother, I know that." Gwen raised a hand toward Rain and turned her face slightly away at Rain's protests. "No, I was."

Rain saw that same guilt washing over Gwen's features. That guilt she was painting, the guilt she felt, too. A universal, unquenchable and impotent guilt.

"You've always been good to me, Gwen."

"Not motherly, though," Gwen said, looking up at Rain squarely. "You just never had a mother and I'm sorry for that. I've seen what it did to my children. Neither of them ever had children of their own. I was absent in every way."

Rain suspected Gwen was dancing around something she would never detail. But equally, she thought Gwen was too hard on herself for not being the über-mom that was expected of women of her generation.

"I think they've forgiven you by now, don't you?" Rain asked.

"Why should they? That's up to them, anyway. Nothing I can do anymore."

They sat in comforting silence.

"Your mother's name was Alice," Gwen said.

"Yes. And?" Rain said, closing her eyes. "Look, it's okay that Daddy never told me about her. She doesn't matter. She gave birth to me, that's it."

"Alice Morrow," Gwen added.

Rain willed her facial expression to flatten, to keep the strange bits of recognition from washing through her while she tried in vain to hold her molecules as they were. "That was her maiden name?" she asked finally.

"No," Gwen said. "She was married."

"Are you sure it's Morrow? Because…" Rain trailed off, glanced up at Gwen.

Gwen sat looking at her calmly.

Rain met Gwen's gaze. "She was married to James Morrow?" she asked, feeling molecules shift.

Gwen nodded.

"What did—," Rain sputtered. "Did they—? It was an affair?"

Gwen rolled her eyes and stood, taking plates with her and clearing the table. Sometimes her gait was crooked and she tilted into furniture as she walked across the room, but she had a kind of grace with her aging body that was unparalleled.

Alone at the table, Rain felt her eyes welling up. They filled, they overflowed, they spilled down her cheeks. She pursed her lips to switch on that lever in her brain to shut down emotion. The lever failed. Sobs pushed against her pressed mouth, pumped at her throat. She sputtered and coughed in a battle with her baser self.

Gwen came back, poured more wine for Rain, and then wrapped her arms around Rain's head and shoulders.

"This is so...so-o s-stupid!" she exclaimed, plastering a crazy smile on her face and looking up at Gwen even as she continued to cry. "I don't know why...why I'm crying!" she said, but then she stuffed her head back against Gwen's soft bosom again.

"I'm disappointed to have to break this to you, but it's a biological thing," Gwen said. "Mothers are no joke."

"How can I need what I never had?" Rain asked, calming herself with logic. "Can you be an alcoholic if you've never had one drink?"

"If a tree falls in a forest...?" Gwen countered. "My mother was the original ice queen," she said. "I used to spend every spare moment I had at my friend Mary's because her mother had a *lap*!" She gently let go of Rain and resumed a position across from her. "My mother never once told me she loved me, never ever kissed me, never held me. My father was much older, and she never spoke about her past, which was murky and veiled—a dancer maybe, although that may have been euphemistic, I don't know... My brother and I went to live with her family after my father died. A distinct and shocking decline in circumstances, that was, though my mother kept the furs and jewelry. Even there, we never learned anything more about her. It never stopped me loving her, though, wanting her, needing her approval. Ridiculous." Gwen shook her head. "Cruel, empty person that she was. Finally, I woke up and begged to be sent away after my brother went to college. One of my older half-brothers helped with that. I think that saved my life."

Gwen raised her glass and took a sip of wine. Then she looked at Rain as though snapping out of a reverie. "Why am I telling you this? Because a non-existent mother can be even more powerful than one who is right there to disappoint you," she said decisively. "I think you need an exorcism."

"Oh, my God!" Rain blurted, laughing.

Gwen smiled. There was a shared sense of humor between these two women, one that they both valued and which linked them together.

"So here it is, Rain," Gwen said. "This is everything I know about your mother. Alice Morrow left her husband, became John's lover, gave birth to their child and then died about a month later."

"I thought she died in childbirth," Rain said.

"The easy explanation for a child," Gwen said. "'Postpartum complications don't really nail down a date. She was from Norway originally. Her maiden name was Gudrid Loss, but she always hated her first name, so she chose Alice when James brought her to the U.S. From Alice in Wonderland."

Rain shook her head, tearing up again.

Gwen waved dismissively. "I'm sorry I'm the one to bring this to you."

They sat in silence a bit longer until they both heard the crunch of gravel under the wheels of Gwen's hired car. Gwen glanced at her cellphone. "I still have a little time."

"She left James Morrow for Dad?" Rain asked. Gwen nodded. "Did James know? Does he know now?"

"He must. They were all friends before things got mixed up," Gwen said. "Remember, it was the seventies."

"Dad was already in his fifties, wasn't he?" Rain asked.

"And very handsome and very broad thinking and accepting," Gwen said.

"What's that supposed to mean?"

"She was a painter. Your father appreciated that, evidently, more than her husband did."

"That doesn't make sense."

"Well, of course, nothing is simple. I don't know why we're always driven to distill things down to truths when there's no such thing." Gwen was oddly cheerful.

"I always thought I'd killed her," Rain whispered.

"Nothing is ever simple," Gwen said. "But anyway, I'm sorry you ever had to think that." Gwen snapped her diminutive Fendi purse shut and looked at Rain for a moment. "John never ever felt that way."

Gwen collected her coat and scarf.

"I always thought…" Rain said hurriedly, trying to get this all in before Gwen left and she would have no more answers. "I always thought Daddy felt a little bit resentful of me, like maybe he tried to make up for being angry for what I'd done to his life."

"Rain," Gwen said. "I know very little, most of which is probably distorted by confused egos, bruised hopes and all that romantic claptrap. But your father and I were together for many years and I loved him with all my heart. One thing I know for certain is how he felt about you. He adored you and considered you perfection in every way. You were a gift from the cosmos, he always used to say. He hadn't known what he'd gotten into with Alice. Might not have chosen that path for himself, but, as things

turned out, he said he found out what real love means. With you."
Gwen kissed Rain on the top of her head. "And, as far as I'm
concerned, he left you to me, and I've decided to keep you. So
I'm telling you what I know, and I'll talk to you about it whenever
you need to. But I need you to keep a phone on. And you need to
come see me in the city. Come for dinner. Let me see you."

Rain remained in her chair, looking down at her wine glass as
she absently ran a fingernail over the foot of the glass.

"See me out, sweetheart," Gwen said. Rain stood and followed
her out.

As she got into the car, Gwen called, "I want to see that larger
work you sketched. Have it ready for me by the new year."

And Rain let go a wide, grateful smile. "I will," she shouted as
the car rolled away into the night. "I will!" She watched the tail
lights fade down the road, grow briefly as they stopped in front
of the factory, then pivot as they turned and disappeared.

The night air felt delicately layered, like some rarified Medi-
terranean dessert, the warms and cools of the air yielding and
slicing each in to each with a nutty smell of drying leaves letting
off atomized bursts of spice and flavor.

Standing out on the porch listening to the sound of the gathering night, Rain took big gulps of night air, tasting its delicate
balance, feeling on the verge as the earth prepared to take the
turn at solstice, at the outer edge of something, her wine-sluiced
veins feeling that thrust, that throw outward of gravity and orbit.
The stars laughed at her, at this great flinging that only pulls back
in again and again.

Rain wanted to hold onto that feeling, despite knowing it
was partly the wine, but she felt certain she was letting herself
feel again. Maybe for the first time since she had moved here.
As she turned to go back in the house, she noticed the box
she'd returned to Morrow weeks before sitting discreetly by the

door again, like a besotted animal returned to the master who'd kicked it. A few leaves had blown over it, so it must have been there for a while. Rain brushed it off and carried it inside.

She cleared the dishes and even put a pot of water on to boil. Feeling almost like a regular human being, she decided to attend to the big box she hadn't yet opened, sitting alone on the table in the middle of the studio.

A little key with a jewel-like key ring hung from the lock. It looked like a refashioned pendant with a bit of its chain holding the key. Rain turned the key carefully in the lock and heard a buttery, metal click.

As she opened it, a beautiful scent greeted her. Inside the box were well-waxed maple, cedar and deep-green, velvet-lined dividers. There was the smell of linseed oil sharpened with a little bit of turp or mineral spirits. But as Rain leaned in and breathed deeply, she thought she could detect something else. Jasmine, vanilla? It almost smelled like some vintage perfume, like Arpège or Chanel No. 5, but it was hard to tell with the complicating mix of raw material in the box.

The old bottles and metal tubes looked handmade. Each top was inset with a jewel or a lump of precious metal. The brushes were certainly handmade: bright brass ferules held luscious swellings of smooth bristle. Sable hair, or something finer, even more perfect, strand by strand.

A thick envelope was bound by ribbons to the lid of the box, sealed with wax and very formally addressed to her.

Rain removed a letter from it, and began to read:

For Rain Loss Morton, daughter of Alice Gudrid Loss Morrow,

Please forgive my cowardice, and please accept this unworthy trifle from me. I've put everything I have and

*everything I kept from her into these materials, which I
hope you will set free into the world. It has taken me nearly
thirty years, but I think I may have begun to understand
a little bit about life and about our sad little efforts to pass
through it with dignity and grace. You do what you can
with what you have, and I hope I can give you more to
work with after I'm gone.*

*At first I was confused by your coming to see me, but, as
time went on, and you never spoke of her, I began to loosen
my iron grip on her memory. I don't know what you can
possibly know of her, having been so tiny at the time of her
death, but I can only assume that you can't know who your
mother was to me. And writing this now, I realize there is
nothing I can say that could convey even a little of that to
you. And so, not being able to turn that most important and
most powerful thing in my life into words, I had to do what
I know what to do with it. Put it into paints.*

*What you surely cannot realize is that she lives on in you.
You are distinctly your own, clearly, but there is some of
her going along for the ride inside you and it pains me very
deeply that you didn't know her. Still, she is there. I have
seen her.*

*Though you deserve to have everything that was hers, I hope
you will understand the form in which I need to give it to
you. Once she was gone, it was clear to me that every material thing in the physical world is simply meaningless. It is
what we do with those things that matters so profoundly.
What we give each other, what we reflect, what we
transmit. The things we build are only worth the building*

of them. Fail there, and nothing you hold in your hand will improve things.

Perhaps it is selfish of me to intervene between her and you, but I tell you honestly that I am only trying to offer what I can of her to you. Please accept her and use her.

I give my labor, I give all I had of her, I give my body and my life. Please carry it forward into the world and find love, acceptance, understanding and reciprocity there.

You are a rare treasure. You are beloved. She is with us now.

In love and gratitude,

James Morrow

La Traviata blared through Rain's tiny, but decent, speakers on the floor of the studio, as she brazenly opened and grabbed tubes from the box. Handwritten in fountain pen on the paper labels wrapped around the tubes were odd descriptions: *jewelry/gold, clothing/blue, china/bone white* and other even more cryptic notations were scrawled there. Each had a stripe of its contents painted onto the label. The colors were rich, though not too brilliant. A few brights in tiny tubes, many whites and a broad selection of strangely earthy tones. It was ridiculous, the luxury in the box, the arch formality of his letter. He thought she had known all along. That she was playing some game with him. She strolled into his life assuming a mild acquaintance between her father and him, looking for, what? Solace?

And now this? Take this woman forward into history? Take him? Him? His body? What did he mean by that? As if she could guarantee anything. As if her works would even survive her, let alone be cared for by museum storage maintenance staff, lent around, displayed. She may have grown up around a cultural icon, but if she learned anything so far in life, it was the slimness of the chances of having your individual voice impact the world. Worse than lottery odds. Didn't she know that? Didn't she?

Rain thought how she had tried to return it, and how he'd messed up the first box, squeezing paints onto her palette, removing the temptation to treat it like what appeared to be. A precious artifact.

She was just going to glob it all onto canvas. The enigma of this gift was only partially explained by the letter, but she began to understand. It was what she ought to do now. What felt right and correct now.

She squeezed the unfamiliar colors out on the palette, tentatively mixing them around to find unusual pairings, tones that set the others off in unexpected ways, textures that worked well with other textures. It was a devil-may-care bravery she employed while dispensing and mixing. So what if these were my mother's paints, or my mother's life somehow reduced to paints?

Here's the thing Rain loved about painting figures and the face in particular. The human mind is fiercely attuned to the most minute vicissitude, the tiniest tweak of muscle in the human face. Even in people we've never seen before, we can sense when they're lying, or in pain, or a little bit guilty. Sometimes we just know that something is wrong. Babies spend serious chunks of time studying faces, learning them, getting the language down. So Rain knew when she had gotten a face right. In painting a face, there are artists who can capture feeling, and there are technicians. Sometimes the two skills meet, but usually an artist leans one way or the other. The feeling artists tend to paint more loosely, catching a flare of emotion like capturing a firefly, delicately and with well-practiced, single passes, rather than a careful molding. The technicians can usually mimic an emotion by getting the image mechanically perfect, though the risk is a tiny sense of vacuousness.

Rain was amazed by the lesser-known colleagues of her favorites, Rembrandt, Vermeer, Whistler and Winslow Homer. The also-rans hanging next to them in museums were sometimes great technicians who did everything right, but somehow still produced dull, flat images. On first glance and by provenance these paintings were quite important. The colors were nearly the same, the brushstrokes every bit as careful and skilled, but the emotion just wasn't there. The tiny fluctuations that tell us a smile isn't genuine are minute muscle flarings, failings to twitch just the right way, and if a painter isn't in control of every miniscule slope and fall in his subject's face, it could all fall apart.

This was one of the advantages Rain found in working with oil paints. Painting was neither a straight and easy loping journey lulled by classical flutes and strings, nor a rock-and-roll, jacked-up expression session. It was not glamorous or straightforward. It was something that engulfed Rain, an experience into which she climbed and lived. Before she had begun a piece, she sometimes wondered how she was supposed to do this. She knew how to be in the middle of a painting, even a little bit about how to finish one, not with a bang but many many many feathery whimpers. But starting a painting. That was scary. Oil paints eased this fear since she could always trowel down an area that was bugging her, that she had overworked or that suddenly turned out to be in the wrong place entirely.

That is the secret of oil paint and one reason this ancient medium has resisted the onslaught of most modern chemistry. It is forgiving. Some paintings, of course, cannot be saved at all, but often Rain found herself adjusting proportion, moving the turn of a lip, raising a nostril by a millimeter. And with just that tiny move, the paint almost moving along the canvas of a piece, she could bring life and vibrance and authenticity to a face. Not that she was going for likenesses. But rather an undeniably real but conflicted emotion she witnessed on that face in that moment.

On those rare occasions when she ran across another shot of the same person, she was often involuntarily critical of the other photograph. Yes, it was the same person, but never the same feeling. She was not painting people. She was painting raw feeling.

A paintbrush is nothing like a pencil, a charcoal or a pen. And paint is not like ink. It has body and dimension and you convey it to canvas not by dragging the brush along the surface, but by gentle sculpting, pushing, laying, pulling and manipulating. The brush is an intermediary between the painter and the paints. The painter stands facing a canvas as its equal, brings the paint as an offering and then works it in as a negotiation: brush to paint, mind to image.

In painting, this process goes from the murky expressionism of childhood, through the control of making symbols ("this is an eye, this is a nose, this is a mouth") back to a fresh way of seeing that is all light and form. It resists parroting symbols, is brave enough to use yellow here and green there and illogical shapes we've trained ourselves no longer to see. There is a kind of bravery when your goal is to represent something recognizable and offer it to the judgment of others; a kind of bravery that pushes you to see the dark triangle under the chin, the utter lack of line at the jaw despite the strong sense of sharpness of the jawline. A bravery in creating a nose from darkened shadows extending down the lip, the shine competing against the lightest pales in the face. Rain thought that perhaps she was starting to understand what her father meant, what "discovery and pleasure" he was talking about, what he said he'd miss.

Over the following few days, plugging away at her paintings, more than a dozen sketches, larger, looser and more expressive with each face she painted, Rain worked her way through the leftover turkey and through the hours of the day and night until she approached an almost normal schedule of sleep and waking. One day, having worked all the way through a night and day until six the next evening, Rain crashed to sleep and then awakened refreshed and wide awake at four-thirty the following morning.

She was pleasantly surprised to find herself approaching a mortal's time clock and scraping the bottom of her pantry: pickled garlic stems, a tiny jar of honey mustard and rolled oats. The rice was gone, she had eaten the quinoa and wheat barley with broths and spices. It was facing the specter of mustard oatmeal with this truly intense and impossibly nauseating condiment, that finally gave her the impetus to leave the house and reconnect to the outside world.

Rain didn't feel like actually seeing people, especially not James Morrow nor certainly Chassie, embarrassed as she was about her last encounter with her. So she decided that what she *could* do was go to the city. Funny that the more populated place felt more anonymous, but it was just that one step closer to the world that she could yet take.

A shower and some surprisingly loose-fitting clothing later, Rain was aboard Metro North and hurtling toward the city, watching the Hudson glitter in the bright, hard winter sunlight. She was crushed among the morning commuters, who were crowded and uniformly silent by the time they'd passed Croton and Spuyten Duyvil. Rain watched a crew team sculling at the head of the East River above the tip of Manhattan, inside the bay-like widening under the Henry Hudson Bridge. She let in the landscape, the rocking of the train, the soothing rhythm of the greenery slipping past and the steadier company of the dramatic wet blue of the sky, the heavy, flat sloth of the river and the bright, rolling clouds that had accompanied her to the city.

When she was about ten, John Morton went through what Rain characterized as her father's Buddhist phase. Although he had retained some of the teachings and the practice of meditation for the rest of his life, Rain remembered this time as a phase since he became overwhelmed with his discoveries. He had even decorated the apartment like a yurt and obsessed about his mind's expansion for a while. He'd also sought the regular company of monks, feeding this or that monk at their family dinners.

So it was at times like these in her life, Rain could hear the voices of these peaceful men come to her with their impressive being-ness and calm. She knew what they would say to her. She knew she would be encouraged to be whatever came so persistently to her, whether that be making images with paint or just doing nothing in particular. Today she was planning to try nothing. They always said it wasn't easy, even while assuring her it was the simplest thing in the world to find your path. Only now did that seeming contradiction make sense to her.

So she walked. Starting from Grand Central over to Lex, then down 34th, crossing over to Third, walking steadily, block by block, the city festooned gloriously for the holidays. She walked with genuinely no intention of arriving where she was headed until she passed 14th, crossed back over Third past Astor Place and found herself at her old coffee shop right below the apartment she'd shared with Karl for almost seven years. She had always thought of it as his apartment, having consciously or unconsciously kept her things discreet and organized and separate in the place, never having claimed more than carefully separated spaces for her toiletries, her books, even the few dishes that mattered to her. They hadn't amassed much as a couple since for their wedding they'd skipped the big ceremony and Karl's apartment had been fairly well set up before she met him.

Rain sat, nursing a latte, even ordering a second before Karl finally came into the place, doing an unintentionally comical double-take when he saw her sitting there. Rain smiled a wan smile at him, wondering whether she'd come all this way just to see him and hoping that it wasn't a big mistake.

"Rain," Karl said. He came to her table and looked around like he was expecting cameras or police or something.

"Hi Karl," Rain said with a big sigh. "Hi," she repeated, smiling genuinely this time.

"What are you doing here?" Karl asked, taking hold of the chair across from her but not sitting down.

"I'm not sure," Rain said. "I guess I just wanted to see you."

He looked at her warily, waved to the barista and then slipped out the front door of the cafe to make a call on his cell.

"They can manage," Karl said, coming back in, grabbing a chair and sitting across from her in one swift move. When he looked up, they both registered a little shock to be seeing each other, at how suddenly and almost unconsciously comfortable they could feel again, but then they both reared back into the reality of their situation. "I like the…" he hesitated, "…interesting hair."

She'd forgotten about it, though it was a little less club-kid now that she'd taken out the blue. "Thanks," Rain said, scrubbing a hand through it carelessly.

"Did you…did you get all the boxes I sent? Was everything there?"

"Even the canned food, yeah," Rain said smiling. "Everything. Stuff you probably should have kept."

"I just wanted to be clean and fair."

"Yeah," Rain said, allowing herself an eyebrow raise as she looked down at her coffee.

"I heard about Ben," Karl said. "I told him he was a prick."

Rain looked up at Karl with a wry smile. "Really?" she said, ready to accept that he actually hadn't, but Karl looked back at her sincerely. In a strange way their splitting up made Rain believe him capable of defending her like that. In reality he probably just contradicted himself to his old roommate Ben, setting up her punishment and then refusing credit or blame for it. "No," Rain said. "No he's not."

"I didn't want him to do that."

"I know," Rain said, knowing.

"I wouldn't have."

"It's okay, Karl. I know."

Karl's coffee was called and he went to retrieve it.

He came back, this time approaching with the more appropriate degree of newly minted unfamiliarity and hesitation. He fiddled with the top on his cup. Rain began to smile slowly, realizing maybe she had been headed there on purpose after all.

"You reclaiming your youth?" Karl asked, gesturing with his chin.

Rain looked behind her.

"The hair," Karl said shyly.

"It really doesn't mean anything," Rain said pleasantly.

"I'm sorry," Karl said.

Rain let that sit for just a moment and then said, "That's alright, Karl. I think everything is going to be alright now." Rain smiled at him again. He wasn't looking at her. "You know, it's funny," she said, "but I think the things you're sorry for are not the same things I'm sorry for."

Karl looked up at her. "I'm not sure I even want to do this Rain. You caught me by surprise here."

"Okay," Rain said. "It's okay. No need for the free-psychoan-alytical-profile thing."

"One per customer, no refunds," Karl said ruefully. Rain laughed, remembering that there had been good things between them. Shared wit and interests.

"I could try talking to Ben again," Karl suggested quietly.

Rain shook her head. "No. No, he was right. I did those paintings just for him. And maybe for you. And I think it showed. They were okay, but they just weren't what I needed to be doing."

"I just wish I…" Karl began.

"…could give me something?"

"…could help…"

"Yeah, well we're getting into the free profile area there, so let's just skip that," Rain said gently. "Okay?"

"Yeah," Karl said, and he brought his gaze up to her, one of those open, connected and hopeful looks. He was stripped suddenly of the veiled resentment, criticism and disappointment he had piled up in recent years, just fresh and present and honest. A zing passed between them, and though she knew they both felt it, she laughed again, thinking that it just didn't matter. Just because you could make that connection didn't mean you should make it. It was all too late. She looked back up at him, shook her head lightly, a whole long silent conversation having passed between them. We could, but where would that leave us, you're right, I'm sorry, so am I, you meant everything to me once, yeah me too, and I thank you for all that, thank you too, goodbye, goodbye.

"I guess you'd better get to your office, huh? They're probably five thick in the hall by now," Rain said.

"Yeah," Karl agreed meekly.

Rain smiled genuinely at him again as Karl rose. "Maybe we could…" he began.

"Nah. I don't think so Karl."

Karl nodded. He left Rain and she watched him disappear toward 4th Street.

RED

so much depends
upon
a red wheel
barrow
glazed with rain
water
beside the white
chickens.

—WILLIAM CARLOS WILLIAMS

Red is the top of the rainbow out at the edge of the spectrum, the limit of our ability to see energy. Heat itself. Both love and war, humiliation and excitement, red is intensity, royalty, a Valentine, the pope, the devil, rouged lips, the bullfighter's cape, the can-can dancer's petticoats, Roxanne's red light, a stop sign, a child's fire-truck, blood, the red red rose, red red wine, Christmas and hell.

Reds were easy to come by in antiquity in the form of red earth clays, though the pure bluer tones were more difficult to master and maintain. Earth, flora and fauna—colormen found sources for reds in all creation.

First, the earths. Clay, crystal and stone. Red Ochre, a clay from Cyprus. Vermillion, from the crystalline cinnabar mined in the Almaden region in southern Spain is composed of mercury and sulfur. And finally hematite, the opaque, stony iron oxide, found mainly in Cyprus—all three types of mineral give warm brownish earthy reds.

The root of the madder plant could be made to yield a combination of alizarine and purpurin, though the purpurin was fugitive. When laked, the madder dye became a highly desirable bluish-tinged red. Roots of the madder plant—a weedy-looking spiky-leaved thing with nothing red about its growth—are dried, crushed, hulled and boiled in a weak acid and then fermented to create a dye, which is then extracted or *laked* by binding to an alum, drying in large trays in a low-heat kiln, ground again into the pure pigment before finally being incorporated into its support of oil.

Those are some of the mineral and vegetable sources of red, but by far the most entertaining of sources was the Carmine or crimson red from the cochineal beetle. That last word is, not surprisingly, left off most descriptions of the pigment source for fear that consumers might find the wearing and eating of insect blood repulsive. The source was referred to as a grain, likely because the tiny beetles look like seeds when gathered in large numbers from cacti where they live. But they yield a bright, clean, indelible red when processed with alum, which was responsible for the red of the British red coats, the blush on ladies' cheeks and lips and the cheery red in many processed foods still being made today. Crimson is a key primary in any color scheme. Red, green, blue or RGB in light. Red yellow and blue in paints. Even cyan, magenta, yellow, black or CMYK, the printers' basics, that magenta being a bluish, red-like crimson.

Red represents fire—fire itself and everything related to fire; power, heat, energy. Early alchemists, sorting through the workings of the world, attempted to name relationships and origins of what they saw as elemental. A hunk of wood, when burned, appears to release fire from inside itself like leaking sap. Thus, the alchemists concluded, fire like sap existed within the wood, only to be released under the right conditions. Here might be why the imagery of the soul as a fire or an inner light came to be.

The details of the final stages were worked out with Samuel Dickerson from the Vanderkill Eternal Rest Parlor. James called Alvaro to his office to witness the signing of documents covering the trickier legal maneuvers required under such unusual circumstances. Dickerson and James' lawyer looked uncomfortable as they sorted out the details. Both men were used to choosing their words very carefully, but they still stumbled over some of the terminology of the transference. Alvaro was unruffled. He took his cues from James who was solidly assured in the details and in the project.

James hadn't been leaving his office during the day, and Alvaro suspected he hadn't been leaving at night either. Crumpled blankets on the couch and a small bathroom with no shower off the back of the office would allow for it. James called Alvaro to the office each morning and walked him through elaborate steps, some of which would have to be performed at Dickerson's. Bones in a metal tank for the crematorium, vital organs discarded except for the heart. Washed in river waters (from the Hudson in this case). Covered in Natron—a combination of salt and soda ash—for forty days, washed again, filled with resin-soaked linens, local Hudson Valley-grown herbs and sawdust from certain wooden pieces from the house. Oiled and painted with resin, scented with myrrh, juniper and thyme. Then laid out in the kiln for forty more days. Ground first in the large chipper, redried in the kiln and finally ground and incorporated into specially prepared oils. This last stage and the preparation of the bone black and white would be performed at the factory, the lawyer having worked a particularly limber legal feat regarding the transformation of decedent into artifact.

Alvaro put his hand on James' arm when he'd finished going over his carefully detailed instructions.

"I will do this for you. But I want you to know," Alvaro began plainly and bravely. He hesitated, "I just..." he faltered, less assured.

"I know, Alvaro," James said, not looking at him. "I hope you understand what this means to me..." he added quietly.

Alvaro let go of Morrow's arm, straightened and stood. "I do understand, James," he said.

James didn't stand, just wiped down his face. "Thank you," he said finally, and he held a quivering hand up toward Alvaro. Alvaro shook it formally. Morrow's hand was thin and papery in the younger man's thick ropey one.

Rain began with the Internet. This time doing something she had knowingly avoided in the months since her father's death. On the plain front page of Google, a simple plane branding ease and pretending simplicity, its primary colors promising completeness, Rain slowly typed j-o-h-n *space* r-a-y *space* m-o-r-t-o-n and began what would be days worth of searching, taking her from university sites to fan sites to off-hand mentions in odd blogs to old newspaper articles.

There were over seven million pages, according to the good robot Google, though dozens of pages in, the results began breaking up her father's name and giving relatively random results. In quotes, his name still brought an impossible several million supposed hits.

He was of another generation. A time before every vicissitude in one's personal life, especially one owned by the public, was as thoroughly documented as overwrought thesis papers on which years of expensive credits relied. In all, Rain found one mention of Alice. It was as though she hadn't existed.

"I told you everything I know, Rain, I'm sorry," Gwen said. Rain was making an effort to call her more frequently, though every time she did Gwen asked mechanically, "When are you coming?" and Rain had either to make up an excuse or name a date.

"Why don't you go talk to Morrow?" Gwen asked her. "Hadn't you struck up a bit of a rapport with him?"

"Oh, I don't know," Rain said vaguely.

"Why not?"

"He gave me…" Rain started, somehow not wanting to disclose this to Gwen. "He gave me some paints and a letter," she said, just finally spitting it out.

"There you go. I'm sure he'd be able to tell you all about her," Gwen said, unruffled.

"Uh…I don't know, he's kind of intense. I must be something terrible to him," Rain said. "He can't have been happy with how things turned out. I must represent betrayal, jealousy. Who knows?"

"You're, what, thirty?" Gwen asked patiently.

"Thirty-one."

"This thing happened over thirty years ago. He knows who you are. You should talk to him."

"I can't!" Rain said plunging her face into her free hand to rub away a rogue smile.

"Rain?" Gwen said, like she was changing the subject. "Rain?"

"Yes?" Rain cleared her throat.

"Don't think too much. Just go see him. You need to brave this. Sometimes you don't get a second chance."

"Okay," Rain said, muffling her voice with her hand still over her mouth.

"Rain, darling, I have to go—when were you coming?"

"How's Thursday?"

"Good. I'll see you at six."

It was pouring rain, a dark, late December Saturday when Rain decided it had been long enough, that she had to face him and that she might never work up the nerve to do it if she waited for the courage to come to her.

Wrapped in bright yellow rubber and Gore-Tex against the cold and sleet, Rain trundled down the slick, muddy road to the factory. She saw that James' office lights were on as she approached, glowing against the dark skies that blotted out the daylight. She took the short-cut across the lawn and went in through an unlocked side door.

As she entered, she could hear voices in the clean echoey space. A woman's voice along with James'. Rain hesitated, not sure whether she might have been intruding, but before she could decide to flee, a small woman emerged at the top of the spiral staircase of James' office, bundling herself in a black, swing coat and a red-and-orange scarf, which set off her bright grey curls fetchingly. She trotted down the spiral staircase and stopped short when she caught sight of Rain.

"I'm sorry," Rain said impulsively.

The woman smiled curiously. "Not at all. You don't work here. Are you a friend of James?"

"No," Rain said. "Yes. I mean, I'm just here to see him. Is he here?"

"I'm Lucy," the woman said with a knowing expression. Rain wasn't sure why this woman was looking so threatening. She wondered whether this might be the lady-friend Anne had mentioned.

"James' girlfriend?" Rain asked quickly. This was the reassurance the woman was looking for, evidently, since the bluster seemed to evaporate from her all at once.

"Friend," Lucy said gravely. "Friend, yes." She took Rain by the arm and guided her a few steps away from the stairs. "Are you his friend?"

"Not in that way," Rain said. "I don't know him very well. He knew my father."

Lucy nodded, looked back up at the top of the stairs. "I'm worried about him. I think it might be affecting his mind."

"What's that?"

"The cancer," Lucy said plainly.

"Oh, my God," Rain said. "I'd heard he wasn't well, but I never thought it was so serious."

"He's sent me away," Lucy announced, looking neither dejected nor relieved. "He doesn't want to see me anymore." Her face put on a brief show of sadness.

Rain reached out to Lucy in sympathy.

"No, it's fine," Lucy said recovering instantly. "It really is fine. It's how we were together. He's released me now. He wants me to remember him in the good years."

"Oh," Rain said, not really getting it.

Lucy nodded. "Can you be there for him?" she asked in a small voice.

It seemed like she was looking for reassurance that she could go. It seemed clear she intended to leave, anyway, but she wanted a pass on the guilt.

"Yes. I'll be there." She patted the woman's shoulder and received a bracing hug. With that, Lucy pulled her scarves over her head and delivered Rain a sad, parting smile.

Rain stood still for a moment, listening to the echoes of the door's slam fade in the quiet. The sharp pattering at the window panes filled the space up again with a wall of sound as the rain increased outside to a gale. Sound, just like color, adjusts its quality depending on what surrounds it, changing in response to the atmosphere, the light, the other colors and sounds in range.

Rain went to the bottom of the spiral staircase and looked to James' office. She called out to him quietly, "James?"

"Yes," she heard him answer clearly, quietly, too. She climbed the stairs.

While he'd appeared a bit wilted at times, and he had seemed delicate ever since she knew him, it was a shock to see him now.

It had been almost two months since she had last seen him. He looked smaller, sitting—half-lying—on the couch in his office. A pillow and blanket lay crumpled next to him. It looked as though he had been living in there.

"Rain," James said. He looked like the painting Monet made of his wife as she lay dying—all flat and almost at a foreshortened vertical in his repose. Whereas she was cocooned in a babylike swath of white, James' legs poked out at odd angles, and the rest of him melted into the furniture, his blanket and couch and the light and shadow around him made this a composition in blacks and tans instead of the hazy whites and grays of that painting.

James remained motionless as she entered.

"Hello James," Rain said, feeling awkward. She stood in the doorway, still bundled in her rain gear. The lights on his desk were angled and shed stark shapes all around the room. "Hi," she said again, trying to regain a sense of ease. It felt like years since she had seen him and she suddenly felt like he was a stranger. Or maybe that this was just someone else. She was nervous. He looked so frail.

"Rain Morton," James said without opening his eyes. "I'm sick. Did you know that?"

"I heard. I'm sorry to hear it," Rain said, stepping over the threshold.

"In my mind, not…I'm not so…can't seem to," James groped for his glasses. "I'm terribly… Did you know, Alice? Did you know your daught—my wi—my moth—your…?" He took his glasses in his hands but neglected to put them on. Just sat.

"I didn't know her," Rain said, approaching him and sitting in a wooden chair facing the couch.

"You have to paint, Rain Morton. Can you paint for me?"

"Why do I have to paint?" Rain asked gently.

"I didn't let her paint. I wanted her to myself. I was… It was me. I did it to her. Chased her…"

"What do you mean?"

"Will you make paintings for me? I'm making paint for you," he said, wilting further with each expulsion of breath.

Rain looked around for a phone, thinking she should call 911.

Morrow opened his eyes. "The orphan and the cuckold," he chuckled hollowly. "The cuckold, the orphan and the suicide."

Rain stood and walked to the office door.

"No! No! Don't go…" Morrow shifted himself up as much as he could. It was as if he were melting away.

Rain halted at the door. She flipped a light switch and turned back around.

He laughed again. "Ah yes. New light. All new colors. You knew that."

"I just wanted to see whether I should call an ambulance," Rain said.

Behind his desk, Rain saw the photograph of Alice Morrow. Her smile was accusing, but charming. The brushes she held toward the camera were worn-out looking, but she looked healthy and alive with wit.

"All new colors on the very same surfaces," Morrow continued, slumping back again. He nattered on atonally. As if he were reciting an old lecture. "Color…merely a phenomenon of light, an interaction between light and the brain. It's nothing, ultimately. Nothing at all. Energy waves triggering electrical impulses in our brains. 'The actions and sufferings of light,' Goethe said it perfectly as usual. A wave and a particle, resisting our impulse to own and describe. We can see only a tiny slice of energy waves all around us, and we make such a big fuss over it.

Such a fuss." His voice trailed in and out. "Like it's real," he said. "Like it's the only thing that's real…"

Rain picked up the phone.

James lay half prone, still propped on one elbow, eyes closed. "You can't even imagine what a tiny slice of the electromagnetic waves—I'm speaking as a scientist now, mind you…the electromagnetic waves that are available…"

Rain dialed.

"…miles and miles of it. Let's see, there's cosmic radiation, x-rays, ultraviolet, then our pitiful share of visible energy, 380 to about 750 nanometers. That's it, a sliver. After that, there's the whole range of infrared and then radio waves, for God's sake…"

She put the receiver back down.

He continued uninterrupted, "…people so convinced of meaning in color, it's absurd. Color has no meaning. It's a pleasure and a balm like food, like good air, a dream. No, it's like food. You need a little of this with a little of that. You need change, you need difference, complements, you see, freshness. An example. Your eye convinces itself of true colors under a candlelight. You still see the tablecloth as white, but it's not white. It's not. What is white? Look at synesthesiacs. I ask you."

Rain heard the ambulance.

"One synesthete is convinced that Tuesdays are dark yellow." Morrow attempted a chuckle again. It was clear he couldn't move. He kept on talking in a garbled voice. "But the next one swears it's purple, for God's sake. He'd swear on ten-thousand, gilt-edged Bibles. And nine is the color blue and the name of Ted is orange and it's completely and utterly nonsense! The random connections in the firings of neurons. Who's to say that my sky blue isn't your puce? We just point to the damn thing and say the same thing when that part of the spectrum beams through our retinae." He laughed again. "Why should one person keep another person?" he went on, as though he'd been arguing about that all along.

Rain went to the landing to meet the paramedics but they were already bustling into the factory. James was still speaking as three large men trundled in dragging brightly colored, plastic cases and a large, orange plastic board.

"Trichromatic, you see? Three types of cones in the eye, three colors to balance and weigh. Having only two leaves one color-blind. Three. You need three."

"Mr. Morrow?" one of them said loudly into James' face as he flicked a tiny flashlight up and down along each eye.

Another wrapped James' arm in a blood pressure cuff.

"Are you the daughter?" one of them asked Rain. She shook her head. Still listening to Morrow speak, Rain was appalled at how dismissive the paramedics seemed about what he was actually saying. She had to remind herself they were not being cold, but competent.

Morrow's lecture was uninterrupted by all the bustle. His words become a bit louder, a bit more dramatic, and were accompanied by a look of slight alarm on his face, but otherwise he continued on unabated, "…such a small part of the brain anyway, and such a small slice of the spectrum of recordable energy is visual in the first place. All just really accomplished by particles scattering white light, absorbing it, scattering it. That's it, that's all I've done. Rearranged particles, sorted them out a little bit…"

"Mr. Morrow how are you feeling today?" the first paramedic said into his face.

Morrow regarded him with some concern in his eyes, maybe a slight bit in the tone of his voice too, as he said to the paramedic "…you'd think something that looks yellow IS yellow, somehow is a yellow thing, but it is actually a thing that is absorbing all of the light that is not yellow…"

"WHAT DATE IS IT TODAY, SIR? CAN YOU TELL ME WHAT THE MONTH IS? WHAT MONTH ARE WE IN?" The paramedic's tone remained polite, but he shouted right into James' face. Morrow seemed to register that he was being asked a question, and appeared to consider answering it, but didn't.

"…and so a yellow thing is really a thing that throws yellow energy back to YOU. Not yellow itself, but all things that are not yellow…"

"CAN YOU TELL ME WHO THE PRESIDENT IS, MR. MORROW?"

Again, no answer was forthcoming. All the while, the men worked full speed, inserting an IV, taping it down on his arm, one of their hands held it down securely while another one fit an oxygen mask over his face, but Rain could still hear James talking.

The paramedic said, "CAN YOU STAND, SIR?"

Morrow's voice droned on inside the clear plastic cup. Little clouds of steam obscured his lips as he continued speaking.

"Okay," one of the paramedics said to the others, "one, two…THREE!" And as the three men, their six arms, the careful support of their six bent legs and three straight backs, lifted James Morrow from his sitting position, across the edge of the couch, Rain couldn't help but see it. See the dramatic gangly pose of David's Morot in his bathtub there for a moment as they swept him onto the orange board on the floor in a fluid, professional, least-possibly-disruptive way.

"Okay, okay, okay," James said from the floor, suddenly more present. He tried to remove the IV from his arm. He finally seemed to be able to acknowledge what was going on in the room. "Okay, okay, okay," he trailed on.

"MR. MORROW. PLEASE RELAX, MR. MORROW. ARMS DOWN. THAT'S MY BOY, THAT'S RIGHT."

The paramedic was gentle and kind despite his shouting and manhandling. Rain, who had been watching from the door, trying to catch everything James was saying, finally let her hand go to her mouth and found her breath catching hard in her throat.

Not for him so much, not for the woman he'd loved or the father she loved or the confused wrecked love between all of them, but for life. Though she'd been orphaned, she'd never before witnessed dying. She didn't know if this *was* dying. Only that it could be dying, and she could see his vulnerability and his hope and firm belief in his continuing to live amidst all the bustle and noise of the three EMTs who had finished their strapping and hooking and buckling and were now hoisting this human being up and out the office door, winding down the spiral staircase and out to the ambulance pulled up on the muddy lawn.

BLACK

*But when I fell in love with black, it contained all color. It wasn't
a negation of color. It was an acceptance... [Black] will give
you the feeling of totality. Of peace. Of greatness. Of quietness.
Of excitement. I have seen things that were transformed into black
that took on just greatness. I don't want to use a lesser word."*

—LOUISE NEVELSON

Black is funereal as mourning, evil as black magic, threatening as a weapon. Black can be witches, bad luck, anarchy, and the theoretical unknowable of the proverbial black box. Blackmail, black sheep of the family and the black dog of depression. The black spot was a death sentence among pirates, their black flag warning of their nefarious intentions. Black hats on the bad guys, the black plague and being blacklisted are all unquestionably negative.

But not all connotations of black lean toward the uncertain or fearful. Sometimes it is taken back purposefully in *black is beautiful*. Black has long-signaled holiness, privilege and good fortune in priests' vestments, limos and black tie, and being *in the black* in business.

Black has a purity that draws many to it, even though the impressionists claimed never to witness true black in nature. And though Van Gogh shunned it, using bright contrasts instead of line, he returned to black just before he died in the form of the scattering black birds in "Wheat Fields with Crows," his last completed work at Auvers.

Carbon black, graphite, charcoal—blacks are the most elemental of art-making materials. The cooled end of a burnt stick is one of the most ancient tools for drawing. Vine charcoal is the most primitive drawing implement and is still common today. Cennini described filling a pot with lengths of vine and sticks, covering it with clay, venting it with a few holes and putting it into the local baker's brick oven overnight. Artists still make their own charcoal, using metal cans fitted one into the other, a metal bucket covered with tin foil, or even by simply wrapping sticks in foil pierced for ventilation and left for hours directly in the embers of a fireplace or grill.

Black or a near black can be approximated by mixing intense hues, but, in an important sense, black is the absence of color. A surface appears black when all spectral energy is absorbed and none reflected. A black hole of course being the blackest thing there is—or isn't—since all energy is pulled into it. The night sky is black where light traveling outward never makes it back.

Rain ran back to the cabin as the ambulance pulled away. Inside, she scrambled into her gear hanging by the door, the rain-proof pants that matched the slicker she was still wearing, the long boots and her helmet. She took the Vespa on the shortcut up through the woods on the path that joins Route 9D a little further south. She couldn't see the lights of the ambulance, but she could still hear it and knew the way to the hospital since it was near the hardware supply store and she had passed it many times throughout the fall. Swearing all along the way that she would finally get herself a car, she pushed the Vespa to its limit through the driving rain. It was that promise to herself that made her realize she intended to stay in Vanderkill.

The rain fell in torrents, forcing her to the side of the road a few times where she sat, abject and soaking, realizing she was too far from home to turn back, too far from the hospital to push forward. It took almost two hours to cover the twenty miles.

When she arrived, Rain locked the Vespa at the front of the hospital near a motorcycle, locked her helmet into the seat, and went to the broad entrance to peel off her wet gear, the exhaustion pulsing through her veins. At the reception desk she asked a grandmotherly lady if a James Morrow was checked in and if she could see him. The lady found him in the computer and directed her to the third floor.

Rain felt dwarfed in the triple-wide elevator. It was room-sized, big enough for three gurneys and moved so slowly you could feel no shift of gravity as it started or stopped.

At the nurses' station, Rain received grave glances when she asked for Morrow, A mixture of suspicion, pity and jadedness.

A tall nurse whose perfectly crafted makeup and tangle of delicate gold jewelry contrasted with her Peanuts-themed scrubs stood reluctantly and pivoted around the desk. "You wanna get a coffee?" she asked Rain. "They're just finishing him up."

"Yes, please," Rain said. "I'd love something hot."

"It's on the way. Here," the nurse said, waving a well-manicured hand toward a break room.

Rain poured the weak but fresh-smelling coffee into a paper cup then looked up to find the nurse holding a large clear plastic bag out to her. "Oh, the…uh…" Rain said, lowering the rumpled yellow heap of her wet rain-gear into the bag. "Thanks."

"Yeah," the nurse said. She kicked some towels around the floor without much amusement, and then gestured Rain to follow her out the other side of the break-room.

"You can sit right there," the nurse said. "I'll see if they're ready." She slipped in through a closed door. Propping it open as she returned, she held up her hand and said, "They'll come out in just a sec. You can go right in when they're finished."

The coffee warmed her slowly from the inside. Rain shoved away the thought that she was going to have to get back to Vanderkill somehow. She had drained the cup by the time three people emerged from the room. One with a stethoscope shot her a look as she stood.

"Are you the doctor?" Rain asked her.

The woman, blonde, very young-looking, brought her hand to the stethoscope she was wearing. "No, I'm the P.A., are you related?"

"No," Rain said, not sure what P.A. actually stood for, and then she screwed up her face wondering at the question again, and then concluded, "No."

"You don't seem sure," the P.A. said through a small laugh.

"I just…" Rain faltered, "recently found out he had been married to my mother. Making him…my stepfather I guess?"

"Uh, yeah?" the P.A. looked down at her clip board and raised her eyebrows. "Is there any other family?"

"Not that I know of…" Rain put her hand up to her face. It was shaking a little so she brought it back down again. She hadn't meant to put herself in this position. She just couldn't see him going all by himself. "I have no idea," she concluded.

"Okay, I don't think you can sign for this, anyway. I need to call his emergency contact. It's his lawyer, I think."

"I'm sorry, you're the…?" Rain said, shaking her head and smiling.

"Physician's Assistant," the woman said. "I'm also in medical school," she added a little defensively, as though Rain were questioning her credentials.

"Oh, I didn't mean to…" Rain began.

"What's that?"

"I just came to see if he was okay."

"He's stable now. You can go in," she paused and then lightened her attitude. "We made him a little more comfortable, but I don't think he has very long."

"Thank you," Rain answered earnestly. "Thank you." She entered the darkened room. It was a double, but the other bed was empty, the lights low.

James was clean and tucked tightly in the sheets. One of his thin arms protruded from the dotted hospital gown with the IV, a cuff and some bandages. The other arm was under the covers at his side. His eyes were closed and he was breathing steadily to the beep of the heart monitor, but somehow he didn't seem asleep to Rain. Something in his breathing wasn't peaceful.

She circled the foot of the bed to sit in a chair by the window and let her bag of wet gear down to the floor. She tossed her coffee cup and it hit the bottom of the trash can with a clunk. Rain was alarmed as his eyelids fluttered and opened.

When he saw her his eyes warmed and squinted slightly with what looked like love and gratitude.

"Al…" he whispered.

"It's Rain," Rain whispered back to him.

"You look so beautiful," James said to her. "So…beautiful. I knew you'd come to me." He closed his eyes again, letting the smile slowly fall from his lips and then quieting again into sleep. Rain sat and looked at him a while longer and then went into the bathroom.

When she returned, his eyes were open again.

"I thought I'd been dreaming," he said quietly, as she rounded the end of the bed.

"How do you feel?" Rain asked.

"I don't. They're good at that."

"Sounds like you have some experience with this," Rain said looking down into her lap.

"They've known me pretty well here for the last year or so," James replied.

They sat quietly for a few moments. Finally Rain looked up to see if he had gone to sleep again, but he appeared to be wide awake. He was looking at her intently.

"A part of me doesn't really believe it," James said. "That perpetual two-year-old inside me doesn't buy that there's such a thing as the end." His gaze steadied on her as he spoke lucidly all of a sudden. "But another part of me, maybe the rest of me, is completely aware."

Rain opened her mouth to speak, but James cut her off.

"No," he said quickly. "I need to ask your forgiveness."

"For what?" Rain said.

"For her, for Alice, I need you to forgive her." James' voice was desperate.

"But I," Rain began, and she pushed out a little laugh. Not meaning to insult him. He was putting such weight on this. "No, I mean, I have no feelings about her."

"I need you to forgive her," James said again.

"Do you need to forgive her?"

"I need you to forgive her," James said.

Rain thought he was fading again and she looked down into her lap.

"I'll do that," Rain promised gently, not looking at him. "I'll forgive her."

James moved his mouth wordlessly like he was tasting something, swallowed painfully and then whispered, "I just want to look. Look at you. Is that alright?"

"Yes, alright," she said very quietly and she looked into his eyes, bravely and silently.

She tried to act courageously, so aware that he was dying, aware that there was something in her face that he was taking and that she was willing to give. But she was also fascinated by his face as it soared and plummeted through emotions, memories, connection, surrender. His mouth was slack, but the skin around his eyes was expressive, pulling in, opening up again. Rain fell into his eyes, the depth of their darkness—it was the exhaustion, she was sure of it, but she was falling into a kind of meditative state, and suddenly she was not sure how long they had been in that dimly lit room staring into each other's eyes, and where she actually was and who this was, but she was sure that he loved her, truly loved her. That he was staring at her for her, Rain Morton, not for the mother she never knew. That staring at her in this way, he was finally relinquishing the hold he had kept on Alice all these years.

"Okay?" Rain asked, very quietly, and James blinked a slow assent. Okay.

He closed his eyes again. He hadn't moved at all, she noticed, and his breathing grew uneven again. It seemed that he was not asleep, but waiting.

Rain leaned back in the chair and instantly fell asleep. She dreamed of love, of Hunter and of Karl, of her first love at summer camp when she was seventeen, of her father, of James, and of Gwen. And of Alice. All the kinds of love in their great variety, but all genuine, all as deeply felt, all as meaningful and real. In her dream there were no boundaries, there was no betrayal, no hurt or abandonment, there was only that same love flowing in and out between all of them, all people, all time and experience.

It was still night when Rain woke up. James was awake, but she couldn't tell if he was really there. She shifted up in the chair and saw that his eyes followed her. She smiled at him and leaned forward toward him.

His eyes welled with tears and he moved his mouth a little, but no sound came out.

"It's okay," Rain said, and she reached out to touch his arm.

His mouth quivered again. "I wanted to…" he said in a scratchy voice.

"It's okay," Rain whispered. "I know, it's okay."

"For you," he mouthed, and then it was just over.

Rain didn't need to hear the monitor's beep to know he was gone. She stood and stepped back toward the window, expecting a rush of people. When none came, she moved toward the door just as the Physician's Assistant and two nurses walked quickly into the room. One of them glanced at Rain and then at the clipboard.

"Uh, it said no, uh…" the nurse began.

"It's okay," the P.A. interrupted him. "She's not next-of."

"Oh," he said. "Do you mind waiting outside?" he asked her.

"Yep," Rain said. "I just need…" she looked over toward the chair and the bag of crumpled yellow lying there at its feet, but then thought better of it and backed out into the hallway.

The nurse shut the door gently. Rain walked back down the hallway to the break-room where a couple hovered over a tray of doughnuts. The woman was hugely pregnant and wearing several hospital gowns. Her partner dithered over the pastries as she teased him lightly.

"No, don't worry about me, go right ahead," she said laughing.

"I won't," he said, wrapping his arm around her broad back and taking hold of her rolling I.V. stand.

"You HAVE to!" she said to him, still laughing. "I need you strong and happy! I can't have you passing out on me again!"

"I didn't pass out!" he insisted.

"You looked like you were going to…"

"I've never done this before," he said.

"Oh, yeah, and I've…"

"No sarcasm, remember?" he said, kissing her on the ear.

"I love you."

"How do you feel?" he said, nuzzling her.

"Just take a doughnut and let's go back to walking," she said, laughing again.

"Okay, just one…" The man stuffed an entire powdered sugar doughnut in his mouth. "Whamph?" he asked indignantly to the woman's shocked look.

Then they saw Rain. The woman laughed. "How 'bout that, huh?"

"Congratulations," Rain said.

"Oh, we're just getting started," the woman said. "Come on, you," she said to the man and they ambled off down the hallway.

Rain fixed another coffee and stared down the hallway toward James' room. A window at the end of the hall glowed bright blue, the night having let go its darkness to the new dawn.

The vines around the front door had been sheared back to nothing. The house itself was nearly empty, all the blank displays stacked neatly by, even much of the furniture was gone. An archival box, about the size of a tombstone, was sitting alone on a table.

Standing in the middle of James' house, Rain looked around. When she spotted the box she walked to it, practically on tip-toe. Inside, Rain found a stack of overstuffed, densely worked sketchbooks and a photo album stuffed with photographs. The sketches were mostly stylized landscapes. They nearly always featured a swath of flat river and a straight slice of train track. Some of the sketches were super-macro details of track, the scraped metal rendered like light itself. Others were abstracted details of light reflecting off water. Notes were scribbled here and there along the pages. Some were just dates, some were inscrutable and poetic. Rain flipped through and looked at the photos, feeling she needed time, hours, years to take them in.

Most of the photographs were of a young Alice. Rain's father appeared in some of the later photographs, in groups of friends, then in portraits.

Rain put it all back into the box and closed it. Glancing around at James' unfamiliar emptied house, she looked at a photograph she had held onto in her hand. It was of James and Alice laughing with John in a moment of perfect balance, before things tipped. A moment of pure light and ease.

James' face was open and carefree in a way she had never seen. Her father was healthy and robust and naïve, too, in a way she had never seen in him. Alice was sylph-like in the picture. Her clear blue eyes alight as she laughed, her bangs blown free of her face. She and James leaned forward toward John enthusiastically and he seemed to take them both in equally in a way Rain knew couldn't last. They looked happy. All three looked equally in love and grateful for each other. Friends who found each other as neighbors. The kind of love that was fierce and passionate and giddy and that eventually cannot be stood.

Rain pushed James out.

His letter and the paints for her were his forgiveness.

THE END

WHITE

Whiteness (is)...the emblem of many touching, noble things—the innocence of brides, the benignity of age ... among the Red Men of America the giving of the white belt of wampum was the deepest pledge of honor...

—HERMAN MELVILLE

White, of course, is not really a color, but neither is it the lack of color. White is all colors. What our eyes and brain perceive as white is really all parts of the visible spectrum reaching our eyes in the same quantity.

White is pure and innocent, white is unnerving and dead. White is open and inclusive; it is the white light of acceptance and forgiveness, and it is the face of fear, ghosts and skeletons. It can represent surrender or an offering of peace. It can also represent the worst kind of hatred when worn (pointy) head to foot. White has no allegiance, more slippery even than black; it slides around meaning and representation while tempting artists despite its poison. Always the biggest tube in the paintbox, white varies in quality, covering power and texture significantly. Many artists continue to use Lead White despite its dangers, since for them, the way lead white moves, how it clings to the brush, holds the stroke, its perfect degree of translucency, the way it takes other pigments—all of these are what painting, what doing art, *is* for them. Asking them to switch to a safer material is like asking Dizzy Gillespie to find another instrument. It's just not at issue.

In 1952, John Cage created the astonishing 4'33", a musical composition built entirely of silence, in response to Robert Rauschenberg's controversial White Paintings of the year before. Of course, Rauschenberg wasn't the first or last to worship white in this way. Malevich's Suprematist paintings were made in 1919, and Robert Ryman has been well known for his work in white since the fifties. But however tempting, it is misleading to read art only through time as though appearing next means anything other than context and behind-the-scenes intrigue. Art is not science after all, it is not about linear "advances," however art historians would convince us otherwise. Art is only tangentially about technology. "To Whom It May Concern:" Cage wrote dismissively. "The white paintings came first, my silent piece came later."

The more memorable description he gave of the white paintings was this: "The white paintings were airports for the lights, shadows and particles." He evoked Plato's famous metaphor of the cave, where human beings were bound prisoners whose lives were lived entirely through watching shadow play on a wall— endlessly naming the forms that they saw there. Socrates asked us to imagine what would happen if a prisoner, not convinced that the shadows were reality, broke free to the outside world. How impossible it would be for the escapee to reenter the cave and convince those left behind of what he had seen.

It is all in the light. Socrates saw that; Rauschenberg saw that. It is all right there in our full spectrum white light. How remarkable that Socrates presages media, the puppet-world of celebrity, the little boxes of shadowplay on which we follow them, and the impossibility of reconciling the things we don't know yet to the things that are right in front of us. Being blinded, paradoxically, might sometimes be the only way we can begin to see

The eye is not a camera, after all, the retina is not film, though they are so often compared. When all the rods and cones are stimulated to the same degree, the resulting sensation in the brain is white. This might explain why a white light is so often reported by those in near-death experiences. Perhaps all the senses, not just the visual ones, are flooded with stimulus at that moment. Perhaps death is not an absenting, but a welling up.

Maybe the body and our flawed mushy sense organs, which string time and experience out into their illusion of variety, are all at once freed from such a stricture, and the soul at that first blinding moment perceives just undifferentiated whiteness. Everything all at once, all here, all now.

> *...And so each venture*
> *Is a new beginning, a raid on the inarticulate*
> *With shabby equipment always deteriorating*
> *In the general mess of imprecision of feeling,*
> *Undisciplined squads of emotion. And what there was to*
> *   conquer*
> *By strength and submission, has already been discovered*
> *Once or twice, or several times, by men whom one cannot hope*
> *To emulate—but there is no competition—*
> *There is only the fight to recover what has been lost*
> *And found and lost again and again: and now, under*
> *   conditions*
> *That seem unpropitious. But perhaps neither gain nor loss.*
> *For us, there is only the trying. The rest is not our business.*
> — T.S. Eliot

An opening at Harris/Gelfman gallery in Chelsea. Large formal portraits of young women standing in front of moody Hudson River landscapes, a slash of train tracks are always in view somewhere in the frame. The figures are life-sized and hold bottles of Budweiser with car keys dangling from their fingers, or they cradle bottles of prescription drugs, tiny glass pipes, lighters, mysterious bunched aluminum foil and spoons. Small details spell out the tragedy or signal possibility and hope. A clear plastic key chain ornament spells M-O-M and is lined with a scribbling of bright crayon. A torn open envelope dangles from a hand from child protective services. A silver NA coin with "30" imprinted on it. And in every portrait, the vestiges of hope in the clear depth of the expression on the subject's face. It's like the artist is trying to save them by preserving that hope each by each.

Displayed under glass is Rain's box of Highland Morrow paints in their hand-made tubes and bottles. It is well used, but still quite abundant. Alongside the box are two small wooden crates of one-of-a-kind Highland Morrow paints. Morrow: *Bone White* is imprinted in the wood on one of them and Morrow: *Caput Mortuum* is stamped on the other. A hand-lettered card dedicates these ultimate and irreplaceable materials to Rain Morton, to art and to the future, and is signed James Morrow.

ACKNOWLEDGEMENTS

First and foremost I thank my husband Seth Gallagher for his love and his tireless belief in me, and my children Ronan and Freya for their love and patience. For me, you are the whole wide world and everything that's in it.

I am so grateful to Chis Sulavik for his passionate love of books, story and the written word, and for his granting that energy and fervid belief onto me and *The Colorman*. And thanks to the brilliant and reckless Amanda Tobier, for her help and expertise.

I thank Patricia Willens for her faith in me, and for putting the seed to the earth. Patricia, along with my other college roommates, Nina Livingston, Mallory Polk and Christine Yeh, have been an ongoing and powerful influence. I thank them each for generously bringing their intelligence, boundless love and specifically varied perspectives on the world to me.

In many ways I wrote this book for the artists in my family: my mother Austine Comarow, my sister Cara Ginder and her husband Bob Ginder. My mother is not only an artist, but an inventor and an innovator, and my thanks to her is woven all through this book. This story began in Bob's loving worship of the deluxe box of Windsor and Newton paints he won in a painting competition, and was fueled by nights in his and Cara's studios in their loft in Tribeca and later in their home on the Hudson River. No amount of thanking could begin to reach what they are to me and how fortunate I feel to have them near. I thank my beloved late grandmother Terry Dintenfass, the art dealer, who introduced me to New York and taught me to live as though I were looking back on it all. My thanks go to my brother Andreas Wood and his wife Clea Montville, artists in film and theater, who have always been so encouraging and inspirational to me. To my father John Wood, an astronomer and optics engineer who taught me through his great love of science that light is the medium that describes everything: thank you. Thank you also to my stepmother Marika Wood, whose dedication to art and to all that is intellectual is unsurpassed, and to my stepfather David Comarow for dedicating his life to his belief in my mother's artwork, and for bringing it out into the world.

I want to thank my hometown for being such a draw for the most interesting people in the world. I am so privileged to find one fascinating and close friendship after another here among artists, musicians, writers, photographers, filmmakers, firefighters, gardeners and chefs. My first loves of grown-up life, Anne Symmes and Steve Ives have that rare and quite telling habit of shining their bright lights onto their friends and colleagues. They have been as close and as intimately supportive as any tight family during the years I have known them, and they were among my first readers; I thank them for their encouragement, love and enthusiasm. I also thank Patty Donohue, Larry Quintiliani and Kristen Sorenson for being deeply sympathetic sounding boards during key periods of working on this book. And to my panel of experts, Kim Conner, John Plummer, Dwight Garner, David Rothenberg and George Saunders: thank you helping me through the tough parts.

A huge thank you to Jean Marzollo, my mentor and a powerful poet, educator and artist. Her generosity, advice and support have been invaluable through this adventure.

Heartfelt thanks to Donald McRae the author, for his unparalleled support and friendship. To Nick Tobier, the artist, early shaper of my experience of art and a great friend for many years: thank you. And I thank art dealer/curator Eric Stark for giving me some of the most intense encounters of art-seeing I've ever undergone, and for generously opening his experience in the art world and in life to me.

I thank John Paine for his insightful rearrangements. Thanks to Emily Church, Isabella Piestrzynska, Nicole Ellul, Heather Marshall, and Spencer Gale for their hard work on behalf of this book. And thanks to Kathleen Lynch, the artist who created the beautiful cover for The Colorman.

I dedicate this book to all artists out there, in all media, of all degrees of exposure, most especially none. Dar Williams put it best: early on in her performing life, she says, she realized with no small degree of awe that audiences "actually want you to succeed," and that this realization can be the source of great courage when pursuing something that makes most of us so vulnerable. May you all recognize and embrace the encouragement and support that is out there for you, and thank you Dar for helping me see mine!

Finally I thank John and Susie Allison, my cultural muses, my security blankets, my partners-in-crime. What they do for me is just like what a great volleyball player does to the ball. That subtle but firm, delicate springing set, boosting you gently but powerfully up until you're perfectly poised for blast-off. Their help has been more than just psychological; I used their house as a writing studio and John Ray was the very first gentle reader of this novel.

THANKS ALSO TO:

The authors of the most fantastic books about pigment, art and color after Cennino Cennini: Philip Ball (*Bright Earth*), James Elkins (*What Painting Is*) and Victoria Finlay (*Color*). Thank you for bringing such a fascinating and mysterious subject to life.

Jamie B., the pigment chef at Art Guerra, New York.

Winsor and Newton for their magisterial and luxurious oil paints.

Natural Pigments and George O'Hanlon, the real colorman of Mendocino County. www.naturalpigments.com

Scott Burdick and Susan Lyon for their amazing oil portraits, and their beautiful and generous website: www.burdicklyon.com

Artist Tad Spurgeon and his amazingly thorough site about painting, paint and color: www.tadspugeon.com

Erika Wood
Cold Spring, NY
July 2009

http://www.erikawood.com/colorman